Praise for the Orchard Mysteries by Sheila Connolly

"There is a delightful charm to this small-town regional cozy. . . .
Connolly provides a fascinating whodunit filled with surprises."
—*The Mystery Gazette*

"A true cozy [with] a strong and feisty heroine, a perplexing murder,
a personal dilemma, and a picturesque New England setting."
—*Gumshoe Review*

"There's a depth to the characters in this book that isn't always found
in crime fiction. . . . Sheila Connolly has written a winner for cozy
mystery fans."
—*Lesa's Book Critiques*

"The premise and plot are solid, and Meg seems a perfect fit for her
role."
—*Publishers Weekly*

"A wonderful slice of life in a small town. . . . The mystery is intelligent and has an interesting twist."
—*The Mystery Reader*

Praise for the Museum Mysteries

"[A] clever, charming, and sophisticated caper. . . . A real page-
turner!"
—Hank Phillippi Ryan,
award–winning author of *The Other Woman*

"Connolly's wonderful new series is a witty, engaging blend of history and mystery."
—Julie Hyzy,
author of the White House Chef Mysteries

Books by Sheila Connolly

"The Rising of the Moon"
Once She Knew
Relatively Dead
Reunion with Death

Orchard Mysteries

One Bad Apple
Rotten to the Core
Red Delicious Death
A Killer Crop
Bitter Harvest
Sour Apples
"Called Home"
Golden Malicious

Museum Mysteries

Fundraising the Dead
Let's Play Dead
Fire Engine Dead
"Dead Letters"
Monument to the Dead

County Cork Mysteries

Buried in a Bog
Scandal in Skibbereen

Glassblowing Mysteries
Writing as Sarah Atwell

Through a Glass, Deadly
Pane of Death
Snake in the Glass

Reunion
with
Death

Sheila Connolly

BEYOND THE PAGE publishing

Beyond the Page Books
are published by
Beyond the Page Publishing
www.beyondthepagepub.com

ISBN: 978-1-937349-96-7

*To the Fabulous Forty,
and particularly Sally and Sandy,
who made this book possible*

Chapter 1

In 1968 Judy Collins sang, "Who knows where the time goes?"
When we were freshmen, you couldn't walk down a hallway in
any dorm on the Wellesley College campus without hearing it coming from stereos in every other room. The title didn't mean a lot to us
then, because at eighteen we had all the time in the world; the whole
future lay before us, with all its possibilities. Now we have more to
look back on than to look forward to—but Judy is still singing.

I had forgotten what a pain in the butt long overseas flights were.
It had been a lot of years since I'd flown to Europe, although back in
college and right after, I'd thought it would be a regular thing. Once,
in another lifetime, I was an art historian, specializing in medieval
churches, but I'd found out pretty fast that there were no jobs available for people who liked to study really old buildings, certainly not
in the foreseeable future. I'd said a regretful good-bye to my dreams
of regular excursions to Aquitaine and Lincolnshire, and come up
with another plan for my life. Not for the last time.

Plan Number Two had included marriage and a child. Or maybe
children, plural, were in the first draft, but by the time our one and
only had turned two, it was pretty clear that the marriage wasn't going to survive, and I didn't think adding another child would make
things any better. We'd stuck together for another decade, citing the
hackneyed reason "for the sake of the child," but in the end we'd decided we were doing her more harm than good and parted ways. By
the time Lisa was in high school, Hugh was history and I'd become
the main breadwinner, since his checks were somewhat unreliable.
I'd never replaced him.

Lisa had survived the whole thing without years of therapy, had
attended a good college, graduated with honors, and was now off in
Chicago and not too close to Mom, doing something even she
couldn't quite define. But she seemed happy when we talked on the
phone, and that was all I was worried about. I'd long since decided
that career planning was overrated, and changing economic and social circumstances had only reinforced that viewpoint. We'd weath-
ered the lean years, although I couldn't say I exactly had a retirement

account. But then, I didn't plan to retire until I dropped in front of my computer keyboard.

But here I was, bound for Italy on the cheapest red-eye flight I could find. Made possible by a small bequest from my late mother, who attached only one condition: do something fun for yourself.

I'd had to think long and hard about what I considered "fun" these days, and how to please me and only me. Then at a college reunion a year ago—one of those landmark ones with a zero on the end—two classmates, Jean Rider and Jane Lombardi, stood up and announced that they were planning a ten-day event in the north of Italy for the following year. No spouses, no kids—just classmates, people we'd known to greater or lesser degrees four decades earlier and in some cases hadn't seen since. They proposed a flat fee, and all we had to do was get ourselves to Italy and all would be taken care of—transport, food, museum tickets, and best yet, planning. I had known both of them slightly and had no idea what kind of organizers they had turned out to be, but the idea sounded like heaven, and my hand was in the air before I could even think—or say thank you, Mom, for allowing me even to consider going.

A year had seemed like a very long time back then. Plenty of time to change my mind, and in fact a number of people had dropped out, citing other obligations or plans or simply cold feet. But there had been a waiting list of people eager to join the group, and the number had held steady at forty. Forty people celebrating the last forty years, after spending four years together in another century, another millennium.

Lisa had all but cheered when I told her. "Live a little, Ma," she said. "Show 'em you aren't dead yet." I didn't know how to take that. I didn't feel old, and I hoped I didn't act old. I took care of myself, ate right (mostly), exercised (sometimes), didn't smoke at all and didn't drink too much (very often), and kept my brain agile by using it as much as I could. Surely I could handle ten days with an interesting group of people and hold my own.

But this was reality, spending six hours wedged in a seat with about two inches' clearance in any direction, breathing recycled air and picking at plastic food. I'd bought plenty to read, but I'd also brought along the record book from our long-ago freshman year. Back then there had been no Internet, no electronic communication, so we'd sent in print snapshots of ourselves—most often those dreadful high school graduation photos—and a short text. Somebody had put them together into a small booklet and sent them to us before we arrived on campus so we could get to know our classmates—the people we would spend the next four years with. I know I was terrified at the time, but I hadn't admitted it, nor had anyone else.

I leafed through the skinny booklet. So many people I'd known well—or thought I had—who had dropped off my radar altogether. So many others I didn't recognize at all—and a scattering of some who had become household names in the forty years since graduation. I paused at my own picture, my hair in a tidy flip, with a headband holding it in place. My sweet, naive little text, which I didn't even remember writing. Had I really thought I would be a biologist?

I had a list of the people who would be on this Italian excursion. No, excursion wasn't quite the right word, but I wasn't sure what was. Trip was too mundane; junket sounded too political. It was a coming together of people from all over the country, to spend ten days together to . . . what? Take stock? Revisit our youth? Indulge in one last blowout before we were too creaky to climb stairs or carry a suitcase? I wasn't sure what the mission was, but I knew I wanted to be there. That kind of spontaneity was very unlike me: I was usually the planner, the organizer, the one who worked out all the details. This time I was going to try to let go and let somebody else worry about all that stuff.

At the end of the flight I emerged from the plane feeling rumpled and sticky and sluggish, in a place where people were speaking something that was definitely not English. I didn't speak Italian, although I had mastered enough other languages to cobble together a few basic phrases, mostly things like "Where is the church?" and "How much?" In my current state I wasn't sure I could string together a sentence in English, much less Italian, so it really didn't matter. I collected my too-heavy bag (I had trouble deciding what to bring, so I sort of brought everything), tucked my shirt into my jeans, and headed through customs. I hoped that the proper documents and a polite smile would see me through. I couldn't possibly look like a terrorist, could I? But what did a terrorist look like these days? If I were planning an attack, wouldn't I want to look entirely forgettable and harmless—just like me?

I had to rein in my befuddled imagination when I reached the head of the line. There, documents were stamped, smiles were exchanged, and I was on the ground in Italy somewhere outside of Florence, free and clear. As airports went, this one was tiny, which was probably a plus at the moment. Now to find the promised ride— because if the driver and a few straggling classmates arriving this afternoon weren't there, I had no Plan B.

With a surge of relief I found the welcoming committee was waiting outside of customs, looking uniformly perky—I figured they must have arrived the day before and slept ever since, because I couldn't imagine being perky at the moment. They waved and smiled and cheered. "You're the last one!" said somebody who looked remarkably like a pruney version of a woman who'd sat next to me in French classes for two years. What was her name . . . Christine? Even with the list and the booklet in hand, I hadn't been able to put a face to all the names. "Time to head out!" she announced. "We'll be there in time for cocktails!"

Donna, that was it. She had always been relentlessly cheerful, although her accent had been atrocious, even after two years of classes. Some things just didn't change, apparently. Which made me wonder, had I changed? How much? Would anyone recognize me now?

Our little covey of classmates trailed out of the terminal building, hauling suitcases on wheels. Mine was the heaviest; as I'd feared, I had overpacked. Like the terminal, the parking lot was surprisingly small, and the van we appeared to be aiming for stood out like a great gray box. I realized that I hadn't given much thought to the logistics of transporting forty people at the same time. If I did the math (slowly, thanks to jet lag) that meant four vans, if everybody got cozy. A caravan of four vans was going to stand out wherever we went— an invading army of middle-aged women.

"I'm the driver," another woman said loudly, over the sounds of planes and traffic. Her I recognized: Brenda something-or-other. We'd lived in the same dorm for a year, and she looked remarkably unchanged. "I only got here yesterday, so this may be an adventure. But we have a GPS that speaks English! Get your bags stowed in the back so we can head out."

We shoved suitcases, backpacks, and totes into the rear of the van, then sorted ourselves out among the three rows of seats. Apparently

Brenda already had assigned someone to the shotgun position, to read maps and road signs—I thought her name was Denise, but it was hard to tell from the rear. It would all get sorted out later, I hoped.

Brenda managed to find her electronic card, money, and the correct exit, and after a few loops through the parking lot we were on the road for . . . someplace I hadn't been able to find on a map. There were a lot of places on our detailed itinerary I'd never heard of. As an art historian, I had once known enough to identify the major cities, and maybe a few of the regions, but the little towns? Not a chance, not unless there was some major monument or work of art there—those places I could name, even if I'd never been there. In any case, I hadn't volunteered to do any of the driving on this trip: I would be hopelessly lost in minutes. Under the best of circumstances I was directionally challenged. The problem had gotten worse in the last few years, and nowadays I really had to stop and think about which way I was going, on foot or in a car. I kept telling myself I was saving room in my brain for really important things, and I could always ask my cell phone or a GPS for directions. That worked—most of the time.

But now I was among friends, or at least women who shared many of the insidious changes that came with age. From a quick scan of the small group so far, no one appeared particularly decrepit, and everyone exuded enthusiasm. But it was early days yet. How would we all feel in ten days?

Damn it, Laura! I reprimanded myself. *You sound like an old biddy, always expecting the worst.* Stress and lack of sleep had brought out all my negative traits; at this moment I was sure I was less intelligent, less interesting, and less successful than anyone else on this trip. Everybody else seemed to know each other, chatting happily away, while I had barely kept in touch with a couple of my college roommates, and with only one exception they hadn't even bothered to come on this trip. Why had I? Was I trying to prove something? To myself? To my daughter?

Stop it. I was here to enjoy myself, in a beautiful country, in the company of interesting, intelligent women with whom I shared a history. All I had to do was relax and go with the flow. I could do that. I turned to my neighbor, whose name I thought—hoped—was Sharon, and asked the logical question: "So, what have you been doing the past forty years?" And talk flowed easily after that.

5

According to our itinerary, we were staying at a place called Capitignano, and the nearest town was called Borgo San Lorenzo. My maps failed to show either, and when I'd searched online, I couldn't seem to find a map that would show both tiny towns and where they were within the country at the same time. In effect, I had no idea where we were, beyond Italy, somewhere near Florence, maybe to the north. I had to keep reminding myself that it was not my problem. Presumably the driver knew where she was going, and I was just along for the ride, so I settled back and admired the scenery. From the airport we took a couple of *Autostrada*—highways I could recognize anywhere, and I enjoyed mentally sounding out the names on the signs. As we drew farther away from the airport, the roads became progressively smaller, and the surrounding hills (or would they be called mountains here?) both nearer and higher, the buildings, mostly stucco or stone, spaced more widely. We went around more than one rotary or roundabout or whatever the heck they were called in Italy, sometimes more than once—there were stacks of signs at each exit from the rotary, and there really wasn't time to read them all until you were already past them. Driver Brenda took it all in stride, even though she admitted she'd been driving the van only since the day before and was still learning the ropes. No one seemed worried. I certainly wasn't; I had handed off responsibility once I reached the airport. Maybe my new mantra was NMP, for Not My Problem.

More small roads, more turns. Olive groves, vineyards, fields and verges strewn with red poppies. We passed a couple of towns that looked surprisingly modern, and I had to laugh at myself: had I really thought that everything outside the cities would be quaint and historic? This was, after all, a functioning country (well, except for the government, anyway) and life had moved on since the time of the Romans and the Renaissance, even though there were plenty of remnants of earlier eras almost everywhere you looked. We were in rural territory now. There were lots of buildings built of terra-cotta-colored stucco, with tiled roofs that often sprouted tufts of grass. The buildings seemed to have grown organically, with additions slapped on as needed until the building sprawled over several levels. Every time I turned my head there was another photo opportunity, although I wasn't much of a photographer and all I had was a point-and-shoot camera and my cell phone. I restrained myself and just looked. I didn't want to see Italy through a camera lens; I wanted to *see* it.

Up in the front Brenda was recounting some story about driving directions. "When I first heard the directions, I was told that I was supposed to turn right across from the big tree. Then the tree fell down in a storm a couple of weeks ago — see? There is it — so now it's turn right across from the dead tree lying on the ground. Who knows how long that will last?" She laughed as she made the right turn onto a road twisting its way upward. It was barely wide enough for two vehicles, much less a car and a monster van, and I shuddered to think what would happen if we met someone coming down. Apparently Brenda shared that fear, because she sounded the horn vigorously at each turn, and there were a lot of turns.

The road climbed steadily, passing a few houses on the lower part of the hill, fewer and fewer as we went higher. Finally we came to a left-hand turn, marked by a single sign nailed to a post: Capitignano. "This is it, folks," Brenda said cheerfully. "Check out the top of the hill." She slowed to allow us to admire the view, and it was definitely worth admiring.

Beyond the ranks of grapevines and the rows of olive trees, the drive — now definitely one-lane — flanked by tall cypresses led to a cluster of stucco buildings seated regally at the top of the rise. The van's engine labored to make the grade, but we finally pulled in at a level graveled area in front of one building, where two other matching vans were already parked. It took a few moments for everyone to clamber out of the vehicle, and then we all stood around, looking, I thought, a bit dazed. Brenda herded us into the building.

"There are information packets with updates on the table there, plus name tags for all of you," she said authoritatively.

I felt a spurt of relief that I wasn't the only one who didn't recognize everybody. Name tags would be a blessing.

She was still talking, so I had to focus. "There's also a sketch map of the property, with the various buildings labeled on it. Your room assignment is in the packet. Some people arrived yesterday and others will be here later. Find your place, unpack, chill out, and we'll all meet at the big building down the hill, at the opposite end from here, for drinks and dinner at seven."

I checked my watch: it was already six o'clock. Midday for me back home, so I should be alert, right? I found my packet and pulled out the map, which showed a lot of small buildings.

"Hey, Brenda, can you point us in the right direction?" I asked.

"What? Oh, sure. Where are you assigned?"

I pointed to a blob on the map.

"Right, the back end of the villa. Go around this building, follow the drive past the tennis court and around the next building, then go down the stairs. Your room is at the back. There's a key in the door, but nobody bothers with them here. Once you get there, you'll see where we'll be eating, right down the hill."

"Thanks," I said dubiously. We all went back outside, dragged our suitcases from the back of the van, and set off in different directions. The wheels of my suitcase left twin tracks in the neat gravel, and I felt like I ought to apologize to someone. I concentrated on keeping my footing—the paths kept shifting from gravel to flagstone to brick to grass, in no particular order. I passed the tennis court, which clearly hadn't hosted a tennis game in quite some time; passed the next building, went around to the back and down a short flight of stairs, and found myself in front of two heavy, ornate wooden doors, one of which had a key in the lock. This must be it. I set down my suitcase with a sigh of relief and turned to check out the scene.

Oh my God. From where I stood I had a one-hundred-eighty-degree view of rolling Tuscan hills, stacked up against the horizon. Small villages nestled in the valleys below; here and there a plume of smoke rose. Clouds drifted across the blue, blue sky. On both sides, more olive trees marched down the slopes. In front of me lay two buildings; the larger one must be where we would be eating. No one was in sight; the only sounds were natural. No cars, planes, electronic devices—just blessed silence. Except for a low buzzing: I looked to my right to see a large tree covered with small yellow blossoms, and when I approached it I realized there were bees feasting on all of them. The whole tree buzzed. I retreated a respectful distance and inhaled the sweet scent of the tree, tinged with a hint of wood smoke and maybe a dash of pine—or was it rosemary? It didn't matter; it was all wonderful.

And it was my home for the next few days. With no little regret I turned my back on the spectacular views and opened the door.

Benvenuti in Italia!

Chapter 2

Once inside the room, my first impression was that it was dark, and I realized that it had no windows. I fumbled for a light switch on the wall next to the door and pressed it, turning on a lamp across the room. It must have had a forty-watt bulb, which didn't help much. The ceiling was high, crossed by massive wooden beams that looked authentic and old. I parked my bag and wandered through a doorway on the right that led to a second, smaller room, dominated by a desk surrounded by bookshelves; there was a high window over the desk. A narrow hall to the left led to a bathroom at the rear. The floors throughout were made of richly ornamented glazed tiles, as were half the walls in the bathroom.

Back in the larger room I contemplated what to do next. There was no sign of Cynthia, my intended roommate, but that didn't surprise me. I didn't want to leave my suitcase in front of the door where we would trip on it, so since I had arrived first, I claimed the sole luggage rack and set it next to the door in the smaller room, out of the way. I opened my suitcase, and as I expected everything was squashed and wrinkled. It didn't seem worth hanging anything up, which I assumed could be done in the high armoire at the end of the hall, and I knew from experience that after a few days the jumble in the suitcase would only get worse. I left the mess as it was. People would just have to take me in wrinkled clothes.

I sat on one of the twin beds and leafed through the information package I'd picked up. Jean and Jane had kept us updated by email over the past couple of months, the excitement level of the emails ramping up steadily, but now it appeared that there were yet more changes, mainly additions to the already jam-packed schedule. We were going to be very busy campers, and I was glad I had brought my most comfortable shoes. This would not be a trip for fashionistas in three-inch heels. Or was I maligning my classmates? From what I'd seen of them so far, comfort had won out over style.

I was afraid to lie down because there was a good chance I'd fall asleep and miss dinner, or at least the drinks and socializing before dinner. I wanted to get there while people were still wearing their name tags, if I hoped to have a chance of remembering anybody at all. I started to remove my jacket—I'd worn all my heaviest clothing on the plane, since the suitcase was bursting already—and then I realized how chilly the room was. Plastered walls, tiled floor—lovely but cold. There was a thermostat on the wall near the door, but when I poked at it nothing happened. Of course it didn't: this was June. Who needed heat in Tuscany in June? No doubt it had been turned off for the season. I quickly abandoned any idea of putting on something fancier for our first dinner together and turned instead to thinking about what layers I could add. Thank heavens I'd brought socks.

After a few more minutes of fidgeting, trying to kill time, I couldn't stand it anymore so I went out in search of some sort of human activity. I armed myself with my camera—I might as well record the spectacular views when I had the time, and while the sun was shining. I stood in front of my door and looked around. Quick inventory, left to right: spectacular view, small building, large building, more spectacular view. I snapped a couple of pictures, then picked my way cautiously down the flagstone path in front of me, stopping every few feet to snap yet more pictures as the view shifted, or the clouds did. At this rate I'd fill my camera's memory card with hills ‍and sky. When I was about halfway down the hill I noticed other women drifting toward the larger building on the right below, and I hurried to join them. First I made sure I was wearing my name tag, in case people didn't recognize me. I'd been half a person more slender forty years ago.

It was clear when I reached the building that I was not the first to arrive—not even close. The double doors opened onto a small vestibule, with a bar on one side, where a forty-something dark-haired man with a five o'clock shadow was dispensing a complicated aperitif involving some red liquid plus slices of blood oranges; on the other side two men and a woman were bustling around cooking. On a table in front of the bar were set platters with appetizers—thin slices of prosciutto, small pieces of toasted bread spread with what I guessed was some form of paté, and more—and I realized how hungry I was when I started drooling like one of Pavlov's dogs. When had I eaten my last meal?

I decided to grab food first, since it was disappearing rapidly, and then a glass of wine. Thus supplied, courtesy demanded I get out of the way so that the next wave of hungry travelers could follow suit, so I followed the crowd up a short flight of stairs into the single large room above. There was a fireplace immediately to the left with a log fire burning briskly, and already a lot of women were sitting or standing around it, many still wearing jackets or windbreakers. A couple of long tables and a scattering of smaller round ones were set for dinner, all garnished with bouquets of wildflowers and grasses, and good smells wafted up from the small kitchen. I wondered briefly how that small cooking space could produce enough food for forty people, but I doubted that we'd go hungry.

I had barely made it up the stairs, juggling a wineglass in one hand and a napkin wrapped around some of the tempting appetizers, when a woman bore down on me. "Laura! Is that really you?"

I looked at her face and drew a blank. I sneaked a look at her name tag and the light dawned. "Connie! You look great!" I meant it: she looked nothing like she had forty years ago, when she had looked like a schmoo, a style not improved by the saggy jeans and sweaters she had favored then. "I saw from the list that you were coming. Let's sit down and you can fill me in on what you've been up to."

"Great," Connie beamed. She waved to a couple of other people. "Hey, Pam, Ginny, come join us." As they approached, she said helpfully, "You remember Laura, right? Art history, wasn't it?" Pam and Ginny gave hopeful smiles, and I was pretty sure they didn't remember me any better than I remembered them. At that point I made an executive decision to forget about learning everyone's surnames and try to keep their first names straight in my head. Luckily, Pam and Ginny sat down with us, and when someone on the staff came around and poured another round of wine, nobody said no. Our chatter followed predictable paths: you look great (did anyone ever say you look like hell?), are you with anyone (apparently it was politically incorrect now to ask if someone was married or even about the gender of a partner), do you have any kids (no pictures, please), what are you doing (more PC talk—it wasn't cool to ask do you now hold or have you ever held a paying job). But as the talk went on, I relaxed. Nobody was here to judge or to claim superiority in her lifestyle choices—and there was a pretty good range, based on what I was hearing. This might actually be fun.

After half an hour of talk, the volume escalating as the drinks flowed, someone suggested that we find seats for dinner. Our group of four filled one of the smaller round tables, so we stayed where we were. I watched the dynamics of the crowd: obviously some old friends had reconnected, or maybe they had never disconnected, but there was nothing cliquish about the seats people chose. All good. And then food started appearing and the talking died down—fast. Everything tasted wonderful—not fancy, but clearly fresh and local. We dug in with healthy appetites, whetted by travel and by the clean fresh air of the Tuscan hills.

Halfway through the main course, out of the corner of my eye I noticed some new arrivals, including my wandering roommate, Cynthia. Past and present roommate, that was. We'd shared an apartment in Cambridge for a few years right after college, surviving each other's company without killing each other, and we'd kept in touch since. But life had taken us in different directions, both geographically and professionally, so we were no longer as close as we had once been. I hoped that this sojourn to Italy would help us reconnect.

The latecomers were greeted by Jean and Jane and made laughing apologies for their tardiness, claiming they had gotten lost, more than once. Not for the first time I wondered how we'd ended up with leaders whose names were so similar, which was bound to cause confusion. This was the first time I'd seen them in person since the official reunion at the college a year ago. I'd known them both but not well.

Cynthia spotted me and made her way over to our table.

"Laura, there you are! Are you all settled in already?"

"I got here a couple of hours ago. You remember Connie and Pam and Ginny?" I waved vaguely at the other women at my table.

Cynthia cocked her head. "I think so, but my head is swimming right now. I'm a terrible navigator—can't tell north from south. Can you squeeze me in at your table? I'll go cajole some food from the hunky staff."

We found an extra chair just as Cynthia returned with a full glass of wine, followed by the guy who had been tending bar carrying a laden plate. She gestured to her seat and he set it down with a grand flourish. *"Grazie mille,"* Cynthia thanked him, and he bobbed his head and all but blushed before retreating. Cynthia dropped into the chair. "Isn't this great? Tell me what I've missed so far, while I stuff my face."

While Pam and Ginny obliged, I studied Cynthia. Back in the day, when we were both young, we'd struck a good balance: tall blonde Cynthia was the charmer, the social butterfly, but with a sharp mind and an eye for long-term strategy. I was shorter and darker, and I was the steady plodder, dutifully collecting footnotes and polishing my thesis. Cynthia had dated a lot of guys, none for long; I had dated not much at all. After we'd gone our separate ways, Cynthia had married twice—that I knew of. The first marriage, for which I'd been a bridesmaid, had ended in a nasty divorce; I wasn't sure what had happened with the second. She did something I didn't begin to understand for a high-tech firm that she'd joined when it was a start-up, and if I remembered right she was now an executive vice president for the same firm, thirty-plus years later. She should have great tales to tell about the evolution of the electronic universe during that time. But she was looking stretched thin now, speaking a little too gaily, focusing high beams on whoever she was listening to at the moment. We clearly had some catching up to do, but there was time enough for that later, when we weren't in the middle of a crowd.

We were halfway through the dessert course and many people's eyelids were just beginning to droop, when there was the sound of a metal utensil clinking on a glass. Announcement time, apparently. I turned in my seat to see Jean and Jane standing at the far end of the long room.

"*Benvenuto, viaggitrice!*" Jean said cheerfully. "I'm so glad you're all here, and I hope you've settled in. I know this place can be confusing, and maybe if I give you the short history it will make more sense. I hope most of you have met the owners, who have so graciously made their place available to us. Please, Barbara and Gerald, stand up so everyone can see who you are!"

A couple only a few years older than our own age stood and waved. American, from what I'd overheard, although apparently they had lived in Tuscany for quite a while. He was a professor, I thought, and I couldn't remember what she did—other than run the place where we were now staying.

Jean went on, "I hope you'll all have a chance to get to know them while we're here. They won't mind if I tell you about the place. This used to be a working farm, but Barb and Gerry were driving around this area years ago and saw it, and they fell in love with it, just like that. They bought it only a few months later. Now, when they first saw it, only the villa up where we parked was habitable. Believe it or not, all the rest of the buildings here, the ones you're staying in, were farm buildings. This one was the hay barn—that's why the brickwork outside the windows is open, to let the air move through so the hay won't rot or explode. The smaller building next door, where several of you are staying, was where the animals were kept. So, yes, some of you lucky ladies are living in a stable for the next few days. Barb has spent years fixing the place up. Now they take guests and some educational groups—and people like us. Let's give them a round of applause for making us feel so welcome!"

Everybody in the room, fueled by wine and good food, clapped enthusiastically.

Jane took over. "Just a few details and we'll let you go for the evening. Rest up, because tomorrow will be a busy day! If you recall your schedule, we're planning to visit several Medici villas in the area—we thought we'd give you an easy day before we took you to Florence and all its wonderful museums. But first thing in the morning we'll be visiting a small monastery that was supported by the Medici. And don't forget—tomorrow night is our murder mystery dinner! Several of our members have been working hard to put this together, and we hope you'll have a good time!"

I'd seen the description of the evening's entertainment on the earlier schedules and I'd carefully avoided volunteering for any part of it. I'm a lousy actress—too self-conscious. Once I thought I would outgrow that, but now I just accepted it as who I was. Let others strut their stuff; I'd watch and applaud.

"Oh, and one last-minute addition that we're very excited about," Jean hurried to add before we all scattered. "Wellesley College Professor Emeritus Anthony Gilbert, who retired to Italy several years ago after more than forty years teaching Italian literature at the college, has agreed to join us on Friday evening and present a lecture on the Renaissance poets of Tuscany." She beamed at the group as if she had just handed us a Christmas present with bows on it.

Maybe it was the wine, or maybe the fatigue, but I wondered if there was just the tiniest moment of silence when Professor Gilbert's presence was announced. I remembered the name vaguely, although I'd never taken a course with him. I had a fuzzy picture of a young man (young—hah! He must have been in his thirties at the time we were on campus) with long legs, who dressed in open-collared shirts and blue jeans, in a day when that was the exception rather than the rule among faculty members. Maybe I was wrong about that lull, for the murmur of conversation resumed immediately.

"We have a lot to look forward to," Jean said, or maybe it was Jane this time, "so I suggest you all get some rest. Breakfast will be served in this building starting at eight o'clock, and the vans will be leaving at nine, from the main house at the top of the hill. *Buona notte!*"

Most people took the suggestion, standing up and drifting toward the front door. There would be plenty of time for talk later, with the luxury of days spreading before us. I looked at Cynthia. "You ready to go? Have you seen the room yet?"

She smiled. "No, I came straight here—just dumped my suitcase outside the door. I didn't want to miss anything. Where did they put us?"

"Just up the hill. I've got a flashlight."

"Ah, Laura—always prepared. Then I'm ready to go crash. Pam, Ginny, Connie—great to see you, and I'm sure we'll see more of each other."

We followed the crowd out into the dark. For once I could lead Cynthia, and I guided her through the dark to our temporary home.

Chapter 3

The flashlight app on my phone got us up the hill without mishap. Even from a distance in the dark I could tell that Cynthia's suitcase was another one that was smaller than mine. What was wrong with me? Why did I need to carry half my wardrobe around with me? I comforted myself by reminding myself that those people who had brought only shorts and T-shirts were going to freeze. Maybe I could rent out my extra long-sleeved shirts.

I opened the door and turned on the light, then stood back to let Cynthia enter. She stepped in and surveyed our domain. "Just like our dorm room, right? I can't tell you the last time I slept in a single bed."

"Bathroom's down that way." I pointed. "I can't testify to the reliability of the hot water." My statement was quickly followed by a god-awful thumping from the other side of the wall closest to my bed. "But I'm guessing that's a water heater, so maybe we'll be lucky."

"God, I hope so." Cynthia dropped onto her bed so hard that it bounced. "Any extra blankets?"

"I haven't looked. Try that bench thingy over there."

She bounded up and pulled open the seat. "Bingo. Are you going to take a shower?"

"I was thinking about it. I was also thinking about wrapping myself in five blankets and crawling into bed. I should have paid more attention to the weather report for this area."

"It's usually wrong anyway," Cynthia said, studying her cell phone. Then she pulled a second phone out of her bag and turned that on. "Lousy reception, thank goodness."

"You were planning to work? And now you're glad you can't?" I guessed.

"Yes, and yes. Those idiots back home can't seem to wipe their butts without my help. And they aren't even kids anymore."

"Are you going to stick it out at this job until . . ." I realized I wasn't sure when "until" was these days. Nobody in our cohort seemed to be retiring at all, much less at any fixed age.

"Until it's not fun anymore," Cynthia said, grinning at me. "But this time in Italy is for *me*, and I intend to enjoy it. You know, kick back, catch up with old friends, et cetera. If the company sinks like a stone while I'm away, so be it. Damn, it's good to see you. How long has it been?"

"A year? Two? Too long."

"You still hard at work?"

"Of course. I wouldn't know what to do with myself if I retired, not that I can afford it. I'm not the type to take up knitting or feng shui."

"Government pensions suck, right?"

"Yes," I agreed—then did a double-take. I couldn't recall ever telling Cynthia what I did professionally, apart from crunching numbers. "Wait, who said anything about the government?"

She grinned mischievously. "You didn't have to, although I must say I was impressed by your artful description of your job that didn't say much of anything. I deal in information technology, remember? I know a whole lot about a lot of people. The things I can tell you about our classmates . . ."

I held up a hand. "Don't, please! I'd rather find out the good old-fashioned way, by talking to them. And why did you feel compelled to do background workups on them?"

"Curiosity. I'm looking forward to seeing who tells the truth about themselves and who gets creative about their own history. Don't worry—I don't have any malicious intent. I was having fun seeing if my early assessments of them had panned out forty years later."

Reluctantly I asked, "And had they?"

"Pretty much. Although you might like to know that the quiet ones have done as well if not better than the ones who made a big splash right out of college. Like you, you dark horse."

"I just keep my head down and keep on truckin'." I smiled at her again. It was a relief that I didn't have to watch my words with Cynthia. With the others, none of whom I'd been particularly close to all those years ago, I could say something vague and turn the conversation to them and what they'd done with their lives. It almost always worked, and I ended up learning a lot more about them than they did about me. And to be fair, I was honestly curious about a couple of things, like why had this group of people opted to gather together now? Of course the location had a lot to do with it, but the group must have self-selected in some way. From what I could tell so far, a lot of these people had barely spoken to each other in college, much less after, so it wasn't just a band of friends taking a fun holiday together. I was looking forward to finding out what the catalyst was.

Or maybe there wasn't one. Maybe everything was just as it seemed and forty women had jumped at the chance to hang out with like-minded women in the sunny north of Italy.

I checked my watch and found I'd forgotten to reset the time. There was a five—no, six-hour time difference, which made it just past ten o'clock where I now stood. Tomorrow would be a busy day, and despite my internal clock telling me it was still early, I thought I should at least try to get some sleep.

"I'm going to brave the shower," I announced to Cynthia.

"You go, girl. If you're not out in half an hour, I'll send in the rescue team."

I snorted and padded down the chilly tiled hallway to the bathroom. I took a moment to study the plumbing, but at least everything looked familiar—hot, cold, a couple of levers to divert the water. I took another minute to chase a couple of long-legged centipedes down the drain (I couldn't bring myself to squish them, but I didn't mind washing them away), then turned on the water, which obligingly became nice and hot. I took a fast shower, toweled off quickly with scratchy air-dried towels, brushed my teeth, and hurried back to the bedroom, where I wrapped myself in a blanket.

Cynthia looked up from whatever she was reading. "Everything works?"

"It does," I said, briskly toweling my hair. "Have you looked at the schedule for tomorrow?"

"I did, and I get tired just thinking about it. One monastery, three villas, and then a home-grown play at dinner. I wonder if our brains will still be working by that time?"

"Maybe that's the point—we couldn't possibly be too critical of whatever they come up with if we're all exhausted," I commented.

"There is that. Wonder what the monastery will make of forty women poking around? I for one can't believe there are still monks in this day and age," Cynthia said.

"What, you can't believe men would actually choose to live without women?"

"I'm trying. I'll admit there are days when a nunnery sounds good—peace and quiet, plenty of simple rules. Think I could find one?"

"It would have to have wireless for you."

"True. But at least that's silent." She stood up quickly. "I'll grab a shower."

"Say hi to the centipedes!" I called out after her retreating back. I burrowed under the covers, pulling a third blanket up to my neck, and tried to read, but I was asleep before Cynthia returned from her shower.

• • •

Of course I woke way too early the next day, although I'd slept like the proverbial dead. Maybe all I needed to do to sleep well back home was drag a fifty-pound suitcase after me all day across a couple of continents. I opened one eye to assure myself that, yes, that was daylight filtering through from the adjoining room. I rolled over to check my clock—whoops, I'd forgotten to reset that too, and the math of adding six hours to whatever it read was almost too much to handle. It was nearly seven, local time, I decided. Too early for breakfast, and I hadn't noticed anything so modern as a coffeemaker in our room. I lay cocooned in my many blankets, listening to Cynthia's quiet breathing, and contemplated what the day and the week would hold.

We were in Italy: check. We had all arrived, apparently without mishap, and were now sequestered in this sprawling estate high in the Tuscan hills: check. Florence was a half hour away in some direction. I listened for a moment for any outside noises but all I could hear was a rather simple-minded wood dove or something like it that kept repeating the same two notes over and over and over . . . I dozed.

The next time I woke up it was half an hour later, and I figured I could justify getting up. I inventoried what I'd brought and decided on three layers of shirts and my jeans. If it warmed up later in the day—one could hope!—I could start peeling off T-shirts. No doubt that would thrill the monks at the monastery.

I took a deep breath and slid my feet out from under the blankets. Luckily I'd slept in my socks, so the cold tile floor wasn't too much of a shock. I tiptoed over to the door and wrestled for a couple of minutes with the heavy iron latch, a task complicated by trying to keep quiet so as not to disturb Cynthia. Finally it yielded and I stuck my nose cautiously into the outside world. Yup, still cold—definitely layers weather. There were signs of stirring at the hay barn slash dining hall down below, which was a good sign.

A muffled voice emerged from the covers. "What time is it?"

I shut the door. "Seven thirty. I think. My body clock has other ideas."

"Where's the coffee?" Cynthia's head emerged from under the covers and she scrabbled to push her hair off her face.

"Down the hill."

"What's the weather?"

"Nippy. Bundle up, dearie."

"Yes, Mother, and I'll take a clean hankie too." Cynthia grinned. Funny how quickly we fell back into our old roles. I'd been the manager, making sure the rent was paid on time and there was food in the apartment; Cynthia had been the gadfly, always on her way somewhere, doing things that sounded exciting. Now and then she had brought home some really interesting men; sometimes I'd found them at the breakfast table the next morning. We had reached a good balance and it had lasted four years, an eternity by postgrad standards. I wondered how we'd work it out now.

I dressed in record time to avoid standing around in the cold. "I'm going down the hill."

"I'll meet you there," came the muffled reply.

I checked to make sure I had my camera in the pocket of my windbreaker. After all, the sun had shifted overnight and the view might have changed infinitesimally. Even though it wasn't yet eight, women were drifting toward the building below in clumps of two and three. I joined them outside the door. It was clear there was a logjam in the lower vestibule, and I made an educated guess that that was where the coffee had been set up. Two people, including the darkly handsome bartender from last night, were busy filling carafes with yet more coffee and passing them over the counter to eager waiting hands.

I smiled at the person next to me, struggling to identify her without looking at her name badge — and then a lightbulb went on. Asian, short, slender and dressed in high fashion (which stood out amid the jeans and running shoes most of us were wearing). "You're Xianling Han — you were an art history major, right?" I mentally patted myself on my back: when we'd first met it had taken me a while to reconcile the spelling of her name with the way it sounded, "Shan ling."

"I was. It's good to see you, Laura. I gather you left the art world."

"A long time ago. You stuck with it?"

"I did. I'm vice president of an auction house now, still dealing in art. You?"

"I'm a quantitative analyst for a large government agency. Not what I expected to be doing." That was where I usually cut the description short. Time to change the subject. "Doesn't this remind you of our dorms?" I asked brightly. "Except I don't think we were so desperate for caffeine back then."

Xianling smiled back. "I know what you mean. It takes a real kick to get me moving most mornings. Good thing Italians like their coffee strong." We inched forward in the coffee queue, only minimally distracted by the announcement that there were hot croissants waiting on the other side. One must have priorities. "Have you been here before?" Xianling asked.

"Here where? Tuscany? Or Italy?" I responded.

"Both. Either."

"The last time I visited Italy was the year we graduated." And we were off, exchanging chitchat until we reached the head of the line and could pour ourselves coffee. It seemed only polite to move out of the way, since the line was still long behind us. We climbed the stairs. "You want to sit over there?" I nodded toward one of the smaller tables.

"Sure. You hold the table and I'll get us some of those yummy croissants."

"Deal." We set our cups down, and then I plunked myself in a chair from which I could watch other people coming in. The cold clear light of morning was not too unkind: most people looked reasonably alert and fit. No makeup among them (myself included), but I wouldn't swear that all the hair colors were entirely natural — but then, neither was mine. Clothing ran to fleece for those who had brought any, or sweaters and/or windbreakers. Sensible shoes all around, if sensible meant high-end running shoes.

Xianling returned with a full plate and two more people. "You know Valerie and Patricia, don't you?"

"Val," "Pat," they said quickly.

I made another quick scan of name tags. "Sure—weren't you in Art 100?"

The other women sat. "Not until sophomore year," Val said, "but I took some other art courses later."

"What was your major?"

"Biology, but not premed."

I laughed. "That was a real distinction back in the day. I started out in biology but jumped ship to art history pretty quickly. Those premed majors scared me, they were so intense."

"They had to be since med schools were taking so few women. Things sure have changed, haven't they?"

We all prattled on as the room filled and the noise level rose. In addition to the marvelous croissants, there were healthy offerings like fruit and granola, which I ignored. If I have a vice, it's an addiction to carbohydrates, especially first thing in the morning. We all refilled our coffee cups at least once. I noticed Cynthia come in—she waggled her fingers at me, then went to join a group at another table.

"What is it we're doing today?" one of my tablemates asked.

"A Medici monastery and many Medici manors," I said, admiring my own alliterative phrase.

"Wasn't everything Medici back in the day?" Pat said wryly. "Seems like they owned most of Italy, one way or another. I wish I'd paid more attention to Italian history, but I never thought I'd need it, and then of course I didn't have time to bone up before this trip."

"Where does the monastery fit?" I asked.

"Wait!" Val said. "I brought the cheat sheet." She fished something out of her roomy bag.

"Just the high points, please," Pat said.

"Okay, okay." Val scanned the sheet quickly. "Hmm . . . was once a convent, renovated by Michelozzo for the Medicis—that would be Cosimo's dad, Giovanni. They slapped their coat of arms all over the place. Wooden crucifix that may or may not have been made by Donatello. Fancy altarpiece by Fra Angelico that got moved to Florence, so we'll see that tomorrow. And there's still a small group of monks in residence there."

I didn't volunteer any information and let the names wash over me. Once I had been on close terms with the greats—Donatello, Fra Angelico, Giotto, Cimabue—but that was long ago, and I had to admit I hadn't given them much thought in years. Save for those few lucky ones among us who had managed to snag jobs teaching art history or working in museums, life had carried us away from art and music and the world of ideas for the most part. I tried to remember the last time I'd crossed the threshold of a museum—and failed. Years, anyway. But if the ambitious schedule we'd been given was to be believed, we'd be making up for lost time tomorrow in Florence, with at least three museum stops planned and a couple of optional ones. Was there such a thing as an art overdose?

Again there came the rapping of a knife on a glass, and we looked up to see Jean and Jane standing at the end of the room. "The vans will be leaving from the top of the hill at nine sharp," Jean said brightly, "so please finish up your breakfast and start making your way up there. We've got a busy day ahead!"

That sounded like an understatement.

Chapter 4

The day proved to be as long as I had expected, but far more interesting. The visit to the monastery surprised me, and by the end of the day I was still trying to figure out why it was also disturbing.

When the name Medici came up, as it did so often in this part of the country, I had expected grandeur and opulence, but the monastic establishment itself was surprisingly small and modest. Of course, in the past its wealthy patrons had embellished it with works from the best possible artists available at the time—for the patrons' private pleasure—but that didn't quite compensate for the small size, and the "good stuff" looked incongruous inside such a plain and simple space. At least they had survived the changes of the centuries, including the ultimate decline of the Medici. I told myself to stop being so critical; it was peaceful and charming and unspoiled.

The most surprising part of the visit was the tour guide: a young monk in full habit, who talked knowledgeably and comfortably about the artworks and artifacts we were looking at. It was only after a few minutes, in response to Jane's direct question (in Italian—he spoke no English) that he told us that he was only seventeen. That hushed a lot of us. I found it hard to imagine many seventeen-year-olds who were so self-possessed, especially when faced with a crowd of ladies old enough to be his grandmother in some cases, and few speaking Italian. But what was more startling was his assurance—and his commitment. He had chosen his path, he told us through Jane, before he entered his teens, and had stuck to it. He'd even convinced the rest of his family to rejoin the Church. Would it, could it last for him? Or at some point would he yearn for a wider world? After all, he had seen so little of life. I had no answer. I just knew that I wouldn't have trusted any path I had chosen at his age to be permanent—and I would have been right, about myself at least.

But the most unsettling part of the discussion came last, translated for us by Jane, whose Italian sounded fluent and authentic to my ears. If Jane had it right—and from the look on her face I wasn't sure if she believed her own translation—the young monk was describing the "discipline" that he imposed upon himself, which appeared to consist of daily flagellation, and maybe worse. In the twenty-first century? From the expressions of the others who were listening, and their sudden silence, it seemed that everyone was having trouble grasping the idea. And the boy — seventeen! — seemed so sure . . . We moved quickly to the cloister and began to take pictures of the ancient well in the center and the cat sleeping in the sun.

When we had seen our fill, our drivers herded us back to the vans. They had told us before we started out that morning that whichever van we chose, that would be "our" van for the rest of the trip. In other words, that group of nine or so people would be our travel buddies. I'd meekly followed Brenda to her van and waited to see who else climbed on board. I saw Cynthia heading off in another direction, but I didn't feel slighted. I wanted to talk to more than one person over the next few days.

Once loaded on board, we set off for the next stop: a (surprise!) Medici villa. Apparently the Medici had roamed the countryside around Florence, picking off nice properties as they went. I had to admit they had good taste. Getting to this villa proved to be something of a challenge: the only road that led to it was barely one lane, but more important, it sloped upward, all the way. If any van showed the slightest hesitancy and slowed, it was an iffy proposition whether they could resume the climb without backing up to a relatively flat section and taking a run at it. Needless to say, with nine people on board, most of the vans did this, more than once.

When we finally made it to the top, we found it was a smallish castle, in the middle of nowhere, but it was nice, and we were told in all seriousness that it had crenellation — apparently that last characteristic was important for status or dating the building or something, for reasons I missed hearing. The castle sat at the top of the hill, and there was no driveway that would take us any closer, so we trudged up from where we had parked at the bottom and arrived at the top panting only slightly.

We were greeted by an older man in a cap — not the owner, but someone who worked for the owner, or so I understood the explanation, which again I could barely hear. It was hard for Jean and Jane to make themselves heard outside, especially when people were spread out along the path, and half of them were busy looking at something else in the opposite direction. I was beginning to feel as though we had wandered into a chapter in a nineteenth-century novel. The aristocracy, the servants, the ancient castle—we visitors were the only anachronism.

We began by touring the terraced gardens, which apparently had been revitalized in the early twentieth century by a romantic-minded Englishwoman, which explained why there were so many roses. And views. I was coming to expect spectacular views everywhere and I wasn't disappointed. Everywhere there were banks of blooming flowers, and exotic trees, and a few olive trees tucked into corners; and then there were the mountains. I took more pictures, but so did everyone else.

Inside we started with a short tour of the ground floor of the house and I was drawn immediately to the kitchen, which opened off the sunny central courtyard. It was magnificent, a funny mix of old and modern, with rows of polished copper pots in all possible sizes hanging on the wall, and then matching rows of copper pot lids, and an immense stone sink—with a plastic bucket sitting in it. The center of the room was occupied by a table that would have seated twenty people easily, made of two massive single boards, with room to spare around it—and there was a flat-screen television hanging in a corner. The collision of past and present was tangible; we were standing in the room where our lunch was being prepared and where who knew how many Medici meals had been made.

The castle was actually still occupied by a family, which presented an oddly uncomfortable situation, although the family members appeared and helped to serve a delicious antipasto lunch prepared by a pair of aged retainers. The youngest family member—a granddaughter?—took advantage of the occasion to practice her English, which was surprisingly good. We were served buffet style, in a long room whose original purpose I couldn't fathom. We collected plates full of antipasti we had just seen being prepared, and after my first bite I was inspired to reevaluate my position on salami, which I liked far more than I remembered. Maybe it was just good, or maybe it was eating it under the watchful ghosts of all those Medici, surrounded by rosebushes and olive trees.

We distributed ourselves in a wobbly oval around the perimeter of the room. Each time we settled somewhere we found ourselves face-to-face, or side by side, with people we hadn't talked to yet, and I wondered idly if there was an algorithm to predict how long it would take the forty of us to sit next to each and every one of the others in the group. Still, I was happy that we would be sticking to the vans we had originally chosen, so we could keep count of our group and not misplace anyone. I didn't relish the idea of trying to explain in English to some sympathetic Italians that I'd been left behind by my tour group. I thought the relevant term might be *perduto* but I wasn't going to bank on it. So far we were sticking together quite well, doing the typical touristy things like oohing and aahing and snapping lots of pictures, of the tower and the roses and each other with the tower and the roses behind. The weather cooperated — still cool, but no rain. More comfortable, in fact, than blazing sun would have been.

After we had eaten we roamed about on our own for a bit, although we'd seen all the high points already. I made a point of ducking back into the amazing kitchen to thank the elderly woman who was still cleaning up. My feeble attempts at Italian produced *molto bene* and *mille grazie*. I didn't know if they were appropriate, but they seemed to get the message across, as the woman bobbed her head and smiled widely.

The printed schedule said we were allowed time for a siesta after we'd driven back from the villa. We quickly agreed that we were all too keyed up to take naps, and nobody was ready to admit they needed or wanted one. Instead we prevailed upon Brenda to take a detour to Borgo San Lorenzo, the nearest town of any size, in search of (what else?) gelato. It wasn't hard to find. We parked on the street near a small cluster of shops and then descended on the tiny *gelateria*, where we provided much amusement for the staff.

But I was on a mission. On my one and only trip to Florence, decades earlier, I had stumbled upon gelato without warning and ordered *nocciola* based solely on the name, since I had no idea what it was and I was feeling brave. The first taste hit me like a baseball bat to the head, and there was no question about the flavor: hazelnut. Uber hazelnut, mega hazelnut. It was spectacular.

Now I wanted to know if my memory was accurate or if I'd magnified it beyond all reason through the passing years. I ordered; I tasted. I think for the first time in my life I understood the urge to swoon. Nocciola hadn't changed, and it was still wonderful. It made me happy to know that I'd have many, many other opportunities to try other flavors of gelato, as well as to revisit nocciola as often as possible. We lingered in the small shop, simply enjoying being there, with no responsibilities beyond enjoying ourselves. The sun was shining and we were in Tuscany eating gelato. Life was good.

Cynthia and I didn't cross paths until we returned to the villa, sated with ice cream and sunshine. We walked in and flopped down in our respective beds almost simultaneously.

"How many more castles are we supposed to look at?" Cynthia asked, her eyes closed.

"A hundred? How many Medicis were there?" I responded, unwilling to move.

"Too many. And they all wanted to put their stamp on everything they touched."

"I noticed that. Like monogramming the silver. Does anyone still do silver?"

"The better question is, does anyone still get married and insist on matching sets for sit-down dinners that will never happen? You know, those big fancy dos with lots of presents?"

"Come to think of it, I haven't been invited to a real wedding in a long time. My daughter's friends seem to have no interest in tying a knot with anyone."

"Smart girls. Oh, sorry—women. They're a lot older than we were at their age. What about your daughter?"

"Aren't they, though? As far as Lisa tells me—which isn't much— she has no interest in getting married to anyone. She's enjoying her freedom." As always, I hoped that wasn't any reflection on what she'd seen of her father's and my marriage, or what came after. I kicked my shoes off and wiggled my toes. "Anyway, my impression was that the Medici had a lot of balls."

Cynthia snorted. "What, you mean all those coats of arms they plastered on everything? You are bad. Wasn't there a handout about the Medicis in that immense information packet?"

"Yes, but I don't remember what it said. I think the bottom line was nobody really knows what those balls were supposed to mean. The Medicis slapped them everywhere, like branding a building. Or maybe just saying, 'I was here and I bought the place.'" We contemplated our eyelids for a few minutes. Then I roused myself to say, "What's on for this evening?"

"I think the encyclopedic itinerary said something about a play."

I'd done my best to forget about that. "Oh, right, the infamous play. You didn't sign up for it?" I asked, somewhat surprised. Cynthia had never been one to suffer from stage fright.

"Nope. I thought it would be more fun to heckle from the audience. You?"

"Not my kind of thing. I will applaud when instructed to do so, but I don't have high expectations."

"How long until dinner? Or should I say drinks before dinner?"

I had to roll over to look at my travel clock. "Half an hour, maybe? Too short for a good nap. Want to go exploring?"

"How about we find a patio with a pretty view and just sit and stare at it for a while?"

"Works for me."

We dusted ourselves off, put our shoes back on (ugh), and ambled out to the small patio in front of our door, where a couple of chairs and a table awaited. We sat and contemplated the vista. I was still trying to make up my mind about whether I preferred the view to the right or to the left. On the right the valley was broad and deep, but there were more mountains on the left. It was a tough decision.

"Why do you think most people came on this trip?" Cynthia asked in a quiet voice.

I thought about why I had decided to do it and realized I was still confused. "You mean this particular group of people?"

"Yes, in a way. I'm trying to figure out the demographic of the group. I mean, they aren't all friends in the outside world, are they? How many of these people have you kept in touch with?"

"Apart from you? Only a couple, and only in a superficial way — you know, sending a holiday card, maybe. I did note that there was a peculiar concentration of people from one dorm freshman year or the year after — mine, by the way — but I don't know if that's significant or coincidental. I think a lot of them stayed there where they started, but I didn't."

Cynthia nodded, not taking her eyes off the view. "I saw that too. But, tell me — is this just an indulgence for most of these women? Are they trying to recapture lost youth? Or trying to figure out whether they have made something of their lives? I mean, as a group we set a pretty high bar, by the standards of the day."

"Huh," I said intelligently. "You mean we expected to go beyond the 'Mrs.' degree? How many reunions have you been to?"

"Uh, three, maybe? Silly, isn't it, since I live so close."

"I've been to the last few. And one thing that has made me sad is that so many of our classmates have said—or written, if they didn't attend—that they were reluctant to come for just that reason: they didn't think they could measure up to those standards. I mean, we have a higher-than-average number of CEOs and MDs and PhDs among us here. I can see that it might be kind of scary."

Cynthia tilted her head at me. "What's even more interesting is how some of these women have reinvented themselves, some more than once."

"Like me?" The shift from art history to my present career was not an obvious or a likely one. But once I'd found my path, I hadn't swerved from it. On the other hand, I hadn't risen very far, but I was content with that.

"Yes, you're one example, but not the only one. Take a look at this group. Do you see any scary power brokers? Any divas? We all seem quite ordinary. So far we've talked about partners and children and where we live, but nobody is throwing her weight around and de-manding, 'Look at me!' So I'd say it's not an ego thing. Maybe we've reached a point where looking back is more important to us than looking forward. Or maybe we just want to reconnect somehow."

"And we had to cross an ocean to do it?" I protested.

Cynthia nodded, once. "Maybe. Here *everybody* is out of their comfort zone. Maybe it's easier to be yourself that way." Her gaze shifted to the building down the hill. "Hey, look, people are arriving. This crowd likes to drink."

"With tonight's entertainment, that might help."

Cynthia stood up. "You are such a cynic. Keep an open mind and see if you can find your sense of humor. You did pack it, didn't you? You packed everything else you own."

In a mature fashion I stuck out my tongue at her.

Cynthia wasn't about to give up. "It'll be fun. You ready?"

"I guess so."

Once again I made sure I had my camera and my cell phone cum flashlight in my pockets, and then we went down the hill to join the growing crowd.

Inside, armed with a glass of white wine and some more lovely prosciutto, this time curled around *grissini*, I checked out the main area. A long banquet table had been set up at the far end of the room, perpendicular to the axis, and all I could think of was Leonardo da Vinci's *Last Supper*. Maybe that wasn't too far from appropriate: after all, this was a Medici murder mystery, and someone at the table would end up dead, and someone else would turn out to be a killer. Or maybe more than one someone—since I had stayed out of the planning I had no idea what the plot was. The designated players started drifting in, garbed in a motley collection of items that could loosely be labeled costumes. I guessed that the players had hauled some of them along with them, squandering precious suitcase space, or had scrounged once they arrived. The members of the group didn't quite match, nor did they hew to any known Renaissance standard, but it looked like people were having fun dressing up, particularly those with outrageous wigs. One person sported a bushy mustache that kept falling off. Nobody seemed to care.

It was close to eight fifteen when people started drifting to tables, including those at the "head" table. I picked a table with yet a different group of people. Cynthia, at a different table across the room, winked at me and turned back to her companions. Food started appearing and more wine bottles circulated. Everything tasted wonderful—nothing like tramping through castles on hilltops to work up an appetite.

And then the entertainment began.

Chapter 5

The performance started gradually. At first, the cast at the large table at the head of the room had been enjoying a meal just like most of us, but at some point they started speaking more loudly and more clearly, and the rest of us slowly realized that something was happening and maybe we should pay attention. The general din in the room diminished but did not stop entirely, and I had to strain to understand what was being said. Our cohort of actors displayed a lot of enthusiasm but a rather uneven range of acting capabilities. As I understood it — in the absence of any sort of playbill or guide — the person in the middle, who had the fanciest outfit on, was the count of something or other (names were particularly hard to decipher); the dumpy lady to his right was his wife, and the woman on the other side was his daughter, who giggled and simpered a lot, even though she declared herself to be an accomplished scholar. The rest of the table, as near as I could figure out, was made up of guests and hangers-on, both male and female, who spoke up in turn to describe themselves and explain their presence. I had a fleeting vision of all of us writing down what we thought was going on and then comparing notes later — I was pretty sure the results wouldn't match well. A couple of servants attended to the head table, dispensing food, drink, and the occasional side comment. Everybody appeared to be having a very good time.

An offstage knocking drew one actor away; she (or he?) returned to say there were callers at the gate or portcullis or whatever the heck the imaginary castle had out front. The Big Cheese in the middle of the table went out to deal with them — and didn't return. Nobody seemed to notice, as they went on emoting in all directions, carrying on real or fake conversations with their neighbors while they tried to keep the pieces of their costumes together. More wine was distributed, to the actors and to the audience. Several more people at the head table got up and wandered around, one or two finally following the missing count (it took them long enough!). Then all hell broke loose when one of them returned and announced that the count was lying dead outside, which resulted in much energetic shrieking from the ladies at the high table. They rose en masse and headed out the front door, followed by half the bewildered audience. Yes, there was the count, lying on the flagstones, liberally sprinkled with ersatz blood, a blood-smeared knife lying next to him. Poor count. At least s/he could stop worrying about remembering his lines.

We trooped back inside and resumed our seats, where the honored guests at the high table seemed only moderately concerned that their host the count was now dead. The head servant (I thought—or maybe it was a guest) came back in clutching a piece of paper, which was apparently a clue to something, but the chatter in the room was so loud that it was hard to tell what it was or what it meant. We'd only begun to digest that information when one of the other guests, a young woman who was apparently pregnant, stood up, flailed around a bit, then collapsed with great gusto in front of the table, apparently also dead (although she seemed to be having a little trouble getting into her role, because she kept twitching with barely suppressed laughter). Some people—including the late count's wife, who was still at the table rather than weeping over the body of her husband—seemed less than concerned that a guest had just dropped dead. The body count was rising fast. Including the count. Had to count the count. I was beginning to wonder how many glasses of wine I'd had, and I was fighting to suppress a bad case of the giggles. I had completely lost the thread of the plot. Was anybody else going to end up dead?

Since the recumbent damsel bore no wounds and hadn't been whacked on the head (unless I'd missed it), someone declared that she had been poisoned by someone at the table. It also turned out that the baby was really a pillow, and that was part of a grand scheme to usurp something from someone, which apparently someone else thought was worth killing for. I wondered if this had made sense on paper, because it didn't make much sense to me. The murderer finally revealed himself: he declaimed for several minutes, explaining everything (only partially audibly), and then all the cast, including the dead ones, stood up and bowed to raucous applause from the audience. And a good time was had by all.

But it wasn't finished yet. One member of the audience, Rebecca, whom I vaguely recalled was a drama critic in the real world, stood up and gave a blow-by-blow analysis of the performance—tongue in cheek, of course—that had many in the room laughing helplessly, including the dead count, who had rejoined the party.

The evening wound down until Jean (not Jane) reminded us that we were catching an early train to Florence in the morning and probably needed our rest. That occasioned another toast to the now-tipsy players. Finally we straggled out into the cool night air and Cynthia and I made for our room.

"That was fun," Cynthia said. It was too dark to tell if she was being sarcastic, and I was watching the path in front of us.

"Well, it was something," I said.

"Oh, lighten up, Laura—everybody had a good time. Isn't that what matters? I for one think it's refreshing to see our gang acting silly. There's not enough silly going around these days."

"If you say so. I think there were a few plot holes."

"Of course there were. So what?"

We arrived at our door. I sighed. "You know, Cyn, I miss having you around to keep me silly. Sometimes I bore myself."

"I'll keep trying. To be fair, I thought the playwrights did a good job of catching the flavor of the era—lots of intrigue, and people pretending to be something they weren't."

"Don't forget the murders, plural."

"Well, that went on too. Why the two, I wonder?"

"Well, if I understood it, maybe, the baby that didn't exist was supposed to be the heir to the count's riches and worldly goods, which means that the pillow stood to inherit a fortune. Wonder how they would have handled that a few months down the line when no baby appeared?"

"So who killed her? I mean, she was killed, right? She didn't die of a stroke or heart attack or the vapors?"

I squinted at Cynthia. "Do the vapors kill? No, don't answer that. I think somebody fed her belladonna, although from what I've heard, the dying part of belladonna poisoning takes more than a minute or two and is a lot messier. You know, vomiting and stuff."

"Hard to stage, on short notice. Consider it artistic license: she was poisoned. So who slipped it to her?"

"Either the count's son—there was a son there, wasn't there?—or his faithful servant, or somebody he paid to do it to throw us all off course. Which worked very well."

"So who killed the count, outside?"

"Uhh . . ." For the life of me I couldn't come up with an explanation.

Cynthia laughed at my confusion. "Oh, come on—admit you enjoyed it."

"Kind of. It was fun watching the actors enjoy themselves. I didn't expect it from a few of the people up there."

"People can change over time. And fun never gets old. What's the agenda for tomorrow?"

"Firenze," I said, rolling the syllables on my tongue. "I haven't been there since right after my senior year. I always thought I'd go back, but then life kind of happened."

"I know what you mean. I haven't done half as much traveling—I mean as a tourist, not just for business—as I always thought I would. I was in Florence once too. What I remember is the Duomo, which you could see from everywhere. The Ponte Vecchio and the goldsmiths there. A place that made incredible lasagna . . ."

"You don't remember the museums?" I asked.

Cynthia smiled. "I remember them as being very large, with lots of art hanging everywhere, most of which was boring. Oh, sure, there were a few high points, but beyond that I was hot and my feet hurt."

"Sounds like the Uffizi," I said. "It's huge. You kind of have to pace yourself and not try to look at everything. If you don't, you burn out fast and then you miss the good stuff."

"Now you tell me. I don't know how many museums I can take tomorrow. I may just find a table out of the sun and a cool drink, and sit and watch the world go by."

It sounded like a nice idea, but I thought I owed it to the former me to visit old friends—Botticelli, Bronzino, Michelangelo—and see if they still meant anything to me. "Dibs on the first shower."

And so we settled in for the night, with a busy day ahead of us.

Chapter 6

I awoke before Cynthia again the next morning and lay there fuming at myself. Why couldn't my body take advantage of this rare opportunity to sleep late? And if I couldn't sleep, what was I supposed to do with my time? Read? It seemed wrong to travel all the way to Italy to read a book that I could read at home. If I practiced yoga this would be a good time to do that, but I'd never taken it up. A stroll around the grounds? Maybe. There were parts I hadn't seen, like a swimming pool someone had mentioned. I could go study an olive tree or a grapevine up close. There was said to be a church dedicated to a local martyr — St. Cresci, was it? — at the top of the hill beyond; he'd achieved his status when somebody cut his head off.

Mostly I wished there was a way to get a cup of coffee without disrupting the staff's preparations for our breakfast. At least today the time for breakfast had been moved up to seven thirty so we could all shuttle to the nearest train station and catch an early train to Florence, where we had a marathon day ahead of us. I was glad we didn't have to drive into the city, at least on behalf of the drivers.

All right, I was looking forward to it, and Cynthia's scoffing the night before had made me see that. Sure, I'd done the museum thing in my distant academic youth, but I was looking forward to seeing some things again, with forty years' worth of experience and wisdom to temper my views. What I wasn't looking forward to was wading through crowds of tourists, and June was prime time for them. But as I remembered it, one could escape the masses by taking small side streets — the ones with no museums or historic monuments lurking on every corner. Florence oozed history in every alleyway, so peace and calm were hard to find.

The queue at the coffeepots wasn't as long today since people had figured out that there was plenty to go around, and they arrived at different times. Nor did the servers mind if we showed up early, bless them. No croissants, though. People were a bit more subdued today, as though saving their strength to tackle the city. Or absorbing as much caffeine as possible in a short time.

The weather looked unpromising, spitting rain, but I chose to believe that it would be better in Florence, which lay . . . somewhere.

Inland, I was pretty sure. Maybe south? After breakfast we cara-vanned to the train station, where Jane and Jean handed out individ-ual tickets. We filed onto a train car and grabbed seats, taking up most of a train car and no doubt terrifying the local population (well, not the teenagers, who regarded us mainly as an impediment to plugging in their cell phones and music players). We emerged into the San Lorenzo station in Florence after a fairly short ride and hud-dled together like a flock of sheep, getting our bearings, until Jean and Jane gathered us up and marched us toward an exit. Then we survived crossing several streets while dodging cars and buses and trooped to our first stop, the monastery of San Marco. The rain had almost, sort of stopped, which was a good omen.

This stop was the one I had most looked forward to, since the one time I had visited Florence, long, long ago, San Marco had been closed for renovations, so I had never experienced the Fra Angelico frescos firsthand. As somebody in the group muttered as we roamed through the monastic hallways, it was like viewing every religious holiday card you'd ever seen, all in one place. I happily admitted that a lot of the images looked familiar, but that was fine with me. What I hadn't realized was that each monk's cell had its own small fresco, either by the hand of the master or overseen by him. I wondered if there had been any competition among novices for the "best" pic-tures — and then I wondered which one I would have schemed for. It was a pleasant way to pass the time, and luckily the place was not too crowded early in the day. It was beginning to fill with groups of students by the time we were ready to leave.

Then on to the Bargello, which housed a lot of sculptures by Big Names like Michelangelo. It was nice because the place wasn't too huge — which I knew the next stop, the Uffizi, was. In the Bargello one could enjoy the artworks up close and personal: no Plexiglas or velvet ropes, and the guards didn't appear terribly concerned that we were breathing on their precious marbles and bronzes. And breathe on them we could have, but we were appropriately respectful, as be-fit Wellesley Women. It was intriguing to learn that on one famous Michelangelo tondo the man himself had finished the face of the Vir-gin, leaving the surface so creamy that I wanted to reach out and touch it, while only roughing out the rest. That kind of detail never showed up in textbooks on art history. You had to be standing in front of it, at eye level, to grasp the nuances. When I'd been here all those years ago, had I done no more than run through the museum and tick off the Important Works on my checklist, without taking the time to really look at them? How sad for the earlier me.

I've always had a sneaking fondness for looking at famous works from unlikely angles (irreverently wondering, what did they do for underwear?). No, I was not searching for whatever hid behind the fig leaf (not that there were many fig leaves in the Renaissance, those came later), but I thought seeing a piece of sculpture from an unusual direction conveyed a lot about the artist. My brilliant observations: most sculptures with feet had a long middle toe, and the sandals they wore would have been useless on a long march; most of the armor depicted would have impeded engaging in a battle of any sort, or even movement. And I still loved the flowered hat on Donatello's *David*, which, the guidebook reminded me, the artist had modeled upon an antique sculpture of the emperor Hadrian's pubescent male lover. Another note said that this had been the first free-standing bronze sculpture of the Renaissance. If that was true, then Donatello had done a damn fine job of it. Whatever the inspiration, the statue was a delight, and I spent quite a few minutes admiring the lovely young man from all sides, even taking note of a discovery made since my long-ago art historical days: David had tasteful golden highlights in his hair. Very nice.

Emerging from the relative cool and quiet of the Bargello, we were dismissed to find food and entertain ourselves until our scheduled tour of the Uffizi a couple of hours later. I looked at a pair of the nearest women, Christine and Rebecca, both of whom I'd known slightly in college. We'd spoken now and then at reunions on campus, and I said, "Food?"

They nodded vigorously, and then Rebecca, with a wicked gleam in her eye, replied, "Gelato."

I grinned at her: a sister under the skin. The heck with art—we were hungry.

It was rapidly becoming clear that if you drop forty women of a certain age into one of the great cities of the world, they will shop— after they've found a bathroom. And they will eat, no matter how hard they might diet at home.

The three of us found a small hole-in-the-wall lunch place with no other Americans in it and ate salami sandwiches and scarfed down bottled water. Then we set off on a gelato quest, led in theory by Rebecca, who had fond memories of an incredible *gelateria* somewhere in the small streets to the east of the Duomo. Finding it proved to be a challenge. Let it be said that having a purpose, whether it is tracking down Michelangelo's *David* or the perfect gelato, is a good thing, because often it takes you places you might not otherwise go (if you don't get run down by a moped on the street). On the other hand, if you and your companions are directionally challenged, you may see the same place more than once as you wander through the twisting streets. Even asking for directions in our broken Italian didn't help, and we kept finding ourselves going in circles when we tried to follow what we thought were the directions we'd been given. But in the end we found a magnificent *gelateria* called Vivoli, which lived up to its reputation. We spent an appropriate amount of time deciding how much to ask for and which flavors, then sat on a bench across the street from it and concentrated on the gelato. It was worth the hunt. And then it was time to go find our museum-bound group once again. At least now we knew the way.

Touring the Uffizi is like jumping into the ocean. You know there's a lot there, but you also know you're never going to see most of it—you're only dipping a toe in. It is vast, but you can't just hug the shore. There are incredible artworks clustered there, if you can find them. And if you can even focus your eyes after the first fifty or so rooms. The only moment that really stood out for me was finding an empty seat facing both *The Birth of Venus* and *Primavera* by Botticelli, and claiming it until the crowds of tourists parted long enough that I could actually see the paintings. I was glad I had waited. The famous Venus was a bit wispy, but Primavera was a babe to be reckoned with. I decided I liked Primavera better.

We shopped our way through the hordes of street vendors selling everything from knockoff suitcases to tomato seeds, back to the train station, collecting souvenir scarves and hats and postcards we'd never send, and then we gathered ourselves together inside the station, where jazz wafted from invisible speakers—or maybe from live musicians in a corner somewhere. We boarded our train without losing anyone. We were surfeited and sated by great art and bargains. All in all, a good day.

Dinner that evening was a somewhat subdued affair. We were, of course, all tired to some degree from trekking from one end of Florence to the other, plus the novelty of the trip had worn off and we were settling into our own rhythms. Happily the groupings kept shifting, so it was possible to spend time talking to people I didn't know well. Cynthia rambled off to one end of the room and sat down at the long table there; I found a smaller table and sat and was quickly joined by two people I hadn't spent any time with yet, Denise and Sharon, and then a couple more. We broke the ice by sharing our happy discoveries from the day and then speculating about what was to come.

"I'm glad tomorrow will be quieter," Denise said. "I think we're touring some local workshops, which should be fun."

"More shopping?" I said. "Florence wasn't enough? Oh, did anyone make it to the goldsmiths?" I felt a bit wistful: I'd been looking forward to seeing their wares, on the venerable Ponte Vecchio, even though I knew they were well beyond my budget.

"Hey," Sharon protested, "all my family demanded that I bring them souvenirs — some even gave me specific orders. But I admit that once I got to the Ponte Vecchio, I had to indulge myself. See?" She reached under her collar and pulled out a lovely pendant on a gossamer gold chain, and I had to sit hard on my jealousy.

"What about the rest of you?" I countered. "What single thing would you like to take back to remind you of this trip and what you've seen?" I looked at my companions. "Don't be shy."

The other women tossed out suggestions and balked at the idea of "only *one* thing." We weren't even halfway through the trip; who knew what other wonders we would see and want to remember? And, of course, would spending money on souvenirs help us do that?

"We don't have to decide right now, do we?" Denise said. "There's plenty of time. I'm looking forward to a little downtime tomorrow afternoon. We have to pace ourselves, because there's lots more coming."

"Don't forget the lecture at four, when we get back," I reminded them.

"Oh. Right." Denise was suddenly very busy cutting up her pasta.

Again, I sensed a curious hesitation. A couple of people at the table exchanged glances; others carefully avoided looking at anyone else. This was odd. "Did any of you take a course from Professor Gilbert?" I asked.

"One, my freshman year," Sharon admitted. "Distribution requirements, remember? Besides, he was hot. Although that's not the term we would have used then. Cute? Dishy?"

"You don't remember him, Laura?" Denise asked. "He must have been in his thirties then, which was young for a professor. Tall, good-looking. And he had charm, however you define that."

"What was his specialty?"

"Renaissance poetry, if I recall — it's been a while. I think the course I took was on Dante. Wonder if he'll be giving the same lecture? After all, this is Dante country, isn't it?"

"My freshman roommate took a course from him, second semester," Connie muttered. "He might have been a hunk, but he could be scathing with his criticism. She never took another humanities class after he ripped apart her term paper in front of the whole class."

"I heard stories . . ." Sharon began. "No, I won't go there. There were lots of stories floating around back in those days, and not all of them were true. It should be interesting to see him again. He must be, what, seventy-something by now?"

"Wonder if he's an old or a young seventy-something?" Denise asked.

"Wonder if he's got a wife, and if she'll come along to keep an eye on him," Sharon retorted, her eyes gleaming.

"A much younger wife?" Denise said, raising an eyebrow.

Interesting. Professor Gilbert hadn't been on my radar, but then, I'd been kind of clueless when I was in college, and I'd never liked swapping gossip. No doubt plenty of stories had sprung up around an attractive young male teacher — presumably not gay — at a women's college. I wondered briefly if Cynthia knew anything about him — she'd been much more tuned in to that kind of thing then. And since. Tomorrow's lecture should prove interesting.

Dinner wound down and I connected with Cynthia once again as we trudged slowly up the hill, my calves feeling every inch of it. I took a moment to look up, with the flashlight off. There were so many stars! I lived too close to the city to see anywhere near this many. An owl hooted somewhere in the distance, but otherwise it was silent. I could smell something sweet—lemon blossoms?—and rosemary.

"Beautiful, isn't it?" Cynthia said softly. "Are you glad you came?"

"I am," I replied in the same low tone. "I needed this."

"Tough times?"

"Not so much tough as blah. Too much same old, same old. Being here is like a jump-start—a clean break. What about you?"

"I just wanted to get away, and to think. Gives you a different perspective, doesn't it, to be surrounded by a couple of millennia of human history?"

"That it does. We should head up—I definitely want a shower."

"It's all yours."

• • •

I managed to sleep a bit later the next morning, which was just as well since we weren't scheduled to saddle up and ride out until nine thirty. Once dressed, I spent some time sitting on my patio watching the shifting light of sun and clouds sweep over the valleys below, and practicing just "being." *Be in the moment, Laura. Smell the roses. Seize the day.* I thought it was beginning to work. When Cynthia was ready, we strolled down the hill to join our colleagues and find coffee, not necessarily in that order. No croissants since that first day, but there was plenty of bread with local honey, in addition to all that disgustingly healthy granola and yogurt. At about nine Jean stood up to give the morning announcements.

"We thought after yesterday we'd have a quieter day today, so we've arranged for a trip to a delightful leatherwork factory in a town near here called Scarperia. The term *factory* is probably an exaggeration—the whole place is not even as big as the room we're in, but they produce some beautiful high-end leather goods there. Sadly, they're one of the last of their kind in Italy. We hope you'll enjoy the tour. Of course, there will be lunch. We'll be back in good time for Professor Gilbert's lecture at four, and he'll be joining us for dinner."

It was a short ride to the town of Scarperia, and we parked the vans next to a plain building on a nondescript fringe of the town. Inside we were met by the heady smell of leather, and we trooped through a small office to the open area where the goods were actually made. Jean had not been kidding: there was one room only, and every inch was occupied, with molds and patterns and hides and bottles of dye and cutting implements and any number of things I couldn't begin to identify. There were a few machines, looking antiquated, but everything was done by hand. There were only four or five employees in the place, led by a charming man who Jane said was past eighty and who took delight in explaining exactly what they did and how they did it—in Italian. I could grasp most of what he said, and Jane translated, but mostly we watched as his skilled hands molded polished leather in rich colors around old wooden forms, or rolled patterns in gold leaf onto a finished product. It was like stepping into a medieval atelier—techniques hadn't changed much in hundreds of years. A perfect time capsule.

And we were the perfect audience. A day before we hadn't known this place existed; now everybody clamored to buy something, anything, which startled the craftspeople (they recovered quickly at the sight of all that currency), and then half of us queued up for the tiny bathroom in the corner, while others split off to find an ATM so they could buy more beautiful leather goods.

We walked to a restaurant a few blocks closer to the center of town, where we had reserved an entire room, and sat down to course after course of amazing food (pasta with three different sauces!). And more than one wine, wrapped up with a shot of intense Italian coffee in a tiny cup, and then we sat there like Christmas geese, stuffed and happy. It was past three o'clock—we'd spent over two hours eating and drinking and talking. I was beginning to get used to the Italian pace of things—and I liked it.

And then it was time to load up and return to the villa and Anthony Gilbert's lecture.

Chapter 7

Like a flock of birds we emerged from our vans and scattered to our various rooms to stash our loot. Yes, I had broken down and bought something—one of the least expensive items in the leather goods place, not that they weren't worth their price—and wanted to take good care of it. We had maybe half an hour before the lecture would begin. I briefly contemplated skipping it, but now my curiosity was whetted: I wanted to see this aging hottie.

Cynthia had followed me in and was sorting through things in one of her carry-ons. "Did you know this Professor Gilbert?" I asked as I sat on the bed waiting for her to finish.

"Only by reputation," she said.

"What does that mean? I heard other people saying things like that."

"I heard he was like a fox in a henhouse. Good-looking single guy with a lot of eager young women worshipping at his feet. Easy pickings."

"Did you . . ." I wasn't sure how to end my question. Cynthia had been a bit more, uh, adventuresome than some of us back in the day. Certainly more than I was. Had she dated him? Or, heaven forbid, slept with him?

She laughed. "Not my type—too obvious, too full of himself. But I knew other people . . . No, I won't name names, and it might not have been true. We all had very active imaginations back then, didn't we? Still, this should be interesting. I wonder how Barbara and Gerry tracked him down? And why?"

"One way to find out. You ready?"

"I am."

This event was being held in what was called the library, which for a change was up the hill rather than down. It was reputed to be the only place on the estate that had a wireless connection. I hadn't checked, but there were usually a couple of people sitting outside staring intently at their electronic devices while ignoring the magnificent scenery behind them. There wasn't anything important enough in my life to require constant checking of my emails; I was on vacation, and the view was much prettier than any computer screen.

Inside the library, folding chairs had been set up in rows facing a makeshift podium. A few women had drifted in and were clustered in the back rows, glancing curiously at the guest of honor but apparently reluctant to approach him. Professor Gilbert was a tall and distinguished man, wearing a very professorial tweed jacket, talking with Barbara and Gerry at the front of the room. I took a moment to study him and I could see that forty years earlier he must have been drop-dead gorgeous. Age had treated him kindly, silvering his hair (still worn a bit long) and adding character lines rather than wrinkles to his face. He scanned the crowd and noticed me watching him, and he turned up the power of his smile. Nope, I'd never known him, but I found myself blushing anyway. Cynthia was right: this was going to be interesting.

People continued to drift in, in ones and twos, until all the chairs were filled and there were people sitting on throw pillows around the perimeter: it looked as though the majority of our group was here. Either everyone was fascinated by Renaissance poetry or they had heard the echoes of long-ago rumors and were curious. Or worse—been fodder for the rumors. At fifteen minutes past the scheduled time, Barbara tallied the room and turned to the professor, nodding at the crowd. He dipped his head in reply, a curiously courtly gesture, and stepped up to the podium. And turned on the smile.

"We won't be needing this, will we?" He pushed the podium out of the way. "Welcome, ladies. I'm flattered that so many of you have chosen to come listen to an aging scholar when so many other delightful options present themselves."

He paused and waited until he was sure he had everyone's attention.

"In the event that you don't remember, I taught at Wellesley College for many years. It was my first professional position, and I never left—that must seem unusual to you in these peripatetic times. But I felt that I had found my home, my niche, and I saw no reason to go elsewhere. I took retirement a few years ago—the New England winters were becoming increasingly onerous and I had purchased a small place not far from here quite some time ago, with an eye to spending my last days on Tuscan soil. Gerry and Barbara were kind enough to invite me to speak to you today, and I am honored to do so."

Again he looked over the crowd, a winsome half smile on his face. "I wish I could say I remembered who among you graced my classes all those years ago, but my memory blurs, save for the words of the poet, emblazoned upon my soul. I won't bore you with my academic prose, but I would like to speak of some of the earlier Italian poets, particularly Dante, who spent time in this lovely region. I do keep up with what my younger colleagues are doing at the college, and I see that there is a course on desire in Italian literature — this is the course I would love to have taught had the times been different then. Of course, one may interpret desire in many ways . . ."

At that point I tuned out on the details and watched the show he put on. He was still handsome — and he knew it. While I had no doubt the course he had referenced did exist at the college, he had made a point of introducing the element of sexuality in his talk, in a room full of aging women, some of whom may have lusted after him from afar — or even acted on it. He could have talked about flower symbolism or the role of the Medicis as patrons of the arts, but instead he talked of sensuality. He knew exactly what he was doing.

I turned to Cynthia. "He's good, isn't he?" I whispered.

"He always was," she replied in a whisper. "He's got our crowd all stirred up, eh?"

I was both amused and horrified by her comment, in equal parts, but she was right. The old letch. Many of the audience were eating it up, but others weren't. Surreptitiously I counted heads: there were several people missing. Taking a nap? Walking in the hills? Or avoiding Anthony Gilbert?

He spoke without notes for over an hour without losing his audience. He was charming, witty, and erudite. The applause when he gracefully wrapped up his talk was sincere, and the follow-up questions lasted another half hour. Finally he said, "Ladies — and Gerry — I mustn't keep you any longer. Your hosts have graciously invited me to share dinner with you and to spend the night, to spare me the drive back over these uncertain roads." That last comment brought a laugh from several people. "Let us continue our discourse over drinks and dinner. Thank you so much for your warm welcome." He turned off his smile and turned away to speak to Barbara, and the energy in the room dropped.

Women stood up quickly and headed for the door. I had a strong suspicion they were going to go to their various rooms and primp for dinner. Cynthia and I left more slowly; Cynthia never seemed to need to primp, and I really didn't care.

Once we were a discreet distance away, Cynthia said, "Well, that was enlightening."

I thought I knew what she meant, but I asked anyway, "What do you mean by that? I assume you don't mean intellectually."

"No, I don't. A nice bit of theater, don't you think? He knew what he was doing back in the day. He knows that some if not all of us know too, or if there are some classmates here who spent their four years in a barrel doing quadratic equations, somebody is bound to fill them in now. He's playing us all and enjoying every minute of it. Frankly I'm amazed he lasted as long as he did at the college."

"Times were different when we were there. Nobody had even coined the term 'sexual harassment.' We were all in a romantic fog anyway — or do I mean hormonal? Do you think he took advantage of any or all of those crushes, or did he know where to draw the line?"

"Since he hung on until retirement age, I'd have to guess the latter. I would like to hope that the college didn't turn a blind eye toward that sort of thing. But I could be wrong. Wonder what dinner will bring?"

"We'll find out soon enough," I said. I had to admit I was curious.

When we strolled down to the dining hall at seven, I smiled to myself: I had guessed right and a number of the other women now sported pretty shawls and makeup. Did we never outgrow that need to preen for a handsome man? My daughter didn't play that kind of games with her male friends, as far as I had seen. But some of us who had come of age in the sixties still clung to vestiges of the old ways: simper and flirt.

Inside I snagged a glass of white wine and insinuated myself into the crowd, all of whom were talking with great animation and many expansive hand gestures. I debated for about two seconds about introducing myself to the Great Man and decided there was no point — I'd never known him and I had no desire to know him now, based on what I'd seen. But I admitted to myself that I was curious to see who *had* known him — and who gave that away by their demeanor, rather than by anything they said.

I ran into Xianling, who was scrolling through images on her omnipresent iPad. "Xianling, are you trying to document the whole holiday?" I asked.

She looked up at me. "The thought had crossed my mind. But I do enjoy simply taking pictures. The professor is very photogenic, I find."

"I'm not surprised," I said.

Xianling tilted her head at me. "Not a fan?"

I shook my head. "I find him a bit too full of himself, even at his age."

"And yet he has his adoring followers still." Xianling gestured toward the group that surrounded him, now that he'd armed himself with a fresh glass of wine.

"You weren't ever one of them?"

"Hardly. Excuse me," she said, tucking her iPad in her shoulder bag. "I think I'll find myself a drink."

After she'd left I joined some of my companions from earlier in the day. "Hi, Sharon. Interesting lecture, wasn't it?"

"Oh, it was!" she gushed. "I wish we could have spoken so openly when we took classes. I feel I missed so many of the nuances of Italian poetry. You never took a class with him?"

I shook my head. "Nope, I took poli sci and psychology instead." Which had proved a lot more useful to me than poetry and literary analysis. "I wonder how Barbara and Gerry knew where to find him. Does he live near here?"

"Closer to Florence, I think, but that's not too far. I wonder what kind of expatriate community there is around here?"

"It sounds as though Professor Gilbert was smart—he bought a place here when things were cheap. So he lives here full-time now?"

"I do indeed," a male voice said behind me, and I turned to find the professor standing there—just a bit too close. "What I said earlier about the winters was one reason, but the truth is that I fell in love with Tuscany when I was an impressionable young man, and my affections have never wavered. It is a beautiful region, don't you think? And you are?"

Here we go, I said to myself, bracing myself against a blast of charm. "I'm Laura Shumway. You may have overheard that I never managed to take one of your literature courses at the college. My loss, I gather. Tell me, is there a Mrs. Gilbert?"

"Not at this moment, although there is more than one ex, I'm afraid. I have never taken well to fidelity."

I wasn't going to touch that comment. "Tell me, Professor — you must have seen many changes in academia during your time at the college. For better or for worse?"

He looked briefly disappointed that I didn't want to play his game, but he rallied quickly. "I applaud the return to frankness. Certainly the Renaissance masters were no prudes, and I'm sure you're aware of some of Shakespeare's bawdier bits. Only now may we talk about it openly . . ."

Points to you, Professor. I had asked a neutral question about teaching and he had diverted it right back to sex. "Excuse me, I think I need another glass of wine."

Sharon was hanging on Professor Gilbert's every word. Nobody noticed my departure.

The head table from the play had been left in place, and at dinner it was occupied by Barbara, Gerry, honored guest Anthony Gilbert, Jean, Jane, and a couple of their closest friends. Once again I was struck by the medieval aspect of it: they were the royalty here and the rest of us were the *hoi polloi*. At least we all got the same food, which, as usual, was simple fare excellently prepared. Accompanied by plenty of wine. Over the course of the meal, the lusty glint in some of the women's eyes morphed into an inebriated stare. Funny — nobody until this evening had overindulged, despite the ample opportunities. Throw in the good — or bad? — professor, and restraint went out the window. I sincerely hoped that he would take himself back to whatever hole he had crawled from and leave us to our activities. There was a reason no men had been invited along on this trip: their presence changed the dynamic of the group, not necessarily in a good way.

Dinner went on, and on . . . The wine flowed, and after a couple of hours the staff brought out something special, a superior local vintage, and it would have been rude to refuse it. It lived up to its billing, and I realized that if I didn't stop I'd be seeing double. I noticed that a few people had drifted out discreetly (and wisely), but the head table was still going strong.

"I think I'm going to turn in," I told my tablemates. "We're looking at a series of Medici castles tomorrow, right?"

"What? Oh, castles, right. Good night, Laura."

I picked my way out of the room, placing my feet carefully on the stone stairs. Outside I breathed deeply of the scented air. Better. The atmosphere inside had gotten a little thick, although with what I wasn't sure. Lust? I giggled at the thought—and was glad I had decided to call it a night. I made my way up the hill to my door, but once there I was reluctant to go inside. The weather had been warming gradually over the past few days, and now the evening was cool but not unpleasant, so I sat down on the patio chair and just listened for a while. I could hear the sounds of happy voices and clinking glasses from down the hill. Funny—in a way I felt like the kid who hadn't been invited to the party. Down below there was still light and conversation, and I was on the outside looking in. But by my choice, I reminded myself.

As I sat, people began straggling out, taking their various paths toward bed. Lights began going out. I saw Gerry come out with the professor; Gerry pointed, and there was much nodding between them. Then Gerry went back along the road to the main building—and Anthony Gilbert headed up the hill toward where I sat.

When he reached my little patio, he seemed winded and was swaying slightly where he stood. "May I join you briefly? I'm afraid I've let myself get a bit out of shape—my place is not so steep."

"Of course." I gestured toward the other chair at the table.

"We never met at the college, did we?" he asked.

Hadn't we already had this conversation? Maybe his memory was going—or he was more drunk than he appeared. "Not that I recall—and I have a feeling I would have remembered. A lot of these women remember you." *Not necessarily for the right reasons.*

"Times were different then," he said, more to himself than to me. "Perhaps I shouldn't have accepted the invitation to come."

There was a slight slurring to his words, although he was articulating very carefully. All those years of academic recitations seem to have served a purpose. "How do you know Barb and Gerry?"

"Gerry and I have participated in a couple of symposia to-gether — I hope you realize he is a scholar of some renown in his field. It was only recently that we discovered we were neighbors of a sort. When your colleague Jean was assembling this delightful event, he thought my lecture might be a nice diversion and reached out to me. Of course I was very pleased — I have such fond memories of the college. Barbara wasn't sure at first — she thought I might put you all to sleep — but I thought it went well. Didn't you?"

"Your audience was definitely paying attention," I replied. To what they were paying attention, I wasn't sure.

"I was so happy to see so many familiar faces . . ." he said, almost to himself. "Well, I suppose I should find my lodging." He stood up and then wobbled, laying a hand on the stone wall of the building to steady himself. I wondered if he could manage the stairs.

"Do you know the way to your room?"

"I believe I'm right above you, but the entrance is on the uphill side, facing the other way. Good night, *bella donna*. It has been my pleasure to make your acquaintance, however belatedly." He walked off into the darkness, grasping whatever handholds he came across, until he disappeared around the corner of the building.

I restrained myself from snorting, because no doubt he would hear. *Bella donna* indeed! The man was incorrigible.

Chapter 8

Cynthia straggled in after I'd crawled into bed and was trying to read the brief histories of the Medici castles we were scheduled to see the next day. I wondered idly what the total count would be. Had those Medici nobles built or seized them all at once or over time, grabbing every castle that tickled their fancy just because they could? What would that kind of power be like?

"Damn, some of those women simply won't stop talking!" Cynthia said, sitting down to pull off her shoes. "I wonder if their spouses or family members have stopped listening altogether and they're hungry for a new audience?"

"Maybe. Are they still down there?"

"A few. The staff was running around turning off lights—I think they want to go to bed. At least there's no rush tomorrow morning. And it's our last full day—after that, Liguria!"

"About which I know next to nothing," I said. "I can't even figure out where it is, or where the boundaries are."

"You probably ignored it because there were no major artists working around there. Or maybe I should qualify that: no visual artists. It's known for its rugged scenery and difficulty of access. Various writers and poets loved the place, maybe because they were trying to escape their adoring fans. Or maybe because all their friends were there. Can you imagine the luncheons and parties, with all the glitterati of the day? Anyway, we're supposed to see where Shelley managed to drown in sight of land."

"The fun never stops, does it?"

"Hey, chill out. This is a vacation, remember? A time when you have fun? You are having fun, aren't you?"

I stuck the papers back in the file. "Actually, I am. Don't blow my cover—I like cultivating a curmudgeon image."

"Whatever for?" Cynthia asked.

"Habit, I guess. Act prickly and people don't bother you."

Footsteps sounded on the floor above us—a first.

"Who's up there?" Cynthia asked, gesturing at the ceiling.

"The great professor. He told me that was his room."

"What, you actually talked to him?"

"He had to walk right by me to get up there, and you know he can't resist flexing his charm."

"Did it work?"

"He called me *bella donna*. I did not melt. Maybe he was off his game — he seemed a bit the worse for drink."

"A lost opportunity. Maybe he'll look like hell by morning sunlight and everyone else will let go of their long-cherished illusions."

Cynthia went into the adjoining room, I hoped to restore some order to the jumble of clothes she had spread over every surface. I didn't envy her the job of repacking when we left, the day after tomorrow. I wasn't exactly looking forward to packing myself — I couldn't even remember what I'd worn and what I hadn't, and it all seemed to expand when I wasn't looking. Our departure seemed so soon — how had it sneaked up on us? With a sigh I turned out the light by my bed and was asleep before she came back into the room. Without benefit of romantic fantasies involving septuagenarian professors.

· · ·

Once again I woke early — would this jet lag never end? I thought I spied sun filtering in from the other room: the weather was certainly being kind to us, after those first few chilly days. I could hear the same blasted dove cooing away. Weren't there any other birds around? A little variety would be nice.

I checked the clock: barely seven. All right, today I would slip out and enjoy the morning, check out the flora and fauna and all that good stuff. I probably wouldn't have the time tomorrow. I was pleased that my creaky body was holding up well — I wasn't used to so much walking, but if I was going to keep on eating at the current pace, I'd better keep walking or I'd have to roll home. Actually all the members of our group were managing the rigorous pace. Maybe those who knew they couldn't handle it had wisely stayed home, but surely there would have been some among us who were in denial and clung to the belief that they could deal with it — or that sheer willpower would prevail. Happily everyone had done just fine, so far. Maybe Liguria would be the true test — I'd read that it was more hills than anything else, at least until you hit the sea.

I tiptoed into the bathroom and pulled on clothes and shoes, then struggled to open the door without rousing Cynthia, not that she showed any sign of moving. Outside the air was fresh and just the right amount of cool—it promised to be a warm day. I saw a couple of the staff heading down to the dining hall, but none of our class-mates were out and about this early.

Where to now? What hadn't I seen? I was afraid if I ventured into one of the groves or vineyards they would be slippery with dew, and my shoes would get wet or I'd fall on my butt. I knew where I'd been, so it had to be somewhere I hadn't been. Maybe I'd go hunt for that mythical swimming pool—not that it was what I considered swimming weather. I stood up and headed toward the right and around the building. Past the ratty tennis court (I thought the space could be better used, since it was unlikely that anyone would be playing on the pitted surface again). Past the library with its siren Wi-Fi. Ah, around the next corner lay the pool. Actually it was surpris-ingly tasteful, a sheet of water reflecting the sky, tucked out of sight from most of the buildings. It looked almost tempting. Almost, if the weather had been about twenty degrees warmer and I had brought swimwear, which I hadn't.

The far edge all but overhung the olive grove below, and there was an uninterrupted view of the valley. I walked carefully to the end of the concrete bordering the pool and peered out, then pulled out my camera and took, yes, a few more pictures of the view. Hey, this was the seven o'clock view, rather than the eight o'clock one or the noon one or the four o'clock one. They were all different, weren't they?

I don't know why I looked down. Past the edge of the pool. Past the stone retaining wall that supported it while still blending taste-fully into the hill. And that's why I saw that the body of Professor Gilbert lay twenty or thirty feet below, sprawled in a way that made it very clear that he was dead. A neck did not usually bend in that direction. I knew immediately who it was. I didn't have to get any closer to recognize the silver hair and the bespoke tweed jacket. Pro-fessor Anthony Gilbert had met an untimely end.

Since I've been reading mysteries since high school, I'd always wondered how I would react to finding a body. I'm told that some women shriek, burst into tears, faint, run around in circles and do other inappropriate and useless things, but that wasn't me. I shut my eyes and opened them again, just to be sure I wasn't hallucinating. No, the body was still there.

It occurred to me that I should sit very still before doing anything else and make sure I wasn't disturbing anything that could be evidence — finally all that reading was paying off. I looked around me. No footprints (except mine), no bloodstains, no obvious weapons. I peeked down at the professor once again: no sign of blood. He could have slipped in the dark and fallen. There were many corners of this beautiful piece of land that were not lit, and someone unfamiliar with the terrain could easily make a fatal misstep. Especially after a dinner accompanied by much wine.

A fall would be the simplest explanation. Why couldn't I accept that?

Because I remembered that curious pause, that little hitch, in the flow of chatter when the professor's lecture had been announced, the uncomfortable glances, the odd comments. Enough little details that I had to wonder if maybe someone had helped him over the edge. One of us.

No one else had appeared yet. Still without moving from my spot, I reviewed what I remembered. When the professor and I had talked the night before, he'd told me he was looking for his room, and I'd heard him — or someone? — overhead not long after that, around eleven, when I was already in bed. Cynthia could attest to that, which meant that I had an alibi. Not that I could possibly need one: I hadn't even met the man until the day before. I had no motive for killing him.

But could I say as much about the other women here?

And why had my imagination gone straight to murder?

But the immediate question was, what was I going to do about it?

I remembered suddenly that I had my camera in my pocket. I should take pictures, in case something was disturbed later. I stood up and peered gingerly over the edge once again, then snapped a few shots, regular and zoom. I looked around me and snapped others, showing the absence of any sign that anyone else had been there lately. I noted the time on my watch, in case anyone asked. I looked up at the windows overlooking the view, to see if anyone else could have witnessed or overheard what happened. None were in a direct line of sight. This side of the main building housed primarily storage or work-related areas, not bedrooms. If this had happened near midnight, it would have been hard to see anything, even a few feet away.

I sat down again to think. One of the resident cats — mouse catchers rather than pets — came out and butted its head against my knee, then lay down, baring its belly to the warmth of the rising sun. I absently rubbed its tummy. I had found a body; it was my responsibility to tell someone about it. To the best of my knowledge, Barbara and Gerry's rooms were in the main house up the hill from where I sat. This was their property, therefore they should take charge. They should know what to do. I assumed someone would have to call the *polizia* or the *carabinieri* or whoever handled deaths in this country — I wasn't familiar with the local pecking order. I should have paid more attention to the details of the Amanda Knox case, but I had never thought I would need such information.

I wondered how it would affect our plans. Or would it? If the professor's death was determined to be the result of a fall, a misplaced step in the dark, then it would have nothing to do with us. If it wasn't an accident, things could get a lot more complicated. I was first on the scene, and I thought that maybe the way I told the story might, just might, set the tone for the police response to this death. Accident or something darker?

I still hadn't done anything. I took a deep, steadying breath. The cat got up and stalked away after something in the bushes. Time to talk to Barb and/or Gerry.

But first I made a phone call. I would have done it anyway, given my job. I wanted to put someone higher up on alert that not only was I the person who had found the body, but I had some suspicions about the manner of death. And I was in a foreign country and I didn't know protocols in Italy. I didn't plan to share those suspicions with my friends here. In fact, I'd try my best to support the accident theory, unless something came along to upset that. This was supposed to be a happy vacation, a reunion of old friends. The death had happened, sadly, but it didn't have to tarnish things for the rest of us. Unless . . . No, I wasn't going to go there.

When I was through with my call, I stood up and brushed off the seat of my pants, then turned and skirted the pool to climb the stairs on the other side. I knocked on the front door of the main house, and it was Gerry who came to the door, fully dressed, his hair neatly in place.

"Good morning, Laura. You're up early. Is there a problem?"

"I'm afraid there is, Gerry. Professor Gilbert is lying dead on the hill below the pool. I just found him."

Gerry's expression betrayed everything it should have: disbelief, shock, then something resembling calculation. "I'd better call the authorities in Borgo San Lorenzo. Are you sure he's dead?"

Based on the angle of his neck, I had little doubt. "About ninety-eight percent. Is there anything I can do?"

"Just keep anyone else from going near the pool, if you don't mind. Are you okay? You seem very calm."

"Don't worry, I'm fine. If anyone does come by, should I send them all to the dining hall?"

"Oh, right, yes. Let me make that call, and I'll see what the police say. Thank you, Laura."

Thank you for finding a dead body on your property? I stifled a laugh: there was such a thing as taking courtesy too far. But I'd done my duty, so I took myself back down the stairs and stationed myself in a chair to block anyone from approaching from the lawn; I figured I'd hear anyone coming from the graveled drive above.

No one had appeared by the time I spotted an official car coming up the long driveway, without sirens or flashing lights. Now what? I realized that since I didn't speak Italian, it might be challenging to ex-plain what I had seen. I had no idea how good Barbara's or Gerry's Italian was. Which left Jane, the only one of our group who spoke con-versational Italian. What the heck was the word for "dead"? I pulled out my cell phone and called up the translation app: *morto, defunto, de-ceduto, spento. Il professore è morto.* Who here would mourn him?

I stayed put while I heard tapping at the front door above, fol-lowed by the door opening and voices, one fast (the *polizia*) and one slower (Gerry). Then a female voice: Barbara must have joined the discussion. Then the sound of booted feet on the stone stairs. I rose and turned to face the newcomer, a tall fortyish man in a neatly pressed uniform, accompanied by Gerry and Barbara.

"*Mi scusi, signora, ma posso parlare con te? Capisco che hai trovato il morto?*"

I knew what he was saying, but I wasn't going to take any

chances about being misunderstood. *"Mi dispiace, signore.* Gerry, I think we need a translator."

"Of course. Barbara, can you go find Jane? She's the most fluent speaker here."

"Right away, Gerry. I won't be long." She turned and hurried down a path. I realized I wasn't even sure where all the others were housed, scattered as they were around the property.

So there we stood—me, my host, and a handsome Italian police-man in a nice uniform, and below us lay the broken body of Anthony Gilbert, professor emeritus and self-declared charmer. Not quite what I'd expected from this vacation.

Chapter 9

Barbara returned quickly with Jane in tow. Poor Jane—she didn't deserve this. She and Jean had put so much effort into planning this event for us all, and I seriously doubted that there was a contingency plan for a dead guest speaker.

Apparently Barbara had briefed her on the basic outline of the situation, and Jane went straight to the senior official and erupted into quick Italian. I stayed where I was, assuming someone would want the details of how I found the body. The policeman, or whatever he was, was scrupulously polite to Jane. Well, why not? She was old enough to be his mother—as was I. Italian men were famously polite to their mothers. Would that help here?

After a few minutes of gesturing and pointing, Jane turned to me. "Can you tell me, him . . . us what happened?"

I ran through the brief story of my early rising, my stroll over to the pool to take pictures of the landscape, and my discovery of the body, while Jane translated quickly. No, I hadn't seen anyone else, unless I counted the cat. No, I hadn't seen any signs of a struggle or a fall—everything had seemed to be in place, although since I hadn't visited the pool before, I couldn't swear to whether anything had changed. I had recognized the body because I had met the man the day before. For the first time. And had spoken briefly to him after dinner, outside my door. And I had heard him—or someone wearing shoes—walking around in the room over my head after that. He appeared to be wearing the same clothes I had last seen him in.

Had he seemed despondent? the policeman asked. I shrugged. Since I didn't know the man, I didn't know what his usual frame of mind was, therefore I had no idea if he had strayed from that the night before. If I had to guess, I would say no. I did not voice my thought that in fact he had seemed to be in his element, surrounded by adoring women. Well, mostly adoring.

Had I heard any voices coming from above? For example, female? I shook my head. I hadn't heard anything except the footsteps, and I had no idea how long they had lasted because I had fallen asleep very quickly. I had pointed the sounds out to my roommate, who had stayed awake longer—perhaps she had noticed something more? I was sorry that I couldn't offer more help, but that was all I knew.

The policeman was looking at me oddly, and I wondered if my calm disturbed him somehow. Would he believe me if I had hysterics? Would that seem more authentic to him? But tears wouldn't help either the professor or the investigators now.

While we had been talking another vehicle had arrived, this one unmarked, and I surmised it belonged to a coroner or medical examiner or whatever passed for one around here. Several men headed down the steep hill with a gurney; one came up the hill to speak with the policeman. I caught only a few words, but they weren't hard to guess at: *collo* probably was neck, and *accidente* was self-evident. So this was already being classified as an accident. Jane started talking again, gesturing down the hill toward the dining hall, and I assumed she wanted to know what she could and should tell the rest of the group, who were even now gathering for breakfast, unaware of the drama unfolding up the hill. The policeman made reassuring noises, and I guessed that the gist of the conversation was that she could tell her friends that there had been an unfortunate accident and the poor professor was no more. And we were free to go on about our business, if a touch more sadly.

That suited me. It seemed a bit peremptory, to declare this death an accident without more detailed analysis, but I had no evidence to contradict their finding. I had to agree that the most likely story was that Professor Gilbert had gone for a walk to clear his head after a heavy dinner accompanied by much wine, and, being unfamiliar with the path, had slipped and fallen. Period.

I must have been drifting because I realized that Jane was standing in front of me with a hand on my arm. "Are you all right?" she asked anxiously.

I nodded. "I'm fine, Jane, really. After all, I didn't know him, and I saw his body this morning only from a distance. I'm sorry that this had to happen to you—you've put so much into planning all this. What comes next?"

"The police will take him away. I'll tell everyone at breakfast, but we're all free to do what we'd planned. They're calling it an accident. Is that all right, do you think? Are our friends going to want to spend a day in mourning or something?" She looked at me anxiously, waiting for an answer.

I was so the wrong person to ask, but she wanted guidance, or reinforcement. "I would say, tell them the bare outline, and say that we intend to continue with the schedule, but that if anyone wants to stay behind here, they're welcome to."

She nodded. "Good, good. I mean, it's a shame, but it has nothing to do with us, really. Come on, let's walk down the hill together. You don't have to say anything about finding him unless you want to. I won't mention it."

I had never known Jane well, but I thought she was handling this unanticipated situation with grace. I would have granted her a moment or two to whine at the gods that had dumped this on her, in the midst of everything else. But I knew that we were all tough women, and we could take it. I was pretty sure some people might ask me questions, maybe later, like, what was it like to find a body? I'd deal with those when they came up, but I wasn't about to volunteer the information. I still wasn't sure how I felt about it.

But I wasn't going to deal with anything without coffee. Jane and I walked down the hill and let ourselves into the dining hall. Jane had a quick word with the staff, a couple of whom crossed themselves. Then they went on dishing out food. The big room was half filled, with more people arriving every minute. I helped myself to a cup of coffee and some tasty pastries left over from dessert the night before, and found Cynthia and one other person I barely knew sitting at one of the small round tables. Cynthia took one look at me and asked, "What's up?"

I shook my head. "You'll hear in a minute." Then I focused on my breakfast. Cynthia didn't press.

Jane conferred briefly with Jean, and it was interesting to watch their interaction without sound. Jean looked appropriately horrified, and then asked the logical question, now what? Jane rushed to reassure her, and Jean ended up nodding in agreement. The plan would go on.

When it looked as though the majority of women had arrived and were seated, Jane reluctantly went to the end of the room, and several people rapped on their glasses or cups until all eyes were on Jane. I sat up straighter in my seat. My table was well positioned to watch everyone's face when Jane said, "I'm sorry to tell you this, but there has been an unfortunate accident. Professor Gilbert was apparently taking a walk after dinner last night. He slipped on a path and fell to his death."

I expected the collective gasp that rose from the group. What I was watching for were the flashes of expression on faces that suggested something other than grief—and there were a few, I noted. I wondered what those meant, and filed the names away for later.

Jane was still talking. "While I am sure we are all saddened by this news, we don't need to let it interfere with our plans for today. If you would like to take a few moments to collect yourselves, we can delay our departure for, say, half an hour. There is also a small church up the hill, if you'd like to take advantage of that to remember the professor. And of course if you'd like to stay here, that's your choice. Is everyone all right with that?"

People exchanged uncertain glances. Most probably had no template for something like this: an unscheduled half hour to mourn the passing of someone they might or might not have known, but had at least seen, very much alive, the night before.

Someone's hand shot up. "Are the police investigating?"

Jean said quickly, "The police are here now, and they have called this an unfortunate accident. We are free to come and go as we like. Anything else?"

Cynthia looked at me and arched one expressive eyebrow in question. I mouthed "Later."

Jane seemed relieved that nobody else had anything to say. "Then we'll meet at the vans at nine thirty. I'm so sorry this had to happen while we're here together, but I hope you won't let it put a damper on your trip. Please, go ahead and finish your breakfast—there's no rush."

My plate was empty but I wanted more coffee. I stood up and walked through the crowd, back to the serving area, catching snippets of conversation along the way. "Think he was alone last night?" "Oh, the poor man." "What a waste." "He was probably drunk." "I knew those paths were dangerous—we should all have been given flashlights." It was a curious mix.

I carried my refilled cup of coffee carefully back to my table. As I walked, I was thinking: nobody knows I found him. Who knew which room he was in? I hadn't, until we spoke after dinner. *Was* he alone, after? Did I really believe his fall was an accident? Did Cynthia hear anything after I fell asleep? How many people in the room had known him back in the day? And how many of those had unhappy memories of him?

I had reached our table, so I sat down. Diane, whom I vaguely recalled hearing say she was a doctor, said, "Isn't it too bad about the professor? But I'm glad Jane and Jean are going ahead with the schedule. I've been looking forward to seeing the lemon garden at the Villa di Castello. I read that it was designed by Cosimo di Medici when he was quite young, and then improved by Vasari later." I gave her a perfunctory smile.

Cynthia, after one more glance at me, chirped, "Oh, that's right — you're interested in plants, aren't you, Diane? Can you tell me anything else about the garden we'll be seeing?"

Their empty conversation carried me through the second cup of coffee, by which time the crowd had thinned. I stood up. "Cynthia, I'm going to go on up and get . . . my sweater."

"I'll come with you. Thanks, Diane, now I'll know what to look for when we get to the villa."

Cynthia and I walked out of the dining hall together, but we didn't say anything until we were halfway up the hill — out of earshot of our classmates. "Okay, what's going on?" Cynthia demanded.

"You were still asleep this morning, so I took a walk, over to the swimming pool. I found the body."

Cynthia gave me a probing look and apparently decided I wasn't emotionally devastated. She knew me well. "Was it awful?"

"No. He'd fallen down the hill, so I didn't see anything up close. No blood or anything, but he was obviously dead."

We'd reached our small patio and I stopped. It might be more private to talk inside, but I wanted to be able to see if there was anyone around who might overhear.

We sat at the small table and I began tentatively, "Cynthia, I told you that I spoke to him after dinner. He was staying in the room right over ours. I heard him, or someone, walking around after I got into bed. Did you hear anything?"

Cynthia was not stupid, and she got my drift immediately. "I heard those footsteps that you did. Are you asking if I think someone was with him? Not that I noticed. But if she — I'm assuming it would be a she — was barefoot, I don't suppose she would have made any noise. Laura, what's going on here? Are you thinking this was something other than an accident?"

I hedged. "It certainly looked like an accident. It was dark, the paths are slippery, and he didn't know the place well. And yet he went out again, after we heard him upstairs. It was clear he'd been drinking—heck, we all saw him drinking—and when we talked for a moment after dinner, he was a bit unsteady. So what happened?"

Cynthia looked around: no one in sight. "You've already jumped right past the part about a nice little tryst followed by a walk to, uh, cool down, right?" Then her expression changed. "Wait—you're guessing maybe he had a little help in falling off that path?"

I took a moment to reflect. I had known Cynthia since I was eighteen, and I'd lived with her for several years. But I hadn't seen much of her in the past couple of decades. I had to decide right now: did I trust her? I had no reason to believe that she had any animus against the professor, but people lied. And people changed.

But I didn't want to do this alone, so I decided that I needed to confide in her. "Yes. When he talked to me he said he was headed to bed—he as much as admitted he was getting old and needed his rest. Although of course he could have lied, although from what little I saw of him, I would have guessed he would be more likely to brag about an assignation than to conceal it. I can't imagine he would decide to take a walk after that. But there's more to it than that. Did you notice the weird undercurrents in the group every time his name came up? I get the feeling some people weren't happy to see him here, that they had some kind of history with him. Not a happy one."

Cynthia nodded. "I know what you mean. I told you earlier that there were rumors about him, when we were in school. That he hit on students. I can't point to anyone in particular, but there were hints. God, we were such babies then! Nowadays if a professor makes an unwanted move, a student would head straight for the administration to report it. And it would probably be in the paper the next day, or on the morning news. But do you seriously think that someone who, uh, suffered his unwanted attentions over forty years ago would take action now? After all this time?"

I didn't know what I thought. I'd never been placed in that position, when I was in college, and I couldn't guess how I might feel about it now, after so many years. Who was I to decide how others would feel? "Cyn, I don't know. Maybe. The shock of seeing him un-expectedly, in an unfamiliar setting like this, could have set someone off—someone who thought she'd put it all behind her."

"What do you want to do about it?" Cynthia asked quietly.

I met her gaze. "I'm not sure. Something doesn't feel right. The police have declared it an accident, so they aren't going to look any further, or at least I think that was what they said. I can't blame them—it looks pretty straightforward: he was old, he'd been drink-ing, he fell. And I'm certainly not going to deliberately mess up this trip for everyone, not after we've been looking forward to it for the better part of a year. But just in case, I plan to keep my ears and eyes open."

"Laura, do you seriously think that one of our classmates came to Italy and murdered the man? Nobody even knew he was coming un-til after we arrived."

"I think it's a possibility that they saw a chance and grabbed it. I will be happy to be proved wrong."

"And if you can't prove anything, either way?"

"Then it will go down as an accident, period. By the way, you didn't happen to take a stroll in the moonlight after I went to sleep, did you?"

A peculiar look flashed across Cynthia's face before she burst out laughing. "You calling me a suspect, huh?"

"Maybe." I grinned at her. "I never assume anything. You had opportunity, and all it would take is one push."

"But I had no motive. I didn't know the man. I didn't like the man, from what little I saw of him, then and now. Besides, if you're going to investigate this, Sherlock, you need a Watson, so you have to trust me."

"I always thought Watson was kind of thickheaded."

"I'm the smart Watson. Am I in?"

"Of course."

"So let's get ready to go admire more Medici monuments. While we're driving, while we're wallowing in art and history, we talk and we listen. Somebody is bound to say something about the professor's death. Good thing you and I are in different vans—we can listen to two sets of people."

"Good thinking, Watson."

Chapter 10

Cynthia had made it sound simple, but I had to ask myself what I thought I was doing. I don't go by gut reactions or woo-woo "feelings." I'm an analyst by trade and by choice. But something about the death of Anthony Gilbert troubled me, and I wanted to know why — without making it painfully obvious what I was doing and why I was asking questions.

Point one: He was a charmer, and I distrust charmers from the get-go. Point two: I'd be willing to bet he had directed his charms at some of my classmates gathered here, based on the curious range of responses to his presence. I wasn't ready to say who, but I'd guess it was more than one of them. More than five? I shuddered at the thought — that would definitely put him in the sleazeball league. Point three: I was angry that he'd somehow insinuated himself into our gathering and then ended up dead. That wasn't fair. This was supposed to be fun, with a bit of a trip down memory lane — good memories only. He'd screwed that up, although since he was the victim he couldn't exactly be blamed — but I wanted to blame someone, and that meant his killer, assuming there was one. I made a mental note to check exactly how he came to be invited in the first place. Whose idea was it originally? Had Professor Gilbert said it was Gerry's?

I wasn't exactly "doing" anything about it. As I'd told Cynthia, all I wanted to do was watch and listen and see what people had to say. That wouldn't be evidence of anything, but it might be suggestive. I certainly didn't want to label any one of the women here a killer, but I had a suspicion that there were a few people who were happy to see the professor dead. I wondered if I should show some of the others the pictures I had taken of the professor's body, sprawled on the ground, just to watch for their reactions. I'd have to be discreet, of course; otherwise I would come across as ghoulish and insensitive. No, probably a bad idea. I wondered why on earth I had taken those pictures in the first place. Because I'd been planning to photograph the landscape, and somehow captured a body by mistake?

No, Laura — you thought there was something wrong with the whole thing, so you took the pictures just in case . . . I made a mental note to off-load them when I had the chance. Did I have any faith in the Italian police? Not necessarily, but I wasn't about to butt into their investigation—or lack thereof. I had no idea which unit was in charge of murder investigations here, or whether it was regional or even national. In any case, it looked as though they were content to do nothing, and I couldn't fault them, exactly. Old drunk man falls down hill—not precisely big news. But if anyone came asking, I'd be ready.

It wasn't clear to me where Cynthia fit. I didn't really suspect her of killing the professor, but I wasn't sure if she was taking this seriously or just humoring me. Still, I knew she could keep her mouth shut, and I could use a second pair of eyes and ears. And from what she'd hinted earlier, she knew I was serious.

Up at the parking area in front of the main house—the only place on the property with room enough to accommodate four oversize vehicles—the drivers huddled over maps and printouts and GPS devices, plotting our next move. I climbed into my seat—on the left, behind the driver, Brenda. A couple of the others were already in the van, waiting.

"What an awful thing!" Dorothy said in a hushed voice, clearly relishing the drama. "Poor Professor Gilbert. Although I suppose he went as he might have wished, in the region he so loved."

I tried not to gag at the saccharine platitude.

"Could it have been a heart attack? Or a stroke?" she went on, with unhealthy glee. "After all, he wasn't young."

"He was fifteen years older than we are, tops," said Ann, throwing cold water on Dorothy's commentary. "He seemed fit enough."

I was debating asking the innocuous question "Did you know him?" when Dorothy beat me to it. "I was in his Florentine Poets class one semester. Did any of you ever take any of his classes?"

"Nope," Ann said promptly. "They sounded kind of sappy to me. I took modern poetry to satisfy the requirements, and contemporary women writers."

Dorothy was not to be deflected. "Anyone?"

Nobody else had, or at least not that they were willing to admit. I decided to stick my toe in the water. "What was he like as a teacher, Dorothy?"

Her eyes gleamed. "Oh, he was wonderful! He made the poets

come alive. I loved to listen to him recite in Italian—it was so mellifluous. Even if you didn't know Italian, you could hear the soul of the poem, the music of the words. He was something special . . ." Dorothy trailed off, lost in her misty memories.

Someone behind me snorted. Dorothy turned quickly. "Do you disagree?"

To my surprise, it was Denise who retorted, "Yes, I do. I took a class with him, and it was clear that he was a good-looking guy talking to a room full of impressionable young women. He ate it up. And I heard he did a little more than that."

Aha, now we were getting to the meat of it.

Our driver, Brenda, climbed into the van and did a quick head count. "Good, everybody's here. Take this, Denise—you're navigator." Brenda handed her a map, plus a printed sheet of instructions. Since the vehicle had a GPS that had worked just fine so far, this was kind of belt and suspenders thinking, but I'd rather we had an idea where we were rather than roaming aimlessly along pretty roads in the Italian countryside.

"Right, Chief," Denise said. "GPS programmed?"

"Check it," Brenda snapped back. "Everybody buckled up? Then we're off!"

We waited while the first couple of vans started making their slow way down the hill and pulled in behind them. We were on our way.

I debated about trying to return to the discussion of the character of the late Professor Gilbert, but then Sharon, sitting next to me, said, "Hey, Laura, there's a rumor that you found the body?"

How had that gotten out? The only people who knew were Jane, Barbara and Gerry—and Cynthia? And the police, of course. Had someone else been watching?

I decided to stick to the truth. "Yes, I did."

"Ooh, was it . . . awful?" Dorothy said in a hushed voice.

"No. He looked peaceful enough, but I wasn't very near to him." The police had confirmed that his neck was broken, but I wasn't going to go into details. Let the other women use their own imaginations.

"The poor, poor man . . ." Dorothy said softly. I was sure if I turned around to look at her, she would have tears in her eyes. But at the same time, I wasn't sure if her sentimental reactions suggested any closer sort of relationship, past or present. She'd always been a bit sappy, I recalled.

"*Media vita in morte sumus,*" she went on. Show-off.

"Gerry must feel terrible about this—I heard he was the one who invited the professor," I tossed out. "How did they come to know each other?" I'd heard one version and I wondered if the stories would match up.

"I heard they met in the States," Ann volunteered.

"I thought it was over here?" Sharon said. "Some local symposium or something."

"Is Gerry an academic too? I haven't had much chance to talk with him," I said. Apart from telling him there was a body in his olive grove.

"I think he used to be. Now mostly he does research and publishes, and manages the property. Maybe he teaches a course now and then, or gives lectures," Brenda said. She might know, since she had arrived earlier than the rest of us and had possibly spent more time with our hosts.

"How did Jane and Jean come to know Barb and Gerry?" I asked, out of general curiosity.

"Didn't you know?" Brenda asked. "Jean's daughter was over here on a junior year abroad and stumbled on the place online. She loved it, and when Jean and Jane started cooking up this trip, she mentioned it. It was available for this week, and when Jean mentioned the Wellesley connection, it was a done deal."

"Barbara went to Wellesley?" I thought I'd heard that mentioned but I wanted to make sure.

"Yes, but before us," someone behind me said.

I probably wasn't going to get any more out of the group without looking obsessive, so I thought I'd let it rest—for now. "So, how many of you have grandkids?"

The topic of grandchildren carried us well until we arrived at Medici villa number whatever. "Poggio a Caiano was purchased in 1473 by Lorenzo the Magnificent, although he did not live to see it completed," Dorothy intoned, reading from her handout. "His son Giovanni—later Pope Leo X—finished it, and the place was used by the Medici Grand Dukes for quite a while. It includes paintings by

Andrea del Sarto, Pontormo, and a few artists I've never heard of. There used to be twin ramps in the front for horses to ride up and deliver people—they've been replaced by staircases. The garden was redesigned in the nineteenth century."

"Thank you, Dorothy," Denise said sweetly. "Brenda, pull in on the left, there."

"Well, I thought somebody might like to know," Dorothy replied, hurt. It looked to me like tempers were a bit short this morning.

The villa was lovely, and not too crowded. The rooms, with their paintings by artists well known and less known, were magnificent and many—so many that it was easy to get lost. I wandered happily, admiring moldings and wallpaper (later additions) and furniture (ditto) and one amazing bathtub. It was hard to imagine living in a place like this, even with scores of servants. But then, it was hard to imagine being a Medici. My sole accomplishment was asking one of the guards standing in the palatial dining room an actual question in Italian: *Dov'è la cucina?* I'm pretty sure she said it was somewhere below where we were standing, since she pointed down a lot while speaking very quickly, and I was left wondering how the staff ever managed to transport the food from the kitchen to the dining room— or if the Medicis ever even ate food while it was still hot, after having been carried through a half mile of chilly corridors.

I ran into Cynthia somewhere in the maze. "Anything new?" I asked.

"Can't talk here. I'll fill you in later."

Several other classmates drifted in. "Isn't it glorious?" Cynthia sighed, quickly changing the subject.

"I have to agree," I said amiably. "Amazing what endless money can buy. Do you think anyone just had fun here? Or were they too busy plotting and scheming?"

"Who cares?" Denise said, coming up behind us. "Just enjoy it."

I turned to her. "How can you enjoy it when you know how it was paid for?" And that led to a discussion of pure art versus artistic context, and patronage, and where the heck the kitchen in the place was, and we entertained ourselves until it was time to regroup for lunch.

Lunch was held in a restaurant about half a mile away, and we all trekked along the sidewalk like a ragged army regiment. At the restaurant we filled the back room, painted a color somewhere between yellow and cream and ringed with large glass windows overlooking a leafy patio. Each table held eight or ten of us, and the food was served family style. We ate, and ate more, cleaning each plate that appeared. The wine bottles circulated. A woman sitting across the table from me held up a piece of bread and contemplated it seriously. "You know, I don't think there's any salt at all in this, and it still tastes great. I wonder how they do that?"

We talked and talked some more. Nobody mentioned the late professor or death, or even the Medicis. Instead, we were still busy filling each other in about the last forty years of our lives. From the bits and pieces I overheard from all directions, people had done a lot of interesting things, and I wondered if I'd have time to talk to all of them, not about the murder but about what they'd done, who they'd become. Funny—when we'd been applying to colleges, in another century, no one had considered that we'd come together like this to see what we'd done with the education we had been given. We'd all worked hard, and it was clear that we'd used what we'd learned in different ways.

It was again past two when Jean stood up and said, "I hope you aren't villa'd out yet, because we've got one more villa to see." A few groans issued from the crowd. Jean ignored them. "At this one we can't go inside the building, but the gardens are spectacular. Everybody powder your noses and we'll hit the road."

After our potty break, we hit the road again. I was totally lost by now. I knew we were sort of circling around Florence, but I couldn't have retraced our steps if you'd paid me. Still, it was kind of nice, not being responsible for any of it. If we got lost, we got lost. We'd get unlost soon enough.

Once again Dorothy treated us to snippets from the detailed handouts as we rode along. "All these gardens we're visiting aren't just pretty—they embody any number of symbolic elements, not to mention showing off some pretty fancy technology with fountains and such. Very formal though—you know, central axes and grid patterns. I guess the fake natural gardens came later."

I was amazed when we turned out to be the first van to arrive at our latest destination. GPS worked! We parked, and once we climbed down from the van we gave Brenda a standing ovation for her achievement. She bowed proudly. Then we strolled back the way we had come until we found the discreet entrance to the Villa Medicea di Castella, the latest in our string of Medici homes. Yup, Lorenzo the Magnificent had owned it but had given it to a cousin also named Lorenzo, and then Cosimo—the one who later became Grand Duke of Tuscany—had restored it. End of history lesson. The formal garden was lovely, with row upon row of lemon trees in massive pots. Who knew there were so many lemon varieties? Big ones, small ones, round ones, lumpy ones, all ensconced in massive terra-cotta pots that the pamphlets claimed were stashed in warm greenhouses each winter. I couldn't imagine trying to move a pot that large. I suspected in the modern world forklifts were involved—but in the past?

The highlight of the garden was an amazing grotto built into the rear wall, farthest from the house itself. It was filled with carvings of exotic animals (who would never have appeared together in life, but still). I was admiring them all (and taking pictures) when Ann came up beside me.

"Interesting—gorgeous and creepy, all at the same time," she said.

"I know what you mean. Did this qualify as entertainment back then? Instead of television, the counts and dukes and assorted guests came out here and contemplated the flowers and lemons and the weird animals?"

"It was a simpler time," Ann said, then giggled. "Oh, look—the rest of the gang finally showed up." She pointed at the people from the other three vans, who were just now straggling in through the entrance. Way to go, Brenda!

Even with all of us meandering around the garden, it wasn't crowded. I climbed the steps to the upper terrace, where I found I could see the airport where we had arrived a few days earlier. Then I leaned on the parapet and lost myself in calculating how many guest rooms the villa might have, and where the heck they put all the servants. What was the ratio of servant to guest, if you were a Medici offering entertainment to your peers? For that matter, where did they park all the horses and carriages?

Cynthia wandered up beside me. "We got lost."

"We didn't. This is nice."

"Yes, it is. Can you imagine living like this?"

"Nope. Does anyone anymore?"

"No one I know. Although I gather that Newport was something like this in its heyday. And I've seen some pretty swanky spreads in Manhattan. All it takes is lots and lots of money."

"Bet it's hard to find good help these days."

"Speaking of help . . ." She stopped, uncharacteristically hesitant.

"What?" I demanded, turning to look at her.

"I should tell you now, I did go out again, after you fell asleep."

"Not to meet the slimy professor, I hope!" The thought was unpleasant.

"No, not him. But I did meet someone else . . . you know the bartender guy?"

"At the villa? What, you got together with him?" I wasn't sure I believed what I was hearing.

"Not just him. He has a twin brother."

I stared at her, and then I burst out laughing. "You've got to be kidding."

Cynthia looked hurt. "Why? I've always wondered about twins . . . Hey, it's not like it's going to happen again. Ever. Call it a last hurrah."

"What happens it Italy stays in Italy, eh? Did they live up to your expectations?"

"Yup, and that's all I'm going to say. But I did learn one thing from the bartender. Our dead professor? He asked for a bottle of wine and two glasses, and one of the twins dropped them off at his room after dinner."

I stopped laughing. "So either he was planning to get really drunk or he was meeting someone. Who hasn't told anyone. Shoot."

"Exactly. Maybe you were right."

Of course, anything resembling evidence was long gone by now. I looked back over the lovely, peaceful lemon garden spread out below us. The Medici may have been schemers and connivers, but it looked like we had one of our own.

Chapter 11

Compared to some, it had been a relaxing day, wallowing in art and gardens and good food. It was bittersweet coming back to the villa at Capitignano because we all knew we were leaving it the next day. After the chilly start, even the weather had warmed for us. When the vans drove up the driveway and parked, the lowering sun cast gold light on everything. In the parking area we milled around a bit aimlessly, reluctant to retreat to our rooms but unsure of what we wanted to do.

"Anybody want to walk up to the church?" Bonnie asked of no one in particular.

"Sure," I said, to my own surprise. I wasn't one to take walks for their own sake, but I wanted to see what lay up the hill—and take pictures of more views, preferably without bodies. Yes, I knew that I took too many pictures of the same things, but I was always hoping for that one perfect shot, and modern cameras made it easy to keep trying.

Nobody felt like joining us, so Bonnie and I set off. I had known her but not well, so I wondered what we'd find to talk about. We had to go down the long driveway to go up the hill to the church, but we weren't in any hurry. The drive bordered the vineyard and was flanked by a row of tall thin cypresses. It was as close as I had come to the vines, but it was too early in the season to see much in the way of grapes, so I contented myself with admiring the orderly rows, neatly staked.

"What made you decide to come on this trip, Bonnie?" I asked as we set out.

She trudged forward intently, watching where she put her feet. "I wanted to do something different. I can't recall the last time I took a real vacation—one just for fun, and just for me. And I guess I was curious to see how we all turned out. You?"

"About the same. I majored in art history but I never got a chance to use it much. I keep trying to remember why I chose that in the first place, other than the fact that I had idealistic—or do I mean unrealistic? — ideas about what the academic world was like. Plus, I thought it meant that I would be able to travel regularly and make it tax-deductible." I grinned at her.

"How'd that work out?"

"Not too well. Couldn't find work in my chosen field, so I found what my parents would have called a 'real' job, and got married, and had a child, and the travel part kind of kept slipping down the list. I haven't been to Italy since right after I graduated, and you know how long ago that was. As for being here, I guess that like you, I kind of wondered if everybody else had taken the same kind of roundabout path as I did, or if they'd managed to stick to their first choices. And how I'd feel if they had succeeded." I stopped myself: that was more frank than I had intended to be. But it was honest: I'd often wondered if I had stuck it out just a little longer in art history . . . No, that was water under the bridge; there was no going back.

"Are you enjoying the trip?" Bonnie asked.

"Yes, I am. I have to say I was kind of worried before I got here — I thought everybody would be more successful than I am, more content with who they are and where they are in their lives. Almost like when I first arrived at the college, you know? Everybody was smarter and more sophisticated, and I felt like such an imposter."

Bonnie flashed a shy glance at me. "We all felt like that, but we didn't know anyone else well enough to admit it, not at first. And it's probably not much different now. You think everyone on this trip has led a perfect life? I haven't, I can tell you. And you know something? The perfect ones probably wouldn't bother coming to something like this. It's the ones with questions who showed up."

I laughed. "Damn it, Bonnie, I wish I'd known you better. But I've learned something about myself since I got here. I thought I'd feel more nostalgic about all the art, since I was an art historian. I've always wondered, what if, you know? But now that I'm here, it's been great to see it, but mostly I have to laugh at the Medicis — they were so into impressing everyone by throwing a lot of money around. Now I guess I take a broader view of the context of the art than I used to. You know, back when I first studied art history, everybody was so busy analyzing style that they never looked at how it came about. I mean, medieval cathedrals wouldn't have existed without somebody to pay for them, right? But nobody ever talked about the finances."

Bonnie laughed. "I hear you. I think students today have a much more comprehensive view than we did. Where did the time go?"

"I wish I knew. Is that a fig tree?" I pointed.

"I think it is—how cool is that? Wonder what else grows around here?"

"Are you a gardener?" I asked, more to be polite than because I cared.

"Nope, no time for it. Besides, everything I touch dies."

"Ditto. But I like to look. I love to see things I've only read about. That thing there looks like a dandelion on steroids, doesn't it?" I pointed to a large yet airy puffball.

We wandered up the hill, stopping to admire a weed with pretty flowers, a group of sheep, and yet another view. We both took pictures of all three. It didn't take much longer to reach the church at the top of the hill. It was deserted, but the door was open. However, the inside was disappointing. St. Cresci might have had his head chopped off, but there was little evidence of his gruesome martyrdom visible. Still, it was cool inside, so we sat quietly for a few minutes.

"Too bad that thing with the professor had to happen," I ventured almost reluctantly, since I'd been enjoying just talking with Bonnie without any ulterior motive.

"He had it coming," Bonnie said with a venom that surprised me. "The gods are just."

"What do you mean?" I turned in my pew to face her.

"Well, I never took a class from him, but one of my roommates did. She told me he was a real sleazeball."

"Like he came on to her?"

"He did that with every girl—excuse me, woman—who didn't have a hunchback and only one eye. But it got worse. If you turned him down, he made a point of cutting you down for as long as the class lasted. He all but called you stupid in front of everyone. You know how insecure we all were back then—it really stung."

"And nobody ever said anything to anyone?"

"Who would they tell? I don't think they'd invented the term *bully* then, for that kind of behavior. Worse, I think we all felt we were at the college by accident, and we didn't want to make waves. As far as I know, nobody ever said anything."

"If you don't mind my asking, is that roommate here on this trip?"

"No. She kind of cut off all contact with the college and the class after she graduated. But it's certainly possible that someone else he treated like that is here. I can't be sure because nobody has talked about it, at least not when I could hear it. Maybe I've already said too much, but I won't pretend that I'm sorry he's dead. You weren't one of his 'girls,' were you?"

"Not me. I never took his class, never met the man until yesterday, and didn't like what little I saw of him. I guess that's a good thing. You ready to start down the hill?"

"Sure. I hear there's a special farewell dinner tonight. With meat."

When I thought back, I realized that we had been eating a lot of pasta here. In any case, the subject of the professor was closed, and Bonnie and I enjoyed a leisurely walk down the hill from the church, then up the hill to the villa. We paused partway up to catch our breath.

"Looks positively medieval, doesn't it?" Bonnie said. "If you ignore a few electrical wires and that tractor over there, it could be any era at all."

"You're right. This whole area feels kind of timeless, until you go into a town, with those fancy modern things like streetlights and trains." I looked up at the villa and worked out where the swimming pool lay. Unlike in the States, there was no fence, no guardrail. Just a flagstone and concrete pavement surrounding the pool that went up to the edge—and to the hill that fell straight down twenty or more feet. But wouldn't a falling body have rolled? Bounced? Wouldn't Anthony Gilbert have tried to stop his fall? Maybe not, if he was drunk or drugged or dead when he went over the edge. "Let's get moving—I think I smell grilling meat."

I stopped by the room to change into a slightly "nicer" shirt, in honor of the occasion, and found Cynthia there. She looked up from her tablet.

"Where've you been?" she asked.

"I took a nature walk, believe it or not. Bonnie and I went up to look at the church."

"Anything interesting up there?"

"Not really. Some pretty flowers and some sheep. You ready to go down the hill to dinner?"

She held up one finger, then tapped the screen a few times and shut it down. "There. I watched to capture a thought before it evaporated. Yes, I'm ready. I can't believe we'll be leaving here tomorrow. This place is beginning to feel like home."

"I know what you mean. And I'm not looking forward to packing, or rather, jamming everything back into my suitcase. How do you manage to travel so light?"

"Practice. Everything I own is black, so it all matches. And I've trained myself not to sweat."

"Yeah, right," I muttered. "Let's go, then."

The mood in the big dining room was hard to read. Everyone was there early, no doubt drawn by the good smells of grilling pork and beef, as I had been. We were midway through our trip, so there was still some excitement about what was to come. But at the same time there was a tinge of sadness: we all knew this part of the trip was ending, and, as Cyn had said, it had come to feel familiar. From what little I'd seen from the handouts, the next home base would be very different. Still, I guessed that people would be glad to put the shadow of the professor's death behind them. Maybe some people more than others?

Dinner was, as usual, delicious, served this time by a trio of young trainee chefs who were getting some on-the-job training. I watched the bartender as he winked at Cyn, and she gave him a bright smile. I had to say, her bucket list was a whole lot more interesting than mine.

Once again the wine flowed freely, and at the end of the meal we mangled singing the college's alma mater (nobody could ever remember the words). Once again I was struck by the strange intersection of past and present: who among us could have foreseen this moment, all those years ago?

And who could have foreseen that we might harbor a killer in our midst? *No, Laura,* I chided myself, *don't think like that.* There was no tangible reason to believe that Professor Gilbert's death was anything but an accidental fall . . . except for a few little facts that didn't quite add up, like that late bottle of wine delivered to his room. Nobody had admitted to seeing him after dinner (except me) — but then, nobody had been asked, because his death had been declared an accident from the start. If there were alibis to be had, memories were fading fast, and at this rate nobody would remember where they'd been only a day or two before. Still, it was not my problem, so why was I gnawing at it? I wanted more than anything to relax and enjoy the evening; I had certainly enjoyed most of our time in Tuscany.

It was close to eleven when Jane and Jean stood up and gave one last try at clinking glasses for attention. It took a while for the din to die down. When it was finally quiet, Jean said, "I hope you've all enjoyed your special dinner tonight. Let's give our chefs a round of applause." Everybody complied very happily.

Then Jane took over. "As you all know, we'll be leaving the villa tomorrow. We'll be stopping at the lovely walled city of Lucca, where we'll have lunch, and then we'll be driving north to the Cinque Terre, which is an amazing part of this country. That's where my family originated. There's a religious procession taking place in the heart of the village, and you're welcome to join in if you wish, if we arrive in time. In the evening we have planned a wonderful dinner at a seaside restaurant, which I'm sure you'll all enjoy."

Jane and Jean exchanged glances. "It doesn't seem right to end the evening without at least a brief mention of Professor Gilbert," Jane said. "He touched so many of our lives when we were in college."

I choked back a snort: I was pretty sure he'd touched a bit more than that.

Jane went on, "But if there's any silver lining to his, uh, passing, it's that he died doing what he loved — teaching eager students — in the country he had chosen to call home. Let us share a moment of silence in his memory."

Heads were bowed — but not all of them. A couple of people looked openly defiant, or looked away. Jane sensed that she should cut the "moment" short, so she said, "Now, let's all get a good night's sleep, because we have another busy day tomorrow. Breakfast will be at eight, and the vans will be leaving at nine, so be sure you're packed and ready to go. *Buona notte.*"

People straggled out of the building, into the dark, reluctant to let the night end. Cyn caught up with me just outside the door.

"What, no tryst with the twins tonight?" I twitted her.

"Nope. Once was enough. No regrets, though."

I envied Cynthia her ability to leave her baggage behind and move forward. I'd always had a tendency to wallow in those blasted what-ifs about what I could have done better, or at least differently, and in some ways I'd come to count on her to drag me out of my introspection. I'd kind of missed that, when our lives had diverged — and my husband hadn't filled the void. But when I'd had to put a good face on things for my daughter, it was Cynthia's model that I usually followed, and sometimes the act became the reality.

As we strolled up the hill, I inhaled the scented night air. "I'm going to miss this."

"It's not over, you know. There are more wonders yet to be seen."

"I know, but I like it here. And it's been interesting, getting to talk to so many people I never knew well. I mean, we share a chunk of the same history, but it's been a long time. I keep trying to step back and look at us objectively. Do we come across as one of those groups of silly old ladies in funny hats to the rest of the world?"

"Of course not," Cynthia said firmly. "And what if we did? We're enjoying ourselves. Who cares what other people think? We don't have to make excuses for anything."

Cynthia hadn't changed — thank God. "I'm glad to hear you say that. Now we'd better go pack. Can I just dig a hole and leave most of my clothes here?"

"Whatever you want — as long as they're biodegradable. Can you imagine what future archeologists would think when they unearthed a cache of eternal polyester?"

I laughed, then intoned, "The artifacts appear to represent an offering to the gods of Synthetic, the focus of a popular cult with many, many followers . . ."

"Exactly," Cynthia said.

Chapter 12

The next morning I was glad that someone was picking up the luggage in front of the dining hall, because I seriously doubted my ability to haul my blasted suitcase over the gravel path and up the hill to where the vans were parked. There were a few small benefits to growing older, I was finding, and having someone young and strong volunteer to carry things for you was one of them. Sometimes. I still bristled when someone assumed that I needed help, but in some cases I wasn't above accepting any help offered. This was one of them.

Breakfast passed quickly — it felt like everyone was eager to get on the road. Maybe a fast break would make it easier to leave such a lovely location, and since we now knew what the standard for accommodations was, I'm sure we were looking forward to the next site. We loaded up the vans and set forth on schedule, headed for Lucca, another place about which I knew next to nothing. And to think that once I had done homework compulsively. I couldn't figure out whether I was simply lazy now or whether I wanted to see new places without somebody else's opinion coloring my reactions.

In the end, my old compulsions won out. I dug out my handout material and read. Lucca: founded by Etruscans, Roman grid plan, remnants of amphitheater, lots of history, yadda yadda, conquered by Napoleon, who made his sister Elisa "Queen of Etruria" for a while. Main sights: statue of Puccini, his home, some nice churches, surrounding city walls largely intact. Manageable size, not too much traffic. Okay, I was ready; I had a general sense of the scope and location of the important monuments. All I needed was some willing accomplices to enjoy them with.

We parked the vans in a lot a short distance from the city so we could admire the walls as we approached. Once inside, we got our bearings and were preparing to follow the herd toward the remains of the amphitheater when that plan was immediately disrupted by the sight of a *gelateria*. My feet veered toward it without any conscious thought — and my partners in gelato, Rebecca and Christine, followed me. My first gelato of the day, and it wasn't even lunchtime. Funny how food kept trumping art for us — both were so good in Italy.

After an agonizing selection process, I returned with my companions of the day to the narrow street that led toward the center of Lucca. None of our classmates were in sight, which was curiously liberating. Spooning gelato in small bites, the better to make it last, we strolled toward what we hoped was a large square in the middle of . . . something, glimpsing occasional views of crenellated towers. Jane had alerted us to the competing towers of Lucca, each one intended to be bigger than the last one built by a rival. Amazing how many they had crowded into a small walled town.

The square when we found it was large and empty, save for an imposing statue—Napoleon's lucky sister? What must it be like to be gifted with an entire town of your own? There were parents and small children playing in the square, often accompanied by a dog. This must be a regular play spot, since there was a small carousel in one corner. Other than that, there were ornate flower beds and a wealth of souvenir shops around the perimeter, which of course we had to investigate. Nothing caught our fancy, although I debated briefly about acquiring a very realistic Glock handgun made of plastic but thought I might have trouble carrying it home. After a while we made a stab at finding Puccini's home—our token nod to local culture—and succeeded in locating his statue in a small square, also surrounded by souvenir vendors. Rebecca entered into intense negotiations with one of them for some lovely cloth-bound notebooks. Christine and I wandered around the corner and sat down at a restaurant shaded by an awning, with a front-row view of the statue of Puccini. This was nice: we didn't have to be anywhere for a couple of hours, when we were going to meet the rest of the group at the cathedral. Once again I flashed back on my sole hectic trip to Italy forty years ago, when I had felt compelled to fit as many monuments and important sites as possible into as short a time as possible, all the while struggling with a ridiculously small budget. It was hard to believe now that there really had been hotels with rooms for the equivalent of five dollars a night, and they were even more or less respectable for a woman traveling alone.

"I like this," I said to Christine after Rebecca had waved at us then wandered off to shop at yet another of the stalls clustered around the square. "Are we ordering lunch?" It had been only half an hour since the gelato.

"Of course," Christine answered promptly, studying the menu. I scanned it quickly: it was clearly tilted toward tourists, but it showed a sense of humor. I ordered what was dubbed a Panini Puccini, along with a carafe of the house wine. If I were to have a sandwich named for me, what would I want in it? Puccini ignored me, staring thoughtfully at the far end of the little plaza. If I'd read the signs correctly, he had lived in a house in the opposite direction, behind his back.

The sandwich tasted good, and it was fun to roll the name on my tongue—close to a tongue twister, especially after a glass of wine. Rebecca returned to join us, laden with yet more bags, and ordered something to eat. We didn't speak much, content to sit and watch the world go by. Was this a way of life in Italy? It was, after all, the Romans who had coined the phrase *festina lente*—make haste slowly. Maybe they'd borrowed it from the Greeks, but it was the Latin version that had caught on—who could pronounce Greek? We observed a few of our classmates strolling past and waved, but they didn't stop and we weren't inspired to jump up and follow them.

"Did either of you ever take a music course in college?" I asked, apropos of Puccini.

Christine shook her head. "Nope. Never fit in my schedule. Do they still have distribution requirements these days? Because that really made for some odd course choices."

"Got me," I replied. "I went for the art courses, but only sophomore year, after I'd heard everyone else raving about Art 100. By then it was too late to fit in Music 100, so I was doomed to remain ignorant of music forever. I did, however, take astronomy."

"I took horticulture," Rebecca volunteered.

"And all this diversity of cultural enrichment has made us better people," I said solemnly. Then we all burst into laughter. That felt good too.

When we calmed down again, I said, "I wish I knew what I was supposed to know about Puccini. He wrote *La Bohème*, right? I've only been to two operas in my life." Too busy going to art museums, I supposed. That had been my priority then, and later life had kind of intervened.

"That's two more than I have," Christine said.

That made me feel better. "Funny—if that statue is accurate, Puccini looks nothing like I thought he would. I figured he'd be some large guy with a beard, sort of like Luciano Pavarotti. The guy here reminds me of Cole Porter."

Christine laughed. "Now I know why I'm hanging out with you—you're irreverent. You don't take any of this too seriously."

Once I had. Once I had believed that it mattered whether Michelangelo finished Statue A before he started Statue B. I could still tell you in what year each part of Chartres Cathedral was completed. And what impact had all that information, so carefully stored in my brain, had on my life? Hard to say, but from this distant perspective, it hardly seemed worth worrying about. Now I was practicing just smelling the roses, enjoying the moment. Art history was filed away in my distant past.

Still, I was forced to admit that it gave me a pang each time we walked into a cathedral. Without thinking I'd find myself ticking off the parts: nave, aisle, transept, apse, crypt; column, capital, clerestory; barrel vault, groin vault. I'd learned my lessons well, and then I'd buried them deep, but they were still there. But I had to wonder: had all the time I'd spent absorbing facts and details interfered with my getting to know the extraordinary group of women I was now traveling with? Back then it had been so much easier to deal with "things" than with people. My loss. How would my life have been different if my priorities had been reversed?

Too late now. Or was it? We'd finished our sandwiches, so I turned to my tablemates and said, "Ready for gelato?"

Rebecca grinned. "Always! Lead me to it!"

Friendship based on ice cream. I could do worse.

• • •

After another couple of hours of pleasant rambling and a brief tour of the cathedral, where we admired the frescos and the elegant and tragic marble tomb of Ilaria del Carretto (or so said our handout, identifying the artist as Jacopo della Quercia) with her sad little dog peering up from under her feet, our group reassembled in the piazza in front of the cathedral, and we trekked back to the gate where we'd entered to return to the vans. Liguria beckoned, specifically a place called Monterosso, which was on the sea. I'd never heard of Monterosso, but our leaders' choices had been spot-on so far. There was talk of a vineyard. Beaches and vineyards all at once? How could anyone complain?

But I did begin to complain—to myself, at least—when we were about halfway to our destination. That was when I realized that I had been lulled into a false sense of security by the lush rolling hills of Tuscany. Leaving Lucca, at first the roads climbed gradually. Then we left the *Autostrada* and the roads narrowed to two lanes, and kept climbing. Then the turns began. I wasn't troubled by motion sickness, and hadn't been since I was a kid; it was looking out the window that was disturbing. I had switched with someone else and now sat in the middle row on the right side of the van, with a nice large window next to me. I was admiring the views, as always, when I realized I was looking at rooftops far, *far* below me. I had no way of estimating accurately, but I figured a couple of hundred feet would be conservative. A spindly metal guardrail a foot or two from the side of the van was all that stood between us and free fall, and it was a long way down. How much did I know about Brenda's driving expertise? How much had *she* known about the perils of the roads when she signed on? I'm sure they looked quite innocent on a nice, flat map, with wiggly green lines suggesting pretty views. And now I'd committed my life and the safety of my limbs to someone about whom I knew very little. I was not reassured.

And the hills—and accompanying valleys—kept coming. I tried closing my eyes for a minute, then decided I'd rather watch my fate approaching than meet it blind.

I didn't say anything. Neither did anyone else riding on the right side of the van. There was an occasional gasp when the turn was particularly tight or we met a bus coming fast from the opposite direction, which they did with alarming frequency (maybe the local population didn't like driving on these roads either and they were all riding in those blasted buses instead). Brenda appeared unruffled, but I was pretty sure her knuckles were white on the steering wheel, and she was wrestling with a large vehicle. I was *so* glad once again that I hadn't volunteered to drive. I preferred my roads flat and wide. Mountains were pretty to look at but not so pretty to drive over.

The ride seemed to go on forever. To distract myself, I tried to recall someone's comment about how the tiny towns strung out along the Ligurian coast were accessible from one to another only by train or by boat—not by road. Now deep in the midst of steep mountains, I could understand that: it would take a long, long time to retrace this route back to the top, then to go down to the next town. I wondered, not for the first time, what the accident rate was around here. Was I carrying any information about contacting my next of kin? Assuming my body survived the plunge with ID intact?

Finally we arrived at our destination—or rather, as close as we could get, given the size of the vans versus the size of the lane that apparently led toward the small town we could barely see way, way below us. We unloaded our luggage and stood around cluelessly, waiting for someone to give us instructions. We also admired the pretty sea views and the pretty vineyard views, all downhill from where we stood. Finally our fearless leaders rounded us up to announce our room assignments.

"Welcome to Monterosso, everyone. Now, listen up," Jane said loudly, struggling to make herself heard. "The following people are staying in the hotel down below in Monterosso." She read off a long list of over thirty names. "You'll have to walk from here, because they don't allow personal vehicles in the town. But I promise your luggage will be delivered to you at the hotel. The ones whose names I didn't call"—which included Cynthia and me—"will be staying up here in the Buranco vineyard, which is owned and managed by a cousin of mine and which produces some very fine wines, which you'll all have a chance to enjoy, I promise. There are three rooms there with different numbers of beds—I'll let you sort out who goes where. You'll be eating your breakfast there. The bad news is, you'll have to take your own luggage down, by that path there." She waved vaguely at a graveled path that wandered down the hill to the left. "The good news is, it's downhill. The good-bad news is that you'll be in great shape after a couple of days of hiking up and down the hill from the town—you'll know what I mean once you see that path. If any of you assigned to the vineyard don't think you can handle the hill, let one of us know or work out a swap with someone, all right? Is everything clear?"

We all glanced around and nodded, more or less.

"Then let's go! Settle in, and those of you up the hill, join us in town for dinner at seven thirty. It's the Belvedere restaurant, on the waterfront, and our group will be hard to miss. If you reach the water, you've gone too far."

"I'd bet we could get lost if we tried," Cyn muttered in my ear.

"I don't think there are a lot of ways to get lost here, unless you're a mountain goat," I responded. "Shall we?" I waved a hand toward the rows of vines spread out below us.

Our motley vineyard band collected our luggage and started wrestling it down the hill, without any clear idea where we were going. I was reminded quickly that wheeled suitcases and gravel do not mix well. By the time we emerged in front of a long patio, we were ready for a break, and we all dropped into comfortable chairs overlooking the vineyard. Some of us were panting, including me. And that had been downhill. I wasn't looking forward to climbing back up from the town after dinner—in the dark. Was everything on a slant in this part of the world?

"Is that the town down there?" I pointed. And down—way down—in the distance I could see the edge of the town. It looked very far away, like a toy village. There was a path leading to it that appeared to be paved, sort of. I wouldn't want to try it in the rain. It was barely possible to make out a few ant-sized people moving around. Access to the sea led through a notch between steep hills, visible on the horizon.

"It appears to be," Cynthia said. "Damn, nobody mentioned we should spend a couple of months training to get to and from our accommodations. This is one wicked hill."

"You don't think you can handle it?" I challenged her.

She grinned at me. "Of course I can. But it might be a slow trip with a couple of stops along the way. To admire the scenery, of course."

"Of course." I looked over our group: there were seven of us. Five had sat down to pant, and the other two, obviously in better shape than the rest of us, had decided to go exploring the rooms. Connie and Denise I had either spoken with or overheard speaking with other people, so I felt I knew them to some extent. Pam and Valerie I knew less well, and I hadn't had an opportunity to talk with Victoria at all. Once again, the fates—or Jean and Jane—had shuffled the deck, giving us a chance to get to know more people, the ones we were with now. Valerie, the most athletic of the crew, had been the first to go exploring the bedroom options, and Pam had gone with her. They returned to the table grinning.

"There's a double and a triple on that end" — Valerie waved back the way we had come — "and a double at the opposite end," she said.

"Dibs on that last one, even if it is the highest," Cynthia said promptly. "Laura, that work for you?"

"Sure," I said. Maybe that would give us some time to really talk, which hadn't happened yet. But I wondered if there was a reason she preferred the more isolated location.

"Okay," Valerie said. "Anybody else want a double?"

People exchanged glances and shrugs, and in the end Connie, Denise, and Valerie ended up in the triple, leaving Pam and Vicky in the double. I thought Vicky looked dubious. I'd noticed her huffing and puffing already, and I wasn't sure whether she would be able to handle the steep paths. We'd find out soon enough.

With that momentous decision settled, we turned our attention to the vineyard. At the end of the patio we had passed by a cluster of large, shiny stainless-steel vats maybe ten feet high that I assumed were used in wine making. Now we found ourselves looking at a hillside of vines that made the grapes that went into those vats.

Oh, my. For once the pretty pictures on the website that we'd seen were not faked or enhanced; this was real. Terraces of vines rose up the hill across from where we stood and olive trees lined the hill below us. In the more sheltered valley were lemon trees and a series of blue boxes that I guessed were beehives. I could hear fowl clucking somewhere down that way as well.

"I think I need a nap before we attack the village," Cynthia said firmly. "Laura, are you ready to settle in?"

"Hey, don't forget the religious procession," Valerie said. "Jane said it was something special."

Cynthia and I exchanged looks. "I've never seen one, up close and personal. What time does it start?" I asked.

"Like, now, probably."

I suppressed a sigh. I had been looking forward to a little downtime. "Okay. Cyn, why don't we haul our bags up and check out the room, and then head down the hill? You guys don't have to wait for us."

"Sounds good to me," Cynthia said. "Come on, Laura." She stood up and started pulling her cute little suitcase toward the opposite end of the long patio. I followed her, hauling my large evil suitcase. I was not looking forward to the twisting concrete steps I could see leading up to our room, but we managed them. There was a charming patio in front of the door, supplied with a table and two chairs. When we entered we found ourselves in a two-bedroom aerie with a windowless bath between.

Cynthia went back to the doorway to pick up a tote bag and now was standing transfixed. "Oh, Laura, come look at this!" she exclaimed.

I joined her at the door. Below us was spread a vista of sky and mountains, town and sea. It was breathtaking. And if that wasn't enough, Cynthia pointed nearly straight ahead and I could see a faint rainbow arching across the valley. I almost laughed, it was so picture-perfect. I could get used to this.

Deep in my purse, a phone rang. Cynthia noticed and cocked an eyebrow at me: I knew she hadn't been able to get any kind of service for days. I kept my expression noncommittal and walked outside to a corner of the patio to answer it. The call was short and to the point, but it was the news I'd hoped not to hear. When the call ended, I sat down at the table on the patio and stared at nothing, thinking hard. Terrible waste of a good view.

Chapter 13

Cynthia had retreated discreetly, but now she came back and sat down at the table. "Trouble? Your daughter?"

"No, not her." I turned over my options in my mind. What I'd just learned affected all of us. I trusted Cynthia, both because of our long friendship and because, thanks to the twins in Capitignano, she had an alibi for the time of the professor's death, even if it was a crazy one. Just crazy enough to be believable. And the Cynthia I had known did not lie. I had to tell her.

"Professor Gilbert did not die a natural death. Or not entirely," I began.

Cynthia kept her expression neutral. "What do you mean? And how do you know?"

"The autopsy showed signs of drugs in his system—not recreational ones. An opiate, a morphine analog."

"You mean, like heroin?"

"Not exactly. More like a home brew. Did you know you could make a soporific from the petals of those pretty red poppies we've been seeing everywhere?"

"No, I did not know that." Cynthia took a moment to think this over. "So somebody brewed up something and slipped it to him? Is that what killed him?"

I shook my head. "No, it wasn't strong enough to kill, but it was strong enough to make him unsteady and probably kind of loopy. It would, however, have made him much more likely to fall, given the terrain."

Cynthia nodded, digesting what I'd told her. "I see. So you're saying someone fed him this stuff either to embarrass him by making him look like an old fool or in the hope that he would fall down and hurt himself?"

"In a nutshell."

Cynthia looked around carefully, but none of our classmates was in sight. "Laura, how do you know this? Can you tell me?"

I looked at her directly. "You know what I do, although nobody else here does. I hope they all believe I'm some mid-level analyst for a boring government office. When I found Professor Gilbert's body, I made a call, because the whole thing just didn't seem right to me. I did not request assistance here in Italy, but I asked that somebody make sure that the Italian authorities did a thorough autopsy, not just a quick look. Otherwise they wouldn't have found what they did."

"Laura, what did you hope to gain? It certainly looked like an accident."

"But it wasn't," I said, feeling defensive and hating it. "I know what you're saying, Cyn. I could have left it alone, let the police call it an accident, and we all would have rolled along just fine. Which is what we've all done so far. I hoped it wouldn't come to this."

"So why did you rock the boat?"

"I just wanted to be sure it really was an accident. And now I'm not so sure."

"So you're saying that someone in our group had a hand in the man's death."

"Looks like it," I said. Cynthia was right: I could have left this alone and we could all have gone happily on our merry ways. But I'd never been one to take the easy route, and if this was murder, directly or indirectly, I wanted to know. What I'd do once I was sure and had an idea of who might have done it, I *didn't* know. I sighed.

"Cynthia, am I paranoid, or did you get the feeling that there were people who weren't too fond of Professor Gilbert? Who weren't happy to see him there at all?"

Cynthia looked away, toward the sea. "I wondered about that," she said quietly. "As I said when it happened, I never knew him, but I told you there were a lot of rumors."

I nodded. "Exactly. I know I've talked to several people who did know him, who took classes from him, or knew someone who did. And most people said what you'd expect. After all, it was a long time ago. But there was still something a little off . . . There were people who looked, I don't know — angry?" We were silent for perhaps half a minute. Then I added, "The police will be sending someone from Tuscany to talk to us."

"That's what the phone call was about? What the hell are we supposed to do?" Cynthia asked.

"That was a heads-up. And before you ask, I can't call the same number and say, sorry, never mind. I started something and now it's out of my hands."

"Who else knows?"

"Nobody, yet. I'm not sure if the police—is it the police, or the *carabinieri*?—even know where to find us at the moment. If they ever track us down, I'm sure they won't be happy. The crime scene is long gone, as is any evidence in the professor's room, and all the suspects have had plenty of time to think up nice alibis."

"This is Italy. You sure they won't just throw up their hands and declare it's too complicated?"

I shook my head.

Cynthia went on, "You're saying it's likely that one of us gave him the drug. Who?"

"I have no idea. I don't know any of these women well. I've been trying to steer conversations to the professor's death without being too obvious, but that way I get only snippets. I think I've heard at least four possible motives. I think there's something wrong. But, Cyn, how do I fix this? I don't want these women to hate me for wrecking the trip, but I don't want to ignore a murder, even if the guy was scum. You think I was wrong to do it?" I asked.

Cynthia shut her eyes for a moment, then opened them again. "No," she said in a quiet voice, "I guess not. Not if he was helped to death. He may have been a jerk, but he didn't have to die. How you're going to explain that to anybody else, I don't know. They will not be happy if their vacation is trashed."

"I know that." I stopped talking and thought for a moment. "I can see one way out of this," I began tentatively.

"What?" Cynthia challenged me. "Wait, are you thinking what I think you're thinking?"

"If that means solving this murder and salvaging the holiday, all before the police or whoever show up, then yes."

"The two of us," Cynthia said dubiously.

"Why not? We're smart women, aren't we? We can figure this out."

"I hope so," Cynthia grumbled. "How—"

We were interrupted by the sound of voices, ten feet below us. "Ahoy, up there! We're ready to go explore the town. You coming?"

I mouthed "later" at Cynthia, and then called out, "Sure. We'll be right there."

We headed down the hill, watching where we put our feet, and arrived for the last part of the procession. The town, packed with people of all ages, sizes and nationalities, had gathered in front of the church to watch for the arrival of the priest and an entourage of other robed priests. The priest in front carried what I recognized from my medieval classes as a monstrance, a sun-rayed disk that displayed the consecrated Host to the spectators. The small procession trod over paths of fresh flowers laid out in intricate designs, which gave color to the cobbled streets. It was strangely moving, and I felt as though I had stepped back into some earlier time. We found our companions, and our little vineyard group watched together in silence. When the priests had marched past the church toward the sea, we followed slowly, looking for our restaurant.

It was not hard to find. No one would ever call our class shy and retiring, and those who had arrived early had taken over the two long tables under the awning in front of the restaurant. Once again, bottles of wine were already circulating. By unspoken agreement, Cynthia and I settled at different tables, and I took a moment to admire the harbor spread out in front of us, with rocky cliffs on either side.

Dinner, once we finally got around to it, was a rollicking delight. The menu was set so we had no decisions to make, and the bottles of wine didn't stop coming. I decided that I had misjudged Italian wine as weak and watery, but here in its home it was light and pleasant. Maybe it was the air, or the soil — or the company. I pitied any hapless tourist who happened to wander into our space: the members of our group were in rare form, and not exactly quiet.

I chose a seat next to yet more people I hadn't talked to, and Cynthia did the same, at the second table. Leaving Tuscany had somehow relieved us of focusing on art history and culture, and I kept finding myself involved in conversations about unlikely topics and was impressed by the unexpected breadth of knowledge of my companions. Then I chided myself: they had all been officially "smart" women forty-something years ago; why should I assume their lives were narrow and dull now? These women were anything but dull. What's more, most of them seemed relaxed and comfortable in their own skin. There was no jockeying for leadership, no deliberate effort to impress anyone else. Nobody tried to dominate the conversation, and there was no "me, me, me!" Some people were quieter than others, but nobody looked unhappy. Jean and Jane had created something really special when they put this trip together.

The light faded slowly and the prodigious quantities of food gradually disappeared. Finally a few women started to stand, preparing to leave. Jane quickly stood up.

"*Attenzione, per favore!* Tomorrow is what Jean and I are calling a day of leisure. That means you're free to explore all or any of the Cinque Terre at your own speed. You have two options for getting around: ferry or train. Or, well, maybe three, if you count the hiking trails, but I've heard they're in bad shape this year—some parts are washed out. Anyway, I'll explain how the public transportation works and help you get tickets if you want. I should warn you, though: the boats are small, and if you're at all prone to seasickness, you might do better to take the train. The villages are only about ten minutes apart by train, and the trains run every half hour or so, so it's easy to get back and forth. Or if you prefer, you can stay here and sleep or read or wander around Monterosso, your choice."

Jean interrupted her to say something in her ear, then Jane resumed. "When you all return, we'll be eating at another restaurant in town here, closer to the church. The day after, we'll be dining in a castle! And on our last night there will be a dinner for all of us up the hill at the vineyard, and I'm sure the lucky few who are staying up there will tell you how beautiful it is. By the way, you'll be drinking the vineyard's award-winning wines, so we hope this will be really special. I'll go into details about the rest of the week later, but tomorrow, just relax and enjoy yourselves!"

People started drifting off in twos or threes. Cynthia and I found each other again and followed the majority of the group toward the hotel. If I recalled correctly—having seen it exactly once, by daylight—the path to our vineyard aerie took off, uphill, from there. We bid good night to several people and then started the trek upward. Once we'd passed the last building—the office for the *carabinieri*, I noted—I stopped to look up the hill. And up, and up. It looked endless.

"Are you going to tell Jane?" Cynthia asked in a low voice.

I glanced quickly around but didn't see anyone nearby. "About the professor? Maybe I'm chicken, but I'd rather not. Let her remain in blissful ignorance a little longer. If the police come calling, we can tell her what we know and then let her negotiate from there. After all, she's the only one among us who can even talk to the authorities. And she can decide what to tell the rest of our group."

"You *are* a chicken, Laura, but I think I agree with you. I'd hate to spoil things for the rest of the group unless it's really necessary." She looked up the hill. "I guess we'd better start climbing."

"Can we take it slowly?" I asked, stopping just short of whining.

"What, you aren't in shape?"

"I live in a flat city. I couldn't tell you the last time I climbed a real hill, or one this long. Besides, we need to talk."

"Why does that always sound ominous?" Cynthia said, leading off at a reasonable pace. At least it was still light enough to see where we were putting our feet and we didn't yet need flashlights.

"God, I hate to think what it would be like if the police decided to keep us beyond our original departure date. That could be a real mess." I was beginning to wonder if I had thought through all the possible outcomes of my impetuous phone call. Sure, maybe somebody had killed the professor, but why did I have the right to shake up the plans for forty people, who had no doubt been looking forward to this vacation for a while?

"Aren't you borrowing trouble? Anyway, all the more reason we should wrap this up quickly, don't you think? I'm sure we can figure it out more quickly than the Italian police, right?" Cynthia said. "So where do we start?"

I checked her face—as much as I could see of it in the dusk—to see if she was being sarcastic. "As soon as we get up the hill," I said, panting.

"We may not be alone up there, you know."

"There is that, although it's better than it would be in the hotel. I think the first thing that has to happen is that you and I go over the list of our classmates and figure out who we feel safe sharing this with."

"Or who has an alibi," Cynthia added.

I hadn't even thought that far, but she was right. But how on earth were we supposed to collect alibis from forty people? "Good point. We start with our friends sharing the vineyard rooms. If we suspect them, it's going to be hard to find any private time to talk."

Cynthia didn't say anything for a bit, although her breath was coming evenly. "So you trust me?"

We both stopped next to a high stone wall with a niche holding a comically small statue of the Virgin Mary. "Yes, I do. Your ridiculous alibi aside, I've known you forever, and I can't imagine you being cowed by the lecherous professor, back in college or since. You would have told him where to get off, in no uncertain terms."

Cynthia smiled. "I would indeed. I never had the chance, since I never took a class from him. You know, I think I blew off any rumors I heard about him because I figured the girls—women—he was hitting on were weak and didn't know how to handle the situation. I'll admit that I was wrong to be so judgmental then—I was an arrogant bitch, wasn't I? But I had no personal animus against Professor Gilbert. Besides, you need me—I'm your Watson, remember?"

"You can be whoever you want as long as it helps us figure this out."

Chapter 14

We'd reached the level but the vines were shrouded in dusk. The sky was a deep blue, and a few stars had appeared. I caught my breath and said, "Let's go up to our patio. That's as private a place as we're going to find and we can see, and hear, anybody coming."

We made the final climb and dropped into chairs at the table. Cynthia rummaged in her bag and pulled out a half-filled bottle of wine. "It seemed a shame to let it go to waste. There are glasses inside." She disappeared into our rooms to look for the glasses, and I took a moment to listen. I heard no human sounds. Maybe our colleagues were still down the hill exploring the town, or putting off the climb.

Cynthia came out with two glasses, filled them, and handed one to me. "*Salute!*" she said. We clinked glasses. "Okay, where do we start?"

"I've been trying to think of ways to narrow the list down. Look, you said you found out about me and what I do, right?"

"Yes. That's what I do, or my company does. Discreetly, of course, and usually for a nice large fee."

So we were on a level playing field, because I had known what she did for a living too: she was a cyber-snoop for hire, a sometime data miner, with a company of computer nerds to back her up. "I won't ask how much of what you do is legal. You told me earlier that you have profiles of the rest of the group, right?"

"I do. Basic ones, anyway, and I could flesh them out if it would help. What do you want me to look for?"

"I think you may need to dig a little deeper. For a start, can you get college transcripts or class enrollments or whatever covers the ground for the people here and determine who did take one of Professor Gilbert's classes? Then we can see who's admitted it and who's kept silent."

"Sure, no problem. Listen, I'm going to have to involve some of my staff. I have complete faith in all of them, and they have no connection to what has gone on here. Is that okay with you?"

"It'll have to be if we want to wrap this up quickly. Okay, so we'll have an idea about who might have a direct reason to hate the guy —

and you'll get grades, right? See who he gave a C or worse to? That could be a blot on an otherwise impressive record and could have had ramifications."

"Sure. And my crew can work around the clock. Of course, some of the women here may have had encounters with the professor outside of the classroom, and that won't show up in any official record. We've been talking pretty much in terms of what we now call sexual harassment, but there were other ways Gilbert messed with people."

"Such as?" I asked. I'd heard a few suggestions and I wanted to see if she'd heard anything new.

"Humiliating them in class, just because he could. Withholding letters of recommendation for grad schools or jobs. That kind of thing is more about power and his ego than about sex."

"Point taken. I know the transcripts won't tell the whole story, but we have to start somewhere. Let's assume that the information can eliminate, say, half the group. That still leaves twenty, in round numbers. For the next step, we need to match up the list with who was physically close enough to Gilbert to slip him something that night."

Cynthia raised one skeptical eyebrow. "Okay, how are we supposed to get that without asking people dumb questions like, Where were you standing at eight fifty-three the night Professor Gilbert died? That's kind of obvious, isn't it?"

"I'm still working on it," I admitted.

Cynthia said suddenly, "Back up a minute. You said someone could make a knockout potion or whatever you want to call it easily using those poppies, right?"

"Yes, or so I understand. So the supply of poppies was right there. What are you asking?"

"Two points. One, someone would have to know something about toxins to realize how easy this would be to make, although obviously you can find everything online these days. I'm assuming it's not some long, complex chemical procedure using fancy glassware, but something more like brewing tea, involving hot water?"

I nodded. "I think so, and we can check. What else?"

Cynthia took a sip of her wine. "If that's the case, then the second point is, someone needed access to cooking facilities in Capitignano. There are only so many rooms that had stoves at the villa. We didn't.

And I can't see anyone hauling an electric kettle around — can't you see the way the people at customs would look at that? But the building next to the dining hall had a full kitchen, and there was another one in the villa over us. Maybe someone could have sneaked into the dining room in the middle of the night to brew something up, but they'd run the risk of being noticed there, and they would have needed some light, which would have been obvious to a lot of people."

"Good thinking. And we don't know that everyone knew about the stoves scattered around, unless they did a lot of visiting among the rooms. So you're suggesting that narrows the pool of suspects down to maybe ten or fifteen of us who were in those rooms?"

"Exactly. When we compare that with the list of Gilbert's students, that should narrow it further. Within a margin of error, of course."

I smiled into the dark. It felt good having Cynthia's help, and her willingness went a long way toward relieving my guilt at having started this whole thing. "This is great, Cyn. So to go back to my earlier point, the next hurdle is to figure out who was physically near enough to the professor to introduce this substance into something he was drinking."

Cynthia leaned back in her chair and contemplated the sky, now rich with stars. "As far as I recall, not that I was paying a lot of attention, he was drinking most of the night. I don't think I ever saw him without a glass in his hand."

"What was he drinking? Wine? Cocktails?"

Cynthia shut her eyes. "Highball glass, I think, but mostly that aperitif my friend the cook kept whipping up. What was it called? An Aperol spritz?"

"Sounds about right. Anyway, the drink was dark enough that it would hide anything that was added. Of course, we don't know what poppy flower tea would taste like, but it had a pretty distinct flavor of its own. I wonder if Professor Gilbert had had it before?"

"Could be," Cynthia said. "The recipe is on the Aperol bottle, so it must be popular. But that doesn't mean he's had it before, or knew what it should taste like. And don't forget the bottle of wine waiting for him in his room. With the two glasses."

"I wonder if that had been opened or if your guy left a corkscrew? Seems like all the physical evidence was conveniently destroyed," I said absently. "So what do we look for now? A chemist? An MD? No shortage of those in this group. Almost as many medicos as art historians."

"Or an herbalist with an interest in natural remedies," Cynthia suggested. "In low doses this poppy tea is a good sleep aid."

"And you know this why?"

"I looked it up online."

"Ah. Well, one other point the lab report provided was that it wasn't a strong enough dose to kill him. He would have to have drunk gallons of the stuff or had some preexisting medical condition that made him sensitive to it. But say someone slipped him this homemade Mickey, enough to make him clumsy, how'd he fall down the hill? After all, the fall happened not far from our window, and it was very quiet there, if you recall. I can't believe I could have slept through something like that. Wouldn't he have cried out? Isn't that the typical reaction if you're conscious and falling to your death? By the way, what time did you get back?"

"About two. So you're saying he had to have gone over the edge before two, because we couldn't both have slept through it? I mean, it might have awakened you, but if you didn't hear anything else you might have assumed that you'd dreamed it. But we couldn't both have done that."

"That's what I'm thinking. Which means what? He was so out of it that he didn't notice he was falling down a hill? Or there was something else going on. I wish I could see the full autopsy report to see if there were any other injuries that didn't fit a fall. But it's probably in Italian so I wouldn't understand it anyway."

"You can't ask one of your contacts?"

"I could, I guess, but I'd rather keep them in reserve in case this gets a whole lot worse. Like if we all end up in a holding cell somewhere. I don't even know where the nearest police administrative center would be. And I'd rather not find out."

"I agree," Cynthia said emphatically. "Your contact is our ace in the hole if we all get arrested. So forensically we're on our own. Somebody—presumably a woman—slips him the poppy tea, gets him drunk on top of that, and pushes him down the hill. Maybe she didn't mean to kill him, but either way he died. Okay, if we put the late-night tête-a-tête on hold, as I asked before, how do we determine who spent any time close enough to him to slip him the stuff? Did your expert tell you how long it took to work?"

"And as I said earlier, more or less, we can't go around asking people, *Did you talk to the professor? When? Before, during or after dinner?*" I protested.

"Probably before, actually. Wouldn't it be more potent on an empty stomach? And why *can't* we just ask?" I wondered if Cynthia was playing devil's advocate.

"I think you're right, about the timing," I said. "It would take a little while to affect him, but if he was seated at dinner and talking, he might not have noticed. As for the other, because asking questions would tip off the killer, or the accidental one. The death could still have been unintentional. Not that I've noticed any one of us going around looking particularly guilt-ridden."

"Who sat at the head table with him?" Cynthia asked.

"I wouldn't want to swear to it. Barbara and Gerry, because it was their show and they'd invited him. Jean and Jane? After that it's kind of blurry, although I know there were other women there. I was at the other end of the room."

Cynthia refilled her glass and stared into the darkness. Then she said, "Photos."

"What?"

"Everybody was snapping pictures, formally or informally. Cameras, cell phones, and Xianling with her ever-present iPad. Surely we could put together an array of pictures that will show who stood or sat near him during the evening?"

"That is an excellent idea, Watson. But how would we get them all quickly?"

"We need an ally, like Xianling. She could claim she's putting together a memory book or whatever and could she please have all the pictures. Like, right away, while everyone still remembers."

"What if people say no?"

"She'll just have to wheedle. We need a *good* ally. I think she could pull it off."

"Which means we have to eliminate that person — Xianling — from suspicion before we ask her to do this."

"Or we'll just have to go with our gut and trust someone."

"Or two someones, if we need some medical advice."

"Yup. Who do you think are in the clear?" Cynthia asked.

"Well, I can't imagine Jean and Jane sabotaging something they'd worked so long and hard to make happen. If we decide they're in the clear, they could help to clear this up ASAP so we can go on playing tourists without it hanging over us."

"But they don't have the right expertise. Expertises. Whatever."

How much had Cynthia had to drink? "Right. Who knew the professor would be making a special appearance, and when did they know it? And the arrogance of that guy, thinking he'd be welcome after what he did to so many women."

Cynthia held up a finger. "*Allegedly* did. No one ever accused him openly. He was never tried for anything. He didn't lose his job. So he had reason to believe that his behavior was acceptable, or not unacceptable."

"Do we blame the college for that?" I asked.

"I don't know if we can. You remember those days, don't you? Nobody knew of terms like *bullying* or *sexual harassment*. We were mostly good little girls who were raised to believe that if a guy got out of hand, it was somehow our fault because we'd led him on. Now, raise the ante and make the guy a good-looking, smart professor. Any girl would have been flattered to be noticed by him. And when he kicked them to the curb, well, guess what—it was their fault again. They just didn't measure up. Throw in a dash of third-wave feminism—we were breaking out of the old restrictions. And the college didn't have in place any mechanism to address this kind of problem then."

I sat back and looked at her admiringly. "That, lady, is quite a speech. You sure you don't have a stake in this?"

"No, I don't—not personally. I'm just reminding you that those were the times, and the times changed. I hope and believe that this would not happen today."

"Amen. Anyway, Gilbert felt free to join us, confident that he would be welcomed warmly. Jerk."

"Well, he paid the price in the end." She drained her glass. "So, now what?"

"You find out what you can about our classmates. Let me think about who else we can bring into this—my head's a little muddled tonight. You planning to tour the Cinque Terre tomorrow?"

"I thought I might. We should split up and talk to different people again. You never know what they might let slip."

"Like a convenient confession?" I joked.

"You wish. But we can verify if they ever knew the professor. And then we can compare that with the real history, when I get it. If someone lies, then we know we've got a problem."

"I can tell you the ones I know knew the professor, so your list just got shorter. You know, you're pretty good at this. Your data collection company—you've worked with law enforcement before, haven't you?"

"My lips are sealed. Confidentiality agreements and so on. And you haven't been exactly up front with your activities either."

"Fair point. But between us we can handle this, right?"

"Of course. *Ministrare, non ministrari.*" The old college motto: Not to be ministered unto, but to minister. All right, then. We were going to take charge of this problem before the police got involved, and we would take care of it.

Chapter 15

Cynthia went inside, and soon I could hear the sound of running water in the bathroom behind me, but I didn't feel like going inside to get ready for bed — it was too nice out here. I tipped the last of the bottle of wine into my glass and sat listening to the night. No sounds floated up from the town, but my fleeting impression had been that it shut down fairly early — no raucous beach parties or people spilling out of bars.

Was it arrogant for Cynthia and me to think we could figure out who had killed the professor? Why not just let the police handle it? Well, for one thing, I felt responsible for starting the whole mess. If I'd kept my nose out of it, most likely it would have gone away quietly. Two, I had my doubts that the local police, or even the national police, would get it right, although I had to admit that my disdain was based more on years of movies and television shows rather than any direct experience with them. But our group of classmates was on a tight schedule, and nobody had planned on sitting around being interviewed by the cops — in Italian, no less. Would the investigators want to talk to us here in Liguria? Or would they want to drag us back to Tuscany and the scene of the crime? Where would we stay? For how long? Nobody would be happy with Cynthia and me.

It didn't take much of this thinking to convince me that if Cyn and I could expedite the process, we should, *pronto*. And we did bring special skills to the table, skills that our classmates most likely weren't aware of. We could use them, quietly, without revealing too much about what we did, how we worked. We could fix things without anybody knowing. At least, that was what I hoped. I had to admit that Cynthia and I were both behind-the-scenes kind of people in our fields, not experienced or subtle interviewers.

Did I feel a need to make things right for these women, whom I wasn't exactly close to? I was surprised that the answer was yes. We had a bond because of our shared past, no matter what had happened since. And so many people, myself included, had been looking forward to this trip; had probably made sacrifices for it, financially or otherwise. To have it compromised by one person's cruel and thoughtless act was not fair.

Had it in fact been thoughtless? A crime of opportunity? Or had someone planned this carefully, maybe for a long time? Who had known that Professor Gilbert lived in Tuscany? Who might have suggested that it would be interesting to invite him to speak at our gathering? That was a question that should be directed to Barbara and Gerry, but they weren't here, and I wasn't even sure how to get in touch with them. Maybe we could ask Jean and Jane if they knew any additional details. But even if the professor had been lured to the villa, who had known what the topography there was, and that it provided so many steep hills and slippery paths?

Too many questions, and not enough time to ask them all.

I heard footsteps crunching on the path below, and then a voice called out quietly, "Hello?"

"Up here," I said, also quietly — I was pretty sure voices carried in the still night air.

A shadowy figure slid up the last set of steps to my patio. It resolved itself into Xianling, who dropped into a chair. Not a hair out of place, and she wasn't even panting. Not fair.

"What brings you up here?" I asked. "It's a little steep for a late stroll."

"Simple — I switched places with Vicky, who was assigned to a room up here. After one walk down to the village, she decided she'd never make it back up, and I offered to take her place. I can use the exercise."

"You'll get plenty, believe me. What's the hotel like?"

"Like a pleasant small hotel, I guess. There was nobody on the streets except a cat when I started walking up. The only odd thing is that they have Manx cats at the hotel — no tails. It's a bit unnerving to meet one unexpectedly. Anyway, I brought enough to handle tonight" — she held up a sleek small bag — "I'll worry about my suitcase tomorrow."

"Welcome to the vineyard, Xianling. Wait until you see it by daylight, you won't be sorry. Have a seat. I'm sorry, but we finished the wine."

Xianling sat gracefully. "Who else is up here?" After I named the others, she asked, "You and Cynthia were roommates in college, right?" she asked.

"We were. And after too, for a couple of years."

"Have you kept in touch?"

"Kind of. As much as with anybody. I hate to admit it, but I'm still having trouble putting names to some of the people in our group here."

Xianling laughed. "I am *so* glad to hear somebody else say that! It's so strange, you know? Some people you'd recognize if you passed them on the street now, they've hardly changed. Others I don't recognize at all, even after spending a couple of days with them on this trip. Do you remember me? I won't be offended if you say no."

"You were an art historian, so of course I knew who you were. But I don't remember ever having a real conversation with you."

"That sounds about right. I think I started on that track before you did, so we didn't overlap in classes."

"Had you noticed how many people are here from the freshman crop in Munger?" I asked. "Funny how so many of us stuck with the first group of people we met the first week at school. Random choice—heck, it wasn't even computer-organized back in those days. Some little lady in a back office in Green Hall sorted handwritten cards, and presto, people became friends for life. And here we are. Bet no one saw this coming!"

"A trip to Italy with these people forty years later? I can't say that I did."

"And yet you signed up. Why?" Why had this elegant and ac-complished woman volunteered to join this motley group of class-mates?

"I love Italy, of course, but mainly curiosity, I suppose. I've stayed close to Jean over the years—that art history connection—but I wanted to see how everyone else had turned out."

"You've been taking a lot of pictures."

"I have. In part, it's a habit, given what I do. I also wanted a re-cord of the event. I'll be happy to share with anyone who wants cop-ies."

"I think I'd like that. Looking at what's on my camera, I seem to concentrate on landscapes and cats, with food coming in third. I have very few pictures of people. I guess I feel embarrassed taking pic-tures of others, even candids. You seem to do it well, or at least everyone has gotten used to it. I love that group photo you took at Capitig-nano."

"That did come out well, didn't it?" She was silent for a moment, then said, "Can you point me toward my room?"

"It's the one in the middle—go past the patio and up. You'll be in with Pam. The others are at the far end."

"Thank you. I'll see you at breakfast then." Xianling stood and vanished silently into the night. I wondered what kind of shoes she was wearing.

I'd missed a good opportunity to ask her about the professor's death—but I was tired, and it had been a long day, and I'd probably just mess it up. I had to think about how I wanted to approach people without giving myself away. If that was possible.

I stood up and stretched. With one last look at the dark land-scape, I went inside.

• • •

Cynthia and I were up early and went down to the main patio to kill time until breakfast started. The staff was apparently trying to drive us crazy because they put out everything else for the meal be-fore they finally set out a carafe of coffee. Cyn and I used our time well, admiring the incredibly lush flowers everywhere. Roses pre-dominated, but there were some impressive lilies, as well as a num-ber of plants I couldn't identify. The fowl down below the vines were making loud morning noises. From what I could hear, there was a mix of species, all producing different sounds. When the table was finally set up and the staff stepped back, Cyn and I helped ourselves to food and coffee, then settled ourselves on the shady interior side of the table, the one facing the view—I wasn't going to waste a minute of the gorgeous scenery.

The others drifted in gradually. "What are you all planning for today?" I asked when a quorum had assembled.

"I want to take the ferry and do the whole circuit of the Cinque Terre. I'm pretty sure this is my only chance to see this part of the world," Denise said.

"Not me," Valerie replied with something approaching a shudder. "I might do one town. Maybe. And I don't like boats."

"Okay," I said neutrally. "I was thinking it might be nice to see one, maybe have lunch there. I mean, how different can they be from each other?"

"You mean, you see one, you've seen them all? And what the heck is there to do in any of them?" Pam demanded.

"No museums," I said. That brought a wry smile from Xianling. "I guess that leaves taking pictures of the scenery and the town, eating, and shopping. And apparently Xianling is the designated official historian for the trip and is taking pictures of everything and everyone."

Xianling shrugged. "It's not a big thing, I do it everywhere. I have a very visual memory, which may be why I went into art history originally."

"Interesting about how your memory works," I said, and meant it. "I think I was always more attracted to three-dimensional things, like medieval churches. So your pictures—does your tablet work inside and out? I haven't seen any flashes."

"It does." She pulled it out of her bag, tapped the screen a few times, and turned it toward me.

"Wow," I said. "Great resolution, great color. But you've also managed to capture people looking natural, which I know is a lot harder."

"Thank you. I've had plenty of practice."

"You've traveled a lot?" I asked, and that set off a conversation that took us through breakfast and a second cup of delightfully strong coffee.

The next arrival was heralded by a flood of fluent Italian, none of which I could follow. I watched as a woman came up the path accompanied by Jane. Jane was having trouble stemming the flow of the other woman's words, even though she tried.

"*Buon giorno,*" Jane said when she saw all of us at the table, watching expectantly. "This is my cousin Loredana—she and her husband own the vineyard here, and when our head count exceeded the hotel's capacity, she generously offered to let a few of you stay up here. She speaks some English. She'll be accompanying us on some of our excursions in this area." Jane made the round of introductions. Loredana was shorter than Jane and radiated energy and enthusiasm.

Her words of welcome poured out in a haphazard mix of Italian and English, but her warmth was sincere. She seemed quite happy to meet all of us, but I guessed from the tenor of the conversation earlier that something was troubling her. And I thought I could guess what it was.

I stood up abruptly, almost knocking over the chair. "Jane, could I speak to you for a moment, in private? And your cousin too?" Cynthia looked at me, and I nodded slightly.

"Uh, well, sure," Jane stuttered. "In the vineyard office?" She glanced at Loredana for confirmation. She nodded vigorously, still looking concerned. So did the others at the table. I'd managed to confuse just about everyone. I was rarely tactful this early in the morning.

Loredana led the way, opening the office door and letting Jane and me in. Then she closed it, and she and Jane exchanged a complex series of glances, accompanied by shrugs. I hurried to begin with explanations.

"Jane," I began, "I didn't want the whole group to hear this. You and Loredana came up here to tell us something, right?"

"Yes," Jane said. "The police called. They think Professor Gilbert's death was not an accident, or not completely. Were you expecting something like that?"

Loredana seemed to be following but was having trouble expressing her own opinions. "*Cara*, I no have words . . . *la polizia, si?*"

I nodded. "Yes, I was. Have you told the rest of the group yet?"

"No. I thought I'd start up here because you were all together. Are you telling me that I shouldn't tell people? Wait—why don't you seem surprised?"

Poor Jane—I'd really thrown her a curveball. "I'm the one who found the body, and let's say I had some suspicions about how he died. What have the police told you?"

"Not a lot, just that they have more questions for us."

"Did they ask that we return to Capitignano?"

"No," Jane said. "They volunteered to send someone here to talk to us."

I tried to work out what that would mean and concluded that they were still fishing, although they knew something was amiss.

"Did they tell you anything else? Any details?" I asked carefully.

"When they called, I handed the phone to Loredana, and she gave it to her husband—you haven't met him yet, but he's a senator from this region, so he has some clout. They told him that somebody had slipped the professor something . . . harmful, the night he died, and it might have had something to do with his fall."

So the police were making progress. I didn't like it. I definitely didn't want them here in Monterosso asking us questions, and I was pretty sure Jane and her family wouldn't either.

"Laura, what's going on?" Jane demanded.

I took a deep breath. "Jane, I . . . asked some colleagues of mine back home to keep an eye on this investigation, in case we needed some assistance. They warned me that it might come to this. Tell me: can Loredana and her husband stall the authorities long enough so that we have a chance to figure out what happened on our own? Kind of under the radar?"

Poor Jane's circuits were reaching overload. I waited to see which issue she would tackle first. In the end she proved that she was a smart woman. "Yes, they can, if I explain it to them. You're assuming you can fix this thing? What if you can't? What happens then?"

I chose my words carefully. "Jane, I'm in over my head here, but I'd like to try to do it. I'd rather not have you tell everyone that the professor's death was . . . not what it appeared. Cynthia and I have been talking this over, and we think we have some resources that will help. Can we set a deadline? Say, if we don't work this out in the next two days, then we turn the whole mess over to the police? Would that get your relatives into trouble?"

Jane thought for a moment, then turned to Loredana and let loose a torrent of Italian; Loredana responded in kind. I could catch about twenty percent of the words, and I wasn't sure who was winning. Finally it was Loredana who turned to me. "We help you. You are friends of Jane, and guests in our homes. We can keep this trouble away from you, at least for a little while. If Jane will allow?"

"Uh, yes, please. If you're sure it won't get your family into trouble."

Loredana gave a dismissive wave. "Do not worry. Go enjoy the Cinque Terre with your friends."

Jane turned back to me. "Well, there you have it. How can I help?"

"I don't know yet, Jane. Cynthia and I haven't come up with a plan yet, and we may need to enlist a few more people. But we'll be discreet about it. Please thank Loredana for me—I know we're asking a lot from her."

"I will. So otherwise, for now I do nothing, and you all will go your different ways for today and you'll ask all the right questions, and we can regroup after dinner?"

"That works for me. We'd better get back before the children get restless."

Back on the patio, all eyes turned toward us when we emerged from the office. "Problem?" Cynthia asked.

"No, everything's fine," I said, trying to sound confident. "I had some questions about, uh"—I struggled for any reasonable excuse—"exporting wine by the case, back home, and I didn't want to bore you all with it."

"Hey, that's a great idea," Connie said. "You'll have to tell us about it."

"We can worry about that later," Jane said brightly. "Right now you should decide what you want to do today. Did you want to visit any of the Cinque Terre?" She looked around at everyone at the table, clearly hoping to change the subject.

"We were thinking about it, but only if it isn't going to rain," Cynthia volunteered. "Do you think it will? And we don't want to see all the towns. Which do you recommend?"

"Don't worry about the weather, it's supposed to clear later. If you want a short trip, Vernazza is closest, and you can take a train—it's a short ride. How does that sound?"

"Fine," Cynthia said. "Is there any Internet connection somewhere around here?"

"Not on the property here. There are some in the cafés and hotels in town."

"All right, then," Cynthia said, slapping her hands on the table. "Ladies, I need maybe half an hour to check my messages down there, and then we can catch a train for this Ver-place and have lunch there." She looked around the table, where nobody seemed to be in a hurry to do anything. "That suit you all?"

Nods all around: apparently we were in sheep mode today, happy to follow anyone with a plan.

Jane looked relieved. "Okay, how about I meet you at the train station and show you how to get tickets? Say, at eleven?" Jane said. "Oh, and it's all the way on the other side of town, so allow yourself enough time to get there."

"I'm sure we can find it," I said. "Eleven sounds fine. Nice to meet you, Loredana. Thank you for looking out for us."

"No problem, no problem." She beamed at all of us. "We help the friends of our cousin Jane, no?"

We finished the last of our coffee, and by the time we were done the sun had broken through the early-morning clouds. Cynthia was the first to stand up. "I'd better go get dressed if I'm going to find that café."

"Can't leave your work at home?" Valerie joked.

Cynthia ducked the question. "It's an addiction. Hey, I rationed myself at the villa in Tuscany, but I'm just not ready to go cold turkey. See you at the station." She walked off toward our rooms.

"You know, it's kind of nice not having the Internet," Pam said. "Or television, or newspapers. Like we've stepped out of time. I could get used to this."

"I know what you mean. It's kind of soothing," I agreed. Actually I wasn't as sure that I could get used to it, but it did make a nice break—and it forced us to talk to each other, without hiding behind electronic devices. But what I couldn't say was that we needed the Internet, just a little, if we were going to take care of this murder problem. "I think I'll walk down with Cynthia—you all go ahead. See you at the station?"

The others nodded and turned to conversation, while I climbed back up to our rooms above. Cynthia was already dressed. "What was that little confab really all about?" she demanded.

"The police are getting warmer, and they want to talk. I told Jane to keep a lid on it, and then we asked her cousin to see if she could stall the police just a bit. She was happy to help."

"Great," Cynthia said, looking unhappy. "The clock is ticking."

"Well, it's better than nothing. I'll be ready in two minutes," I said.

"Fine. Think I'll be able to get printouts at whatever café we find? Or maybe we don't want to have any paper copies around—what if somebody else found the lists?"

I was busy pulling a clean shirt over my head. "Cyn, I think you're overreacting. And whatever your team back home has collected, all we need at this moment is a list of people we can prove knew the professor back in school, right? One of us can pull that up on our cell phone."

"I guess." She slipped her tablet into her bag.

We started down the hill ten minutes later. I had to admit I much preferred going down to coming up, but that was the price we paid for the view. We went past the hotel where our friends were staying, but Cynthia understandably did not want to use the Internet there in case anyone noticed what she was doing. So we went hunting for somewhere else and found a small café near the church, where for the price of a cappuccino we could have half an hour of access. After ordering, Cynthia dug in quickly, connecting with her office and downloading some files, or so I guessed, watching her. She glanced quickly at one of them, nodding.

Finally she said, "I think this is what we need right now, although there's lots more information. Anyway, it looks like maybe a third of us here took one of Professor Gilbert's classes. There could be more if anyone started the class and then dropped out before the cutoff date, but at least we've narrowed things down a bit. And we know we're two of the people who didn't cross paths with him."

"So we need to ask a dozen or more people if they knew the professor?" I said.

"Let's think about it. What we need next is to collect the photographs. Did you bring a computer?" Cynthia asked.

"I'm afraid I did. I've tried not to use it so far." I hated to be completely out of touch, although I was proud of abstaining as long as I had.

"Well, it's a good thing you did. That means you can collect the photos."

"Why me?" I protested. "I'm lousy at asking people to do things like that."

She looked at me with a wicked gleam in her eye. "Because you have no connection with Professor Gilbert, so you can go all gooshy and say you think since we were the last Wellesley women to see him, we ought to set up some sort of memorial tribute or something in his honor. And then you sit back and see what people say, or if they don't say anything. You won't have to fake anything. Then you just upload them to your computer and we can look them over later. Ask for any picture that includes the professor. We need to see if we can figure out who was close enough to him to slip him something."

"There must be hundreds of pictures!" I protested.

"Stop whining. I told you, focus on that one afternoon and evening. The sooner we start, the sooner we'll have the information we need."

I had a sudden brainstorm. "You know, there's a way to cut the process short," I said.

"What? Ask for someone to confess?"

"No, not that. I was talking to Xianling last night, after you went in. You know, she's been carrying around her tablet and taking pictures constantly. Is she on that list of people who took a class?"

Cynthia looked down at her list and scanned it. "Nope."

I felt a welling of relief. "Then let's ask her to help." When Cynthia started to argue, I raised a hand. "Don't worry, I'll offer her that pathetic excuse you came up with, but I don't think she'll resist. And she seems to be pretty observant, in addition to taking good pictures."

"Sounds good, then," Cynthia admitted. "Is she coming along to Vernazza?"

"I think so. We'll know soon enough. Are you ready to find the train station yet?"

Cynthia snapped her tablet shut and drained her coffee. "Ready. It's thataway, isn't it?" She waved vaguely toward the sea.

"Just follow the waterfront. There should be signs."

As we walked, I reviewed Cynthia's plan. In some ways it made sense. By talking to people, we would get the pictures we wanted *and* I could observe how people reacted to the mention of the professor's name and the whole idea of a memorial piece. But I thought that Xianling's stash of pictures would in fact be more useful to us, assuming she had covered the right time period. At least her photos would be large and easy to decipher. "Do you think having Loredana and her senator husband intervene is going to help or hurt?"

Cynthia shook her head. "I have no idea how local politics and power work—you'd know more than I would. But it may have bought us a little time while we sort things out. Nobody's said we can't do what we planned today. So we'd better work fast."

"Agreed."

"Where is this flipping train station?"

I pointed. "Right there. The door where Jane is standing, looking worried."

Chapter 16

Jane was standing outside the main entrance to the station as we straggled in. She shepherded us inside and up the stairs (once again, everything seemed to be on a steep hillside, and the station was no exception), where we found the rest of our breakfast companions, and then she bought us tickets and handed them out like we were schoolchildren. "Now, I've given you round-trip tickets, rather than an excursion ticket. You did all want to go to only the one place?" she asked anxiously.

Everybody nodded dutifully, and Jane looked relieved. "Be sure to validate your ticket—you stick it in that machine on the wall over there and it stamps it. Maybe nobody will check it on the train, particularly since you're going only one stop, but better to be safe than sorry because they'll fine you if you don't. Vernazza is the next stop down the line, so it won't take long to get there. You can take all the time you want once you're there. Is everything clear?"

"Like crystal," I said. "Don't worry, Jane, we'll be fine." Somehow we had managed to muddle along for forty years on our own, and I was pretty sure we could handle a ten-minute train ride, even if it was in Italy. "Where did everyone else in the group decide to go?"

Jane shook her head, as if worried by the scattering of her flock. "They're all over the place—some took the ferry, others set off earlier by train to try to see as many towns as they could. A couple even decided to try the cliff walk, although I warned them that some parts have crumbled and fallen recently. You may run into them in Vernazza, if they find they can't go any farther. Oh, here's your train! Have a nice day!" Jane watched us as we all clambered aboard the train and she waved at us as it pulled away from the station, into a tunnel.

I looked at the others and we all broke out laughing at once. "You'd think we were in the third grade," Valerie said.

"She's just looking after us," I said. "You know, none of us speaks Italian. I have no clue what to do if anything goes wrong."

"In case you need to know, *aiutarmi* covers most circumstances—it means 'help me!' But nothing will go wrong," Cynthia said firmly. "We are going to a charming town, where we will stroll about and admire the scenery, so beloved of travelers before us, like What's-His-Name, the famous English poet. Then we will find some authentic Italian food and enjoy a leisurely meal. And then we will shop. It will be the perfect day."

The way she described it, it would be, if it weren't for that annoying problem of hunting for a killer. But Cynthia was doing a great job sketching the scene—no pressures, no worries, just some old friends having lunch in a lovely town in Italy.

And it *was* beautiful, as quickly became clear when the train emerged from the tunnel and slowed at the train platform in Vernazza, despite some wind and drizzling rain. We climbed down from the high train steps and stopped a moment to get our bearings. I did a quick head count: all the vineyard people except Pam were here. Then Connie announced, "I think I'll check out that hill path. I'll catch up with you later."

Now we were five, and luckily Xianling was one of them. From what we could see, there was only one road, which led down to the sea. We wrapped our raingear more closely around us and followed that, and, yes, found the sea. We stood on the jetty, watching waves crash over the rocks along the shore and the clouds scud across the sky.

Denise pointed. "Look, there's a boat coming in."

It had to be the regular ferry, but as Jane had warned us, it was a pretty small boat. As I watched its approach, I was glad I wasn't on it. There were a couple of familiar faces from our group: they waved but didn't disembark. They were all bundled to the eyes with waterproof gear. The boat bobbed vigorously, and people climbed on and off by way of a couple of wooden planks that looked none too safe. We were still watching as it pulled away again and grew smaller in the distance, riding up and down over the swells.

"I want to climb up a bit and get some pictures." Denise waved at the path carved from sheer rock, with a rope serving as a railing, that wound up a spire of rock.

There appeared to be a castle at the top, but I didn't feel like exploring it. "You go ahead—we'll wait here."

Cynthia and I watched as Denise, Xianling, and Valerie made their way up, clinging to the handrail. Halfway up they all stopped and started taking pictures in all directions. I took a picture of them taking pictures. They took pictures of us waiting at the bottom, taking pictures of them. This was going to be one extremely well-documented trip, from all angles. I hoped that our Tuscan stay had been as well covered.

"Tell me again—are Valerie and Denise on the list?" I asked Cynthia.

"They both are." She pulled out her cell phone and showed me the screen with the list of names. "Seen enough?"

"Yup. When they come back down, we can go look for lunch. We can pick a relatively quiet place and lead into our questions gently. I just hope we'll have enough time to talk to everyone we need to before the police swoop in," I said. I suppose it could have been worse: at least we were conducting this off-the-record murder investigation while consuming Italian food, most of which had been excellent so far. It all seemed so incongruous—although maybe it shouldn't have, after all the Medici entanglement we had been wallowing in the prior week. Plotting and scheming seemed to come with the territory.

Cynthia looked troubled. "Let's see how this goes."

"One more thing. Are we allowed to have fun while we interview murder suspects?"

Cynthia sneaked a quick look at me to determine whether I was joking. I was. Wasn't I? But we needed to eat, and I didn't want to pass up an opportunity to enjoy seafood this close to the sea.

"How was it?" I called out as our friends descended and approached us.

"Cold, wet and windy," Denise said. "But great views. There's this big yacht anchored out there a ways—wonder who owns it?"

"We can only guess. You ready for lunch?"

"Sure. It's been at least an hour since our last meal. Let's see what we can find."

We strolled up the main street, peering into eateries. A lot had tables and umbrellas set out in front, on the plazas, but it was too cool and breezy to tempt many people. In the middle of the village I glanced up a flight of stone stairs: there seemed to be a restaurant partway up, away from the noisy street. "Let's check this out," I said, leading the way.

When we reached a landing we found a bustling restaurant on the right and a smaller room served by the same kitchen on the opposite side, with three or four tables, all empty. It seemed warm enough, and out of the wind, and the privacy was perfect for our needs. I moved toward the nearest table that would accommodate all of us; the others followed, and we all sat down. A young waitress came out and distributed menus and asked something about drinks. I think. Somehow we ended up with *acqua frizzante* — sparkling water back home.

When I looked at the menu, my eye lighted on a seafood risotto, but it required at least two people to share it. "Who else wants to try this?" I asked, pointing.

"Oooh," Cynthia breathed, taking in the list of ingredients, which was impressive (even I could speak "food" in Italian). Denise and Xianling followed suit, and Valerie ordered some kind of pasta with pesto, with a promise to share. The handsome waiter who came to take our order nodded enthusiastically and told us the risotto would take some time. Or more precisely, he said, *"Venti minuti* — you wait?" Nobody minded.

When he'd gone back to the kitchen, we all relaxed into our chairs. I couldn't see another tourist anywhere. There were plusses to eating in out-of-the-way places like this; even though it was no more than twenty feet from the main thoroughfare, it felt far removed.

"So, what do you think?" I threw out the challenge.

Denise asked, "About what? This restaurant? Vernazza? The Cinque Terre? Liguria? Italy?"

"Yes," I said, laughing. "At least you've identified where we are. I had trouble finding any of these places on a map. You can answer whichever you like."

Valerie volunteered, "This has been an amazing trip."

"I agree," Xianling said. "I never would have found any of these places on my own, and I've traveled quite a bit. I would not have thought to look for some of them. Like that leather place — that was extraordinary."

Everyone agreed. "There are definitely advantages to having organizers who know the area well," Cynthia said. "And the vineyard! I keep pinching myself to make sure it's real. It's such a treat to be able to stay in the middle of it."

"I know what you mean," I told her. "I feel like I've walked into a Travel Channel show, only it's real."

Reluctant though I was to change the mood, it was time to get started on our so-called investigation. I began with a soft question for the group. "Tell me, how well did you know all these other women at school? Or have you gotten to know them since?" I asked.

That carried our conversation along nicely until the waiter reappeared, cradling a large earthenware casserole dish with both hands, well covered with hot pads. *"Caldo! Bollente!"* He set it down carefully on the table, where we could see rice in a rich red sauce bubbling furiously, the whole blanketed with a layer of mussels, with other bits of seafood peeking out. Needless to say, all talk stopped as we did justice to the dish, which vanished quickly. We were reduced to sopping up the last remnants with some crusty bread when the waiter reappeared. *"Caffè? Dolci?"*

"Caffè, per favore," I said, and the others nodded. *"Nessun dolci."* I looked around the table. "Maybe gelato later?"

"Sure," Valerie said. "I didn't know you spoke Italian."

"I don't, not really. I have a vocabulary of about twenty words — dessert being one of them, you notice. But I'm good at imitating accents."

"I'm terrible at languages," Denise said. "Remember we had to take at least one at college? And two if we were headed to grad school? You must have done that, Laura."

I nodded. "Two years of German, which I've never used. Funny, the hoops they made us jump through in those days. Now I hear you can make up whatever major you want — my daughter did something like that."

"How old is she?" "What's she doing now?" And we were off on a tangent, discussing our children, or our siblings' children, until the coffee appeared — a couple of mouthfuls of intensely dark brew. I was getting very fond of it. And I needed my wits about me now, so the jolt of caffeine helped.

Time to get down to business. "Terrible thing about Professor Gilbert, wasn't it?" I said. "Did any of you know him?"

"I told you, Laura, I took a class from him," Denise said. "I thought he was too full of himself. He loved to quote Dante in Italian, which none of us understood at all. It sounded pretty, but what were we learning? It was more about him showing off his noble profile against the backdrop of autumn leaves."

Valerie gave a bark of laughter. "You've got that right. But I guess that style served him well — he had a long career, didn't he? I mean, he was tenured, back when that meant something."

"He sure did," Denise said, her voice surprisingly sharp with bitterness.

We all turned to look at her. "Why do I think there's a story behind that?" Cynthia said quietly.

Denise looked away. "I was a Romance languages major, so I ended up taking a couple of classes with him. Plus he was my senior thesis advisor, which was cool at first — until I found out he was ripping off my ideas. A year after we graduated I saw all my thesis arguments laid out in an article in a prestigious journal, and I didn't even get a footnote. I'd put money on it that the article counted heavily on his tenure application, that publish-or-perish thing."

"What did you do?" I asked.

She shrugged. "What could I do? It was published, with his name on it. If I'd complained after the fact, he could have said that I had absorbed my ideas from him. It would have been my word against his, and he was the professor while I was a lowly first-year grad student. So I did nothing. In the long run it didn't hurt me much — I found other areas of interest to work on, and I got tenure about ten years later."

"It doesn't seem right, though," Cynthia said.

"All's fair in love and tenure battles."

Her last statement might have left the door open to talk about the "love" side of things, but the waitress chose that moment to present *il conto*, and we got sidetracked trying to figure out how much of a tip to leave. In the end we were generous — that waiter had been very cute, and he'd had to carry that really heavy hot bowl.

I was coming to realize that it was not going to be easy to get the answers we needed, or at least not quickly. We gathered up our possessions and descended the steps, letting our meal settle. I was going to remember that risotto for a long time. At street level we stopped to look around and found several more of our classmates wandering around and checking out the nearby shops. We came together, then split apart again in different configurations — Xianling to take more pictures of the shoreline, now that some of the mist had cleared, Denise and Valerie to shop for souvenirs.

Cynthia and I found ourselves alone again. "Well, that was interesting," I said, when we were out of earshot of the others. "I had never considered that Professor Gilbert might be a plagiarist as well as a letch."

"My opinion of him shrinks by leaps and bounds," Cynthia replied. "But Denise has had a successful career in her field. She holds a named professorship at a major university. Do you think she'd risk all that just to get back at him now?"

I knew that Cynthia had already collected the information on the post-college paths of our classmates—she must have a good research team back home. "I'm not going to guess about what she might do. I suppose it's another kind of violation, having your brainchild stolen from you. But I agree—it seems unlikely that she'd nurse a grudge for forty years, when she's clearly moved past it."

"Obviously she recovered professionally. But for others . . . sexual violation has more lingering effects," Cynthia reminded me. "It can create real problems in establishing emotional intimacy in relationships. Once the damage is done, it's hard to repair—not like forgetting about a purloined paper."

"You sound like you speak from experience," I said. There were areas of Cynthia's life I'd never probed too deeply.

She shook her head. "Not personally, no. But the more you learn about people, particularly the way I do, the more you recognize patterns. Anyone who's been raped or molested—too many never quite get over it. And in that area, I doubt even Wellesley women are exempt."

I was pretty sure she was right. And while I'd never been a victim myself, I'd been part of any number of late-night dorm conversations where women had admitted to being forced to go further than they had wanted. Oh, usually they would put a brave face on—after all, we were all newly liberated women then, and the rules we'd grown up with were changing fast. But sleeping with a professor would have been in a whole different league.

"It's a lot harder to lead a conversation toward asking 'Did you sleep with Professor Gilbert?'" I said.

"I know. But we have to try. Anyway, I'd put a 'probably not a suspect' label on Denise, and Valerie claims not to have had any personal interactions with the man, so if I don't find anything from the background checks to contradict that, I'd let her off the hook. And we think Xianling is in the clear. Which means we have only ten or so left to go. Shall we shop?"

"Of course — as long as there's gelato."

So Cynthia and I played tourist for a while, poking around little shops, looking for nothing in particular. While most of the stores seemed reasonably authentic, the price tags suggested they knew their clientele, and it wasn't local. I recalled that large yacht anchored in the harbor. I didn't find much to tempt me, until I wandered into a small shop specializing in silver jewelry. I tried on a few rings, but when I slid one particular one onto my hand, I spontaneously said, *"Perfetto. Quanto costa?"* The girl named a reasonable price, and I walked out with the ring on my finger. An ideal souvenir — distinctive, yet very easy to pack. And I would remember when and where I bought it every time I wore it.

After another hour or so, a group of us kind of drifted together in the middle of one of the plazas. "Time to head back to Monterosso?" someone asked.

"We thought we'd try hiking it," someone else said, and others nodded enthusiastically. I shuddered at the thought of trying to hike those high rocky crags.

"If you're not back by sunset, we'll send someone out to look for you," Xianling said.

"Don't worry," Donna, apparently speaking on behalf of the hikers, dismissed her comment. "Dinner's at seven thirty, right? We'll see you there."

The rest of us dutifully trooped back to the train station, stopping every twenty feet or so to take more pictures.

Maybe I could ask my questions at dinner. Not subtle, but we had to move this forward somehow.

Chapter 17

It was late afternoon when we all straggled back to Monterosso. Most people cheerfully trotted to their hotel to stash their new acquisitions. We came across Connie and Donna, who had actually beaten us back and were now raving about the incredible UN community they had found along the hiking trail, meeting people from an amazing range of countries in a short distance. Cynthia and I looked at each other.

"It's a long way up that hill to the vineyard," I said.

"I know."

"But it's a long time until dinner," I went on.

"Yes, it is."

"So what are we going to do to fill two-plus hours?" I demanded. Cynthia was being suspiciously agreeable but not contributing to this conversation.

"Internet café," she said firmly.

Not my first choice, but I didn't have the energy to argue. "Will there be pastries?" I asked hopefully.

"If you want. Come on." She led the way back to the café where we'd stopped in the morning.

We sat down and ordered—this time I had a large *caffè Americano* and a plate of biscotti—and she logged on quickly. When the coffee arrived I took a large swallow, then dunked a biscotto in the coffee and munched on it. "Have you noticed how much time we spend eating on this trip?" I mused. "Or talking about eating? Or planning for eating?"

"Well, the food has been extraordinary, wouldn't you say? Luckily we spend even more time hiking up and down hills, which more than makes up for it," she said absently, her eyes fixed on the screen of her tablet.

I gave up trying to make conversation with her and let my mind drift, watching people walk by outside the café. A couple of our classmates wandered past but they didn't see us, and I didn't try to attract their attention. I could see the façade of the boldly striped church from where I sat, and catty-corner from it a smaller church that someone had said was dedicated to the victims of local shipwrecks. I had peeked in briefly to catch a glimpse of the rather grue-some skeletons among the carvings inside. Time seemed to slow and I had to catch myself from nodding off.

Finally Cyn gave an exclamation of disgust.

"Bad news?" I asked.

"No news at all. I think we've mined all the online data we can for the moment. Now, if we wanted to know something about some-one who graduated ten years ago, and her history at the college, we'd have much better luck."

"Oh, poor us," I drawled. "We're going to have to rely on actually talking to living, breathing people."

"That's not my strong suit," Cyn said.

"It's not mine either, but do you see any choice? We could drop this whole thing and let the Tuscan *polizia* do their thing—but that could take weeks or months, unless Loredana and her important husband can divert them, or maybe pay them off, or give them a few cases of wine. Maybe that's the best case, because if the police are honest, we might be stuck here for a while until this is settled. On the other hand, we can try to solve it ourselves in the tried-and-true fash-ion of Miss Marple, using the subtle interrogation techniques we're so bad at. And we've got only two more days to do it."

"Don't be so cheerful," Cynthia replied.

"Don't be sarcastic," I retorted. "What do we do?"

She sighed. "We do our best, for the next two days, and if we haven't sorted it out by then, it's out of our hands. Oh, and we run hither, thither and yon sightseeing like crazy all the while, stopping for enormous meals accompanied by lots of wine. Sounds like some weird kind of relay race, doesn't it? Solve a murder while collecting as many souvenirs and photos as you can. The clock is ticking."

"Not exactly ideal conditions for heart-to-heart talks."

"Nope. But it's what we've got."

We sat silently for a couple of minutes, drinking our coffee, think-ing of something—or nothing. I signaled the waitress for another cof-fee. After all, I still had a couple of biscotti left.

Cynthia grabbed a clean paper napkin and fished in her bag for a pen. "Okay, here's what we've got," she began as she sketched out what I recognized as a Venn diagram. "This circle"—she poked her pen in it—"is the group that we know took a class or had some other direct association with Professor Gilbert, and we know this either from them directly or from what my people have found. This circle" — another poke — "is the people who had access to some means to brew poppy tea while we were at Capitignano. I refuse to contemplate anyone finding the right poppies back home and sneaking the potion into the country, especially when nobody knew that the professor would be speaking."

"Agreed. Would a microwave work?"

"Damned if I know. But the only places with microwaves are the ones with kitchens anyway, so it's moot. The third circle is the people who knew enough about medicine or herbs to know what to do with those poppies at all."

Her diagram did add a certain clarity to the muddle we faced. "And if you want to make it a pyramid, there's a circle — or do I mean a sphere? — of those people who were in physical proximity to the professor that evening and had the opportunity to slip him the tea, no matter who made it. Which we hope to learn from the pictures we want to collect. You know, it could have been a couple of people working together — one to brew and one to slip it into the drink." I had to laugh. "Have we managed to narrow down any one of these categories?"

Cynthia looked frustrated. I suspected she had thought her information hunt would yield a fast result. "Not a lot. We've got the list for Circle A, although we're assuming there are no outliers, like he seduced someone because he saw her from afar in Schneider and fell in lust. We can ask Jean or Jane about Circle B, because there was a limited number of rooms or buildings that had any sort of a kitchen, and I refuse to believe that anyone cooked this up over a campfire. We have a list of professions, which will help with Circle C — who had the relevant knowledge. And as for Circle D, you're supposed to be collecting the pictures, remember?"

"I told you, I think Xianling is our best hope. I've never seen her when she didn't have that tablet in her hand, taking pictures, so she should have just about everything covered. Otherwise, when have I had the time?" I protested. "And we've got only two days. That's just not going to happen."

"Then mine whatever Xianling has, and then focus on anyone else who was taking a lot of pictures. Otherwise we're going to be stuck asking around to see if anybody noticed what cologne the professor was wearing."

It took me a moment to figure out what she meant, and then I looked at her and burst out with giggles. "Yeah, that'll work. Or maybe something like, did he have that mole in the shape of Sicily behind his left ear removed?"

"Ooh, you're good. *Was* there a mole?"

"I have no idea. Fine pair of sleuths we make."

"Speak for yourself. Besides, you started this, you with your innocent little phone call to the higher powers."

I almost expected her to stick out her tongue at me. But she was right: I felt responsible. Of course, I was the one who had found the body, but I could have handed it off to the local authorities and left it there. But noooo, I had to get in touch with my contacts and make sure the autopsy was thorough. My instincts had been bang on, but I had created a lot of complications for a lot of people, and now I had to wonder if I had done the right thing. "How about we look at that list of professions? That might be the shortest."

Cyn eyed another page on her tablet. "We've got five current or retired MDs, but only Christine and Valerie admit to knowing the professor."

"Specialties?"

"Ob-gyn, no surprise, given the times."

"A medical doctor might not be the only category to look at. What about people who are pursuing alternative medicines? A late-life conversion? They could know about herbal remedies, if they're into holistic medicine or natural remedies. Although they might not be familiar with poppies that grow only in Italy. Unless they're the same as California poppies."

Cynthia tapped a few more keys. "Close enough, although it's not clear whether the California ones are strong enough to have much effect. The Tuscan variety has a much longer track record for medicinal uses. Anyway, neither of the MDs lives in California where the poppies grow."

"But they might have, once. Or gone to school there. You can check that."

"Yes, I can." More tapping. "Nope, neither one, at least not that I can tell from the information I have. What else you got?"

I was coming up empty. "You know the Amanda Knox case, right?"

"Who doesn't? Face of an all-American angel, but the Italian authorities tarred her as a sex-crazed slacker. And they're still arguing over whether she did it."

"Exactly. And in that case they had physical evidence, even if they bungled it. What do you think they'd make of our case?"

"I'd rather not find out. It could take years, and there'd be a cloud hanging over all of us. We don't want that."

"No, we don't. So we've got to make this right."

"I'm with you on that. What next?"

"You're asking me?"

"Yes, I am. I'm the info gatherer."

"I thought I was!"

"Nope, *I'm* Watson. You found the professor—he's your problem. I stand ready to be awed by your brilliant deductive reasoning. So?"

Funny, in our past years together, Cynthia had always taken the lead. When had that changed? Now I was in charge? I had to think this through. "If this were a crime novel, we'd gather all the cast together in the last chapter and make the big reveal. Or hope that the culprit gave herself away as we led up to it."

"Well, worst case, you've got the setting all lined up—the big dinner in the vineyard on our last night. All the suspects gathered together. If we haven't figured this out before that, you can stand up and announce, 'The killer is . . .' and see who runs screaming into the night."

"That might be a bit extreme, especially if I have nothing to back it up. But if all else fails, I can throw the question on the table and see what happens."

Cynthia looked at me sadly. "I wish I could say I had a better idea, but I don't."

"Okay, then I'll talk to Xianling and ask her to put together whatever she can, and we'll see if that adds anything to what we know. If we're lucky we'll have something before the banquet."

"Big if," Cynthia said. "You know, being Watson isn't as easy as it looks. You want more coffee? Or you want to shop?"

"I will happily look for souvenirs that weigh less than two ounces, until it's time for dinner." Anything was better than hiking up that hill, only to turn around and come back in an hour or two.

So we shopped, and I allowed myself to buy one deliciously scented bar of soap. And after shopping we wandered over to the restaurant, where people were already congregating. Once inside, we were divided among different tables in different rooms, and even if I'd wanted to ask some discreet questions, the noise level made it impossible. When I'd figured that out, I relaxed and just went with the flow. It was a pleasant dinner, not as good as some, but tasty. It was nearly dark when we finally exited the restaurant, and I could hear the sea nearby.

Cynthia and I looked at each other. "Ready for that hill?" I asked.

"I guess. Where are our sister vineyardites?"

"Is that even a word? I think they're still inside. You want to wait?"

"Not really. You and I are pretty evenly matched—we both start panting at the same time."

"Yeah, about halfway there. All right, let's go."

We passed the church, now dark, although some of the cafés on the plaza in front of it were still doing a good business. We continued up toward the hotel, passing under an arch. At the *carabinieri* station, a lone tabby cat sat on a low wall and washed its face. It ignored us. Then came the long dark hike, and I swear it was at a forty-five-degree angle. Or at least an angle that grew steeper each time we climbed it. We huffed and puffed our way to the top, then dropped into the chairs on our little patio.

"What . . . about . . . mosquitoes?" I panted.

"Haven't . . . seen . . . any . . . here," Cynthia replied.

We waited a minute until our breathing leveled out. "Another thing nobody mentioned: bring bug spray. Think we could have gotten it into the country?"

"If it was small enough. The more important omission was mentioning the hills."

"You've got that right. I wonder if anybody would have bowed out if they had known how much climbing they'd have to do. I mean, unless you have a topographic map, you don't even think about it. Unless you're visiting Switzerland. Or Nepal."

"Maybe the lazy and the feeble ones self-eliminated and are sitting at home patting themselves on the back and knitting."

"Hard to do both at once," I commented. "Damn, I don't want to get old."

"We aren't old, we're mature. Wise. Seasoned."

"Yeah, right. I hope somebody shoots me if I get too decrepit to do something like this. I had a friend back at college whose grandparents kept taking grand trips abroad into their nineties. I still have their old steamer trunk in the attic, and it's covered with shipping labels for wonderful places. I think it's full of my mementoes now—nothing as grand as theirs, I'm sure. Anyway, I always thought that's the way I wanted to live, just keep going and doing the things I enjoyed until I dropped in my tracks."

"How does the gene pool in your family look?" Cynthia asked.

"So-so. My grandmother was ninety-four, but my mother died of cancer in her seventies. My father was eighty."

"Not bad. You've got a few good years left in you."

"I hope so. You?" I asked.

"My mother's still alive, and living on her own. My father's been gone for a decade. But I take care of myself, when I'm not glued to a computer monitor."

I could hear the sounds of our hilltop companions making their way up the path. I looked at Cynthia, but she was lost in her own thoughts. I was too comfortable to move, so I remained silent and waited to see what the others would do.

Chapter 18

I had expected the others to peel off to their rooms on the far end of the patio, but instead they kept coming until they were directly below where we sat.

"Ahoy? Permission to come aboard?" Valerie called out.

"Aren't you mixing up your metaphors? The sea's the other direction. But sure, you're welcome to join us."

Valerie appeared first, clutching a bottle of wine, which she held up. "I come bearing offerings." She turned to her lagging companions. "Come on, guys—it's only a few more steps."

Connie and Pam appeared next with Denise, and when we were all seated, the little table was crowded. Xianling wasn't with them. The newcomers exchanged glances.

Then Valerie spoke. "We know what you're doing."

Now Cynthia and I looked at each other, alarmed. "What are we doing?" I asked cautiously.

"Trying to figure out who killed Professor Gilbert. We want to help."

Well, that cat had escaped its bag and was now howling for attention.

"Who else knows?" Cynthia asked.

"Just us—as far as we know. We haven't talked about it to anyone else. It's hard to find a quiet place and enough time to talk privately, as I'm sure you've noticed."

"Believe me, we've noticed," I said. "So you think someone killed the professor?"

"Don't you?" Valerie asked. "I'm just not buying the idea that he just fell down the hill and died. Too many people in the group hated him."

So it had been that obvious to her? Had it been to any others? I wondered. "You know who?"

Our companions shared looks. "I can guess," Pam said. "I'm a pretty good observer. And I have a near-photographic memory. By the way, I'm a lawyer."

I glanced at Cynthia. She nodded.

"I think there's a question I need to ask, before we go any further. Which of you took a class with Professor Gilbert? Or had any interactions with him in any other way?" I thought it would be kind of a test. I still wasn't sure I had complete confidence in these women, but on the other hand, we were running out of time and we had to trust someone.

Valerie spoke first. "I was in one of his classes."

Then Connie. "I didn't take one, but my roommate did, and it wasn't a good experience for her."

"That's putting it mildly," Pam said. "I took a couple of classes with him, and I thought he was slime. But you already knew that, Cynthia, didn't you?"

Cynthia waited a few moments before answering, studying Pam's face. Finally she said, "Yes, I did. We did. Denise?"

"You've heard my story," Denise said. "He plagiarized my research and called it his own."

"You checked us all out," Pam stated bluntly.

"Yes. I wanted to narrow down the list of suspects," Cynthia said. "And I wanted to see who would lie about it."

While Connie and Valerie looked unsettled by the revelation, and Denise just nodded once, Pam seemed pleased. "Fair enough," she said. "Yes, I took one of his classes. I thought it was fluff. I thought he had an ego the size of Texas. I got a respectable B-plus in the class and never took another one in that department. He never made a pass at me or bullied me or made fun of me—I might as well have been invisible. Hey, I know what I look like, and what I looked like then. I wasn't his type, and that was fine with me."

She looked like an ordinary and, yes, forgettable person, as she had forty years ago. "But you knew back then that there were others who did get that kind of attention from him?" I prompted.

"Sure there were, and it was obvious to anyone who was looking for the signs. Some of the women in the class were practically drooling over him. Most of them found an excuse to stay after class and ask him some really important questions, alone, of course."

"You aren't suggesting they were asking for it and they got what they deserved, are you?" Cynthia demanded.

"Of course I'm not," Pam snapped. "We were all young and stupid and impressionable, and he was hot. Things happen. People move on."

"Well, it looks like somebody didn't," I countered.

"Quite possibly. Look, do you know the dropout rate for freshmen in our year?" Pam demanded.

"I do," Cynthia said, and named a number. "And that doesn't include the transfers to the men's colleges that went co-ed around that time."

"Okay. Some of those women left for academic reasons—they just couldn't cut it. Some for social reasons—they felt like they didn't fit in, or they couldn't hack being at a college with only women. Some for financial reasons. And some—a small percentage—bailed because creeps like Gilbert messed with them. But having said that, most of the women he, uh . . . well, you know what I mean—most of them got over it and him and went on to graduate and lead happy and successful lives. How many of our class do you think had or have the potential to be killers?"

"Two," Cynthia fired back promptly. "One spousal abuse, case dismissed, and one psychotic break."

"Damn, you are good, given what you have to work with here," Pam said admiringly. "So how do you profile someone who waits forty years to seek revenge? Was it planned? Was it a spur-of-the-moment thing, where just seeing the guy again unexpectedly brought back a whole lot of repressed memories and she just snapped? Who knew where he was, the night he died?"

"Hold on—you're going too fast," I said. "Let us tell you what we've worked out so far, and then you can tell us what you can add and what the next steps should be."

Cynthia slid her napkin diagram across the table and outlined what we'd been discussing since we returned from Vernazza. Pam nodded, looking impressed, then passed it to the others. "Good start," she said. "If you eliminate the two of us here who took a class—that's Circle A—then you've narrowed it down to fewer than ten people. I can't answer for B, because I didn't spend any time visiting around other people's rooms when we were in Capitignano. I saw people at meals and in the vans, and that was pretty much it. As for C, the poppy stuff, ask Valerie."

Cynthia eyed her. "Right, you're a doctor."

"I was," Valerie nodded. "I retired three years ago."

"And now you're a holistic medical therapist," Cynthia said.

"You know about that?" Valerie looked startled.

"You need a license, don't you?"

Valerie nodded once, processing the fact that Cynthia knew.

Cynthia pressed on. "From what I've read, the poppies haven't changed in the last three years, or even three millennia. What can you tell me about their effects? Assume I've read a Wikipedia article and take it from there."

"The petals of the Tuscan poppy contain substances that aid insomnia," Valerie explained, "and that red poppy we've been seeing everywhere — the same one the Impressionists loved to paint — is very slightly narcotic. The amount of active ingredients is minimal, so to determine an exact dosage is next to impossible. It could be kind of hit or miss. It has a long history, as you've observed, and has been used in herbal treatments for a wide range of ailments, mainly to treat the respiratory system and the nervous system."

"I'd say you know quite a lot," I said. "It sounds pretty benign. Does it have any toxic effects?"

"There's no morphine in it, if that's what you're asking. Ingested in a moderate dose, it would make you sleepy. If you took too much, it would make you sluggish and might cause trouble breathing."

"How much would it take to incapacitate someone?" Cynthia demanded.

"Without an underlying condition? More than he or she would be willing to ingest. Certainly more than the amount someone could sneak into a drink. I assume that's what you're thinking."

"So it's not a poison per se," I said. That squared with what the autopsy had shown. "If it was just a moderate dose, what would the symptoms be?"

"Sleepiness. Lack of alertness. Maybe physical clumsiness. Nothing dramatic like vomiting or fainting."

"Okay," Cynthia finally spoke, after a long pause. "Let's lay this on the table. The autopsy shows that Professor Gilbert had the active ingredient from Italian poppies in his system when he died. Somebody knew how to extract that ingredient from those widely available poppies, although it probably doesn't take anything more sophisticated than hot water and maybe some vinegar. Somebody managed to slip it to him without anyone noticing. It could have been enough to make him thick-tongued and clumsy. Would you agree so far?"

"That sounds about right," Valerie said, meeting Cynthia's gaze.

"And we know the professor was a vain man and would have been embarrassed to be stumbling and mumbling in front of a group of ladies. How long does this stuff take to work?"

"I'd say there would be symptoms within the hour, although there are a lot of variables."

Connie spoke up suddenly. "Cynthia, you're suggesting that somebody gave it to him in time to make him look like a fool at the dinner?"

Cynthia nodded. "Maybe. Or that could have been the idea. Did anyone notice him acting unusual, or different after than before?"

"Since we hadn't seen the man in forty years, how were we to know what 'normal' was for him at his age?" Pam demanded.

"He seemed to be fine when he gave his talk in the late afternoon," I threw in. "So this poppy cocktail had to have been given to him either right before then, or not long after, say, during cocktails."

"Which narrows our timeline, right?" Connie said.

"Exactly," Cynthia said. "All right, Pam, you say you've got a good memory: who was sitting at the head table with him?"

Pam looked up at the ceiling and shut her eyes. "Barb and Gerry, of course. Jean and Jane—Jane took at least one course from him, but you probably already know that. That's five. Uh . . . okay, it was a table for eight, so the rest were Brenda, Rebecca, and Virginia. Does that sound about right?"

Nobody contradicted her.

"None of whom had taken a class with the professor," Cynthia grinned. "Now I'll make it harder. Who was hanging around him before dinner who didn't end up at the table?"

We all looked at each other. "A lot of people," Connie said.

"There were forty of us, not including Barb and Gerry and the waitstaff," Pam said. "Are you talking a quarter of us? Half?"

"Closer to half than a quarter," Cynthia replied, "but not everyone was close enough to put something in his drink. So call it a quarter."

I noticed that Cynthia didn't mention our quest for photographs of the appropriate times. Maybe she still wasn't sure she trusted the women in front of us?

"Are we eliminating the employees?" Pam asked. "I mean, Horny

Tony Gilbert could have been sneaking over to Capitignano from wherever he lived and getting it on with the cook."

I said slowly, "I thought someone said that Gerry was the one who invited him, and he'd only recently learned of both the Wellesley connection and the fact that he was living nearby. That kind of rules out the staff. Agreed? Look, if we don't eliminate somebody, we'll never sort all this out," I said with asperity.

"Okay, okay—we'll assume the most likely scenario, in the interests of expediency," Cynthia said.

"Cyn, you can talk plain English, right?" I said. "We have only enough time to explore the most obvious solutions. Somebody slipped Professor Gilbert a Mickey, probably during the cocktail hour, with the goal of making him look like a doddering old fool. A few hours later, he fell off a hill and died. What happened in between dinner and kaboom?"

"That other bottle of wine," Cynthia said. When our vineyard-mates looked blankly at her, she explained about the chilled bottle of wine and the two glasses that had been delivered to the professor's room after dinner. And that I'd seen him on the way up to his room, which further narrowed the killer's window of opportunity.

"So . . . what? Wouldn't he have had to drink the poppy juice earlier than that?" Pam asked. "How did he seem to you when you saw him, Laura?"

"I didn't know the man, but I would have said he'd had a little to drink—most of us had. He was walking steadily enough, but he was kind of . . . effusive? He was talking to me in Italian, and he called me pretty lady."

"Inconclusive," the lawyer responded. "What about the combined effect of wine and the drug, Valerie?"

Valerie said, "I wouldn't recommend it, but the combination wouldn't be toxic, if that's what you're asking. From what Laura says, he seems to have been in control right after dinner, or maybe slightly drunk. Maybe the stuff simply didn't work. Or the dosage was wrong. Or maybe it hadn't had time to work. Or maybe he'd drunk less than someone expected because he knew he had a late date."

Cynthia turned back to Pam. "Do you remember who left the dining hall when? Alone or with a group?"

"Sure." Pam proceeded to recite the list, in order of exit. I decided that if I ever needed a lawyer, I'd call her first. "Which is not to say that they didn't go out again later."

I glanced at Cynthia, who nodded. "Cynthia did."

"Did you see anyone else?" Connie asked eagerly.

"Yes, but no one connected to the professor or his death—I went in a different direction," Cynthia said. "Besides, we were together for . . . quite a while, which covers the period of the fall."

Connie waited a moment, but Cynthia did not elaborate.

"What about you, Laura?" Valerie asked. "Wasn't he staying in the room right above you? Maybe Cynthia wasn't there, but did you hear anything?"

"I heard some footsteps overhead—tile floors, you know, and the sound carried. But I crashed pretty quickly. I didn't even hear Cynthia leave, or come back. I certainly never heard any voices. I couldn't swear whether he had a guest."

Pam picked up the thread again. "Do you think you would have heard the sounds of a struggle? Or a scream? After all, he fell not far from your window, and sound carried at night at that place. Did you take a sleeping pill or anything to knock you out?"

I shook my head. "Believe me, I didn't need anything—all this exercise is plenty to knock me out. But I want to think I would have heard anything like a scream. I didn't hear anything, ergo he went quietly."

"No signs of bruising, defensive wounds, broken nails?" Pam directed this question at Cynthia.

"What, you have the autopsy report, Cynthia?" Valerie exclaimed.

Cynthia looked at me, but I shook my head slightly; her cover might be blown, but I wasn't ready to share what I did with the rest of the group. "Yes," Cynthia answered. "There were no injuries not consistent with the fall."

"So, to sum up," Pam began, "Professor Gilbert was found dead subsequent to a fall, with no injuries that can be attributed with any certainty to a human hand. He had ingested a poppy solution that may or may not have affected his behavior or coordination. We may infer that he had a late assignation, but we have no idea with whom, and nobody has come forward to admit being with him. And possibly a dozen of our number have a motive to seek revenge against him. He could have been killed, or helped to die, by any one of them — or a combination of more than one."

"*Murder on the Orient Express*," I said suddenly. "Everybody did it, or at least that's the way it looked. Do you really believe that multiple people were involved?"

Pam shook her head. "Too elaborate, and too much planning required. Besides, no one knew he would be there until we arrived, which wouldn't leave much time to plan and brew up the poppy stuff and arrange a late assignation with the man. I'm just playing devil's advocate. But it is possible."

Cynthia yawned. "Hey, gang, can we go to bed soon? Unless you want to upset the apple cart and blow off tomorrow's schedule."

"I'd rather not do that," I said. "It would be a good day to try to talk to people because we can go around in small groups. And there are more of us now to do the asking. But what do we need to know?"

Silence for several beats. Then Connie said softly, "Who had a kitchen when we were staying at the villa. Who knows herbs. And who hated Professor Gilbert."

Yeah, that about covered it.

"I agree with Cynthia," I said finally. "We need some sleep. We can meet at breakfast and see if daylight helps. Thanks, guys."

The others headed off to their own rooms. When our new allies were out of range, I asked Cynthia, "Do you trust them?"

"Laura, I don't know what I think anymore, but I think we have no choice with these people here. Let's get some sleep and regroup in the morning."

"Agreed." Damn, I still hadn't had a chance to talk to Xianling. I'd have to catch her in the morning and hope she had enough time left to pull together what we needed.

Chapter 19

I was continually surprised at how well I slept in Italy, but I assumed it was all the unusual exercise I was getting. If I stayed much longer, my calves and thighs would be rock-hard.

But as soon as I woke up, my brain started spinning. We had little time left to clear up this murder before we were all scheduled to leave. Of course, it was entirely possible that we could all go our separate ways without the police interfering—they hadn't placed any restrictions on us yet, and then we might never know if there was a resolution. But leaving the professor's death an open-ended question didn't sit well with me: it would cloud our memories of this trip, leave a bad taste in our mouths. It had been too lovely (apart from that unfortunate corpse, the one little fly in the ointment), and Jean and Jane had put far too much work into making it happen to let it end like that. So we would have to fix it if we could. But how?

No sound from Cynthia's room. I tiptoed into the bathroom, brushed my teeth, then pulled on some light clothes and went out to sit on the patio and watch the sun burn the mist off the valley. It looked so pastoral, so innocent.

Pam came up the cement steps, her feet silent in rubber-soled shoes. "Hey," she said quietly and took the chair across from me. "She still asleep?" She gestured toward Cynthia's room.

"I think so. You have something to say to her?"

"Nope, I'm happy to talk to you. You two aren't, uh, together or anything, are you?"

"As a couple? No, nothing like that. We've been friends forever, but I don't see much of her these days. Why?"

"Just asking. I like to know who I'm working with. You know I figured out what you two do."

"And what do we do?" I said noncommittally.

"You're an 'analyst'"—she made air quotes—"at a government agency that shall be nameless. Cynthia is a data miner, and she's good at it. That's why I wondered if you'd worked together."

"Not until now," I said. She'd gotten us right, and it wasn't worth asking how or why. "Did you tell the others?"

"They don't know. But we all agree that you two are our best hope of getting out of here on time — with my help, of course."

"You said you're a lawyer, right?"

"I am. If you want to know what kind of lawyer, ask your sleeping buddy."

"In the interests of saving time, let's say you're as good as you say you are and leave it at that. Do you have any suggestions?"

"I think you're doing it right — and you're using your heads, not running around stirring things up. You've defined the parameters well: motive and means. Odds are good that someone is lying to you and everyone else, but the question is, does that matter? Can you figure this out anyway?"

This woman was certainly intense. "I'd like to hope so. We still have to work out which people really did have a motive, no matter what they tell us. We know there were twelve people who took a class from Professor Gilbert. Some took more than one. But he can't have hit on everybody — you're a case in point. There may be more people who connected with him outside of class, but there's no way to track that, so we're sticking to what we can verify. So how do we weed out the — for want of a better word — rejects and figure out who had a real motive?"

"The 'unselected' or the 'unchosen' would be a kinder term," Pam said. "And it wasn't always a sex thing. Sure, he had his share there, but he could be cruel in other ways."

"After he'd scored and then dumped them?" I asked.

"Some, maybe, but not all. He enjoyed showing off, and he enjoyed exposing other people's ignorance. He didn't have to sleep with a woman to screw her, you know."

"Embarrassment as a motive for murder? Give me some examples." I wasn't sure I bought into her theory.

"Remember the times. We were so young, so vulnerable then. To be ridiculed in a class by a professor you admired could be devastating. And hard to forget."

"Maybe." I tried to remember any major faux pas I'd been called out on in a class and failed. I'd always been solidly in the middle — no highs or lows. And I'd had a good eye for artistic styles, which carried me a long way in art history classes. But I'd known shier, quieter girls in the dorm; I'd come across more than one crying in the shower, but I'd never asked why. Maybe I should have.

"All right, say we want to follow up on that. Cynthia should have the grades for anyone who stuck it out in his classes. Should we be looking at anyone who received a C?"

"It's an idea."

"So now we've got sex, plagiarism, and ridicule to think about."

"Great way to start the day," Cynthia said, coming through the door. "Talking about me?" She sat down at the table.

"How much did you hear?" I asked.

"A lot. You make lousy conspirators. Or maybe it's just so quiet up here that all sounds carry. Do you realize we haven't heard a plane in days? And you know a car is coming long before it shows up."

"There are, however, some very loud chickens," I said. "So, Cyn, you have anything to add?"

"I think you've got it right. Do you want to split up the list by possible offense? Like, which ones he slept with versus which ones he embarrassed? Or just go with alphabetically?"

"What's on the schedule for today?" Pam asked.

"What, you haven't memorized it?" Cynthia twitted her. "All I remember is the food. Lunch at some town called Sarzana, tea at some relatives of Jane's somewhere else, and a big dinner at a castle somewhere. And more driving around between the aforesaid. We should eat breakfast before someone drags us off to the vans."

"I assume there'll be some open time at the first event, if not the second one," I said. "The problem is leading up to discussing the dead professor, if people don't want to talk about him."

"We could just be direct about it," Pam said. "You know, 'I think there was something funny about Professor Gilbert's death, and so do the police. What do you think? Who would want him dead?'"

"Oh, now we're a 'we'? Pam, are you signing up for the investigation? And we've already got a Sherlock and a Watson."

"If you'll have me, I'm in. I'll be Mycroft," Pam said.

"Welcome, then, Mycroft. So, what if we put the question to people and they don't say anything?" Cynthia asked.

I threw up my hands, then stood up. "Solving murders is not part of my job description, and I'm making this up as I go. I'm going to grab a quick shower and get dressed so we can go eat. You two, continue brainstorming."

I went inside. While I showered, I turned over the idea of welcoming Pam into our tight little group. Would the other four come with the package? I suppose some small part of me had hoped that Cynthia and I could figure it out on our own and save the day—which I recognized as both vain and selfish on my part—but I had to admit that Pam brought some new and useful skills to the mix.

When I emerged from my room, ready for the day, Cynthia was alone on the patio. "Where did Pam go?" I asked.

"To rouse the others so we don't miss breakfast."

"What do you think of her? And her plan?"

Cyn shrugged. "I don't have a better one. If you're asking a different question, I think we need her. With so little time, we have to trust someone. Of course, I'd rather declare everybody honest and aboveboard, but I'm not sure that's the best way to go."

"She knows about our, uh, professions."

"I'm not surprised. She's smart. Maybe sneaky too. But we can use the help."

"She said Professor Gilbert didn't even notice her."

"Well, he'd have to have been SuperStud to score with every student. He was picky, and he had plenty of pretty girls to choose from."

"Maybe that's a motive—being dismissed as not attractive enough, not good enough to sleep with. Maybe Pam has been trying to compensate and prove him wrong for decades."

"I doubt it." She shook her head. "How could this one man be so toxic? And nobody said or did anything? How many others like him do you think there were?"

"You mean randy faculty members? I can't say. It never happened to me. And I'd really rather think that he was the exception to the rule, and that most academics are nice enough people just doing their jobs, and if they're lucky, they love their subject and try to pass that on to students. Do you think that's possible?"

"I hope so," Cynthia said firmly. "I don't want to see our college, or any college, for that matter, then or now, as a seething pit of depravity."

"Heaven forbid!" I said. "I always hoped it was about learning something, although that could include learning about yourself, not just academic subjects." I stood up. "So let's go get breakfast."

The others were already assembled, helping themselves to coffee, yogurt, fruit, granola and so on. I went for the bread. What can I say? I like carbohydrates. And caffeine. From the meaningful looks darting between them all, I surmised that Pam had filled them in, but no one said anything to Cynthia or me. Fine: now we were six—seven if Xianling came on board—and if each of us talked with three other people . . . that would just about do it. We should find a time to compare notes later in the day.

But I still had one more task. "Pam, was Xianling showing any signs of life when you left the room?" I asked.

Pam shrugged. "She likes her beauty sleep. And she doesn't like breakfast. She's fine. Why?"

"I need to talk with her—I've got an idea." I got up and approached the room Pam and Xianling were sharing, then knocked quietly at the door. After several moments, Xianling opened it, looking absurdly well put together for someone who had just gotten out of bed. "Can we talk?" I asked.

"Of course." She stepped back to let me enter.

I came straight to the point. "I need to ask a favor. I think it will help us figure out how Professor Gilbert died."

Xianling nodded once. "Go on."

I outlined my rather vague plan to have her collect as many photographs as possible. It sounded lame to me, but we were fast running out of options. When I was finished, Xianling looked over my head, thinking. Then she returned her gaze to me.

"I think I can do that. I'll have to work out a method for assembling whatever photos I collect into one file, but that shouldn't be too difficult, and there probably won't be a large number. Not many people were concerned with capturing pictures from that evening."

I hadn't even considered that, but I was relieved. "Thank you. I wish we had more time, but we don't. At least we'll all be together today."

"That we will. The others of our group up here know what you're asking of me?"

"Only Cynthia. The rest know the general outlines of what Cyn and I have been doing."

"That's fine. I'll see you in a few minutes."

I was being dismissed, but I didn't mind. As I rejoined my vineyard companions, I spotted Jane coming up the hill, accompanied by Loredana.

"Good morning, everyone," Jane said, cheerful as always. "Today we're going to visit Lerici, a lovely seaside town much favored by the English literary community in the nineteenth century. Virginia Woolf, for example. And Percy Shelley drowned in the harbor there. We will be driving, so please stick with your usual vans—we'd hate to misplace anyone now! Then we will regroup and go to Sarzana, where we'll have an al fresco lunch featuring one of my favorite regional foods, *farinata*, which is kind of a chickpea pancake, except it tastes better than it sounds. Then later in the afternoon we will visit another town, Montemarcello, where generations of my family lived and where a cousin of mine has a house. She's an artist, and we'll be having tea at her home. You'll have a little time to explore the beautiful coastline there, and the views are magnificent. And finally, we'll be treated to a wonderful dinner at a castle. So, enjoy! We'll meet at the vans at eight—and this time it will be a short climb up the hill for you, because we're leaving from where we arrived! Just take that path there—it's not far. See you in a bit!"

Loredana smiled and nodded but didn't add anything. She was a very cheerful presence, whether or not she understood what we were doing and saying most of the time. She and Jane turned and marched down the hill to inform the others at the hotel; they were talking a mile a minute in Italian again. I was tickled that for once the hotel dwellers were the ones who would have to do the trekking uphill, not us.

We passed a pleasant half hour over breakfast. The sun shone; the flowers were blooming mightily; and the coffee flowed. And then it was time to head back for the vans, for the next leg of our journey. I wasn't looking forward to the steep road out of our valley, but a couple of millennia of Italians seem to have survived it, so I'd just have to deal with it.

The drive to Lerici was lovely—once we got out of the mountains. Lerici was lovely too, what we could see of it. Clearly a whole lot of people thought it was lovely and had arrived well before us and scarfed up all the parking spaces. Parking four oversized vans in Italy is a challenge under the best of circumstances; parking them in a crowded seaside town on a sunny summer day is a nightmare.

After a slow loop around the town, our little caravan accepted the inevitable and started looking for a parking garage or lot somewhere away from the beach and the heart of town. We went around and around, and at the same time up and up. Finally, on a hill (with, as usual, a lovely view) we arrived at a garage entrance without the dreaded *Pieno* sign, and turned in. The first van collected its ticket from a machine and headed down into the bowels of the garage. Our van was second. Brenda pulled her ticket from the machine; the crossbar went up and we began to go down, until we were interrupted by a loud crash, followed by Brenda's "Oh, shit! Oops, sorry, ladies."

We stopped. She put the van in park. We looked around and realized that some part of the bar mechanism had just blown out the back left window and it was now scattered in a million tiny pieces (thank heavens for safety glass!), both inside and outside the car. It was toast. "Shit, shit, shit," our driver said again. I agreed with her choice of epithet. "Anybody hurt?"

We exchanged glances. "No, we're fine," said someone from the backseat.

The car that Jane had borrowed from Loredana pulled up behind us and stopped (having no choice). We climbed out of our van; Jane climbed out of the car. We all stared at the damage. Then Jane pulled her cell phone out and called somebody, while the rest of us wandered aimlessly around near the entrance to the garage, admiring the view so beloved of Shelley and friends. It was very pretty. We took more pictures. I'm pretty sure Shelley had never tried to park a humongous van in his favorite town — and he hadn't had much better luck with a boat. Although to be fair to the poor man, various sources suggested that he was suicidal, incompetent, or had been hijacked by pirates who didn't recognize a poet when they saw one. Or maybe he was murdered. It was anybody's guess. So said Jane's meticulously detailed handouts.

A car emblazoned *Polizia Mobilia* pulled up. Jane went over to speak to one of the men in the car — a chat that lasted less than five minutes, when the *polizia* car pulled away. Apparently our shattered window was not important enough for them to worry about; their suggestion was to contact the rental agency. Right.

Jane stood there, taking a few deep breaths, and looked at the rest of us, who were waiting for guidance. Finally she said, "Screw Lerici. Let's go eat lunch."

We applauded.

We climbed back in the vans, maneuvered until we were turned around in the right direction (without damaging anything else), and took off for our next meal. Our van was now well ventilated, and every time we went over another bump more glass tinkled onto the roadway. We kept going—what else could we do?

My seatmate, whom I didn't know well, leaned toward me. "This is almost a badge of honor. You realize that one of the other vans gouged the entire side panel on the first day?"

"I hadn't heard that," I answered. Not that I was surprised.

"Oh, yeah. And another one ripped off a rear bumper in a parking lot, but they just shoved it back in place and moved on. I think our window tops both of those."

"Definitely. Much more impressive."

Wellesley women do not panic. We cope.

Chapter 20

Sarzana was a ghost town when we arrived at the height of the afternoon siesta. I thought that antiquated custom of taking a couple of hours off in the middle of the day would have long since vanished from modern Europe, but I was wrong. The town was charming but there were no people on the streets and most of the shops were closed.

Luckily, once more Jane and Jean had booked ahead, and we took over the entire area covered with an awning in front of a small restaurant. Those of us who had been passengers in the van that had suffered the window debacle were still a bit keyed up about the event, and those for whom it was news, or who hadn't witnessed it directly, were eager for the details. Our vineyard group, less Xianling, whom I spotted at a table at the end talking to someone, exchanged glances and wordlessly distributed ourselves at different tables. I hung back just a little, waiting to see how the groupings sorted themselves out. I was lucky when several people whom I hadn't spent much time with yet landed at one table, and I snagged the last seat there.

We sat and ordered cold drinks. Luckily lunch was once again preordered, so we didn't have to think about it. What we did was talk, like a flock of noisy sparrows. I realized I was presented with the perfect opportunity. As one of the survivors of the Window Disaster, people *wanted* to talk to me, and I could pretend to be as rattled as I chose. Which was not very, since I had been on the opposite side of the van, and by the time any of us had figured out what had happened we'd also realized that the only victim was the poor van—no human casualties. But for my own ends I could push it just a little, and that small catastrophe opened up the door to talk about the bigger one (although one fading in our collective memories) of Professor Gilbert's death.

Once we were seated, Bonnie leaned forward and said, "So what happened to the van?"

I fought the urge to say something like, *It wasn't that big a deal,* as I normally would. Instead, I needed to play this up, not play it down.

I matched Bonnie's posture, leaning forward as though conveying confidential information. "You saw how tight a turn it was? Well, you know that Brenda was driving. She collected the ticket from the machine and she was moving forward slowly, and I guess there wasn't quite enough room to make the turn, so some part of the equipment clipped the rear windows and it, like, exploded into a million pieces!" All of which was true. I just wasn't used to gushing quite so much.

"Wow! Everyone was all right?" Pat asked.

"Yes, luckily. That safety glass works just the way it's supposed to—there were lots of tiny shards but no sharp edges. And the window was all the way in the back, not next to anyone, and most of the glass fell into the luggage part. What was really strange was how big a bang it made. It sounded like we'd run into a wall."

"Oh, my," Pat breathed. "What did you all do then?"

Well, we didn't panic—but I didn't say that out loud. "First, Brenda said a few words she hadn't used before. And then she apologized to us for cursing." Everyone laughed at that. "Then we pulled over and checked out the damage, sprinkling glass along the way. Which we've been doing ever since."

"If I'd been Brenda I would have refused to drive another foot," Rebecca said emphatically. "Is she okay?"

"She is a trooper, more mad than scared. And it really wasn't her fault. That driveway simply wasn't big enough for those vans." Just like most of the roads in most of the towns we'd driven through. "Back home I bet there would have been warning signs and disclaimers plastered all over the place. Anyway, I think all the drivers should get medals after this. I know I wouldn't want to try it."

A chorus of agreement followed. All right, I'd set the stage. "You know, I wonder if this is part of a string of bad luck—one that started with Professor Gilbert's death."

"You mean, like we're cursed or something?" Rebecca asked, raising a skeptical eyebrow.

I shrugged. "I don't really believe in that kind of thing, but you have to wonder . . ." I paused and let them do just that for a bit—and I waited to see if any of them would speak out.

"I've heard that his death wasn't exactly an accident," Bonnie said carefully. I wanted to cheer.

"Didn't Jane say something about the police looking into it?" Donna responded.

"Don't the police look into any death around here? Or is that only back home?" Christine chimed in.

Even better than I had hoped. Now it was time to nudge this conversation back on track. "Did any of you know the professor?"

"I signed up for his class," Donna said, "but I dropped it. I thought he was a pompous ass, and I was there to learn something, not admire his cheekbones." I made a mental note to check if she was on Cynthia's list.

"But they were nice cheekbones," Christine sighed.

"You took his class?" I prompted.

"Yes. Just the one. It was kind of lightweight, but I didn't have to work hard, which was good because I was taking a lot of premed courses at the time."

I made another mental checkmark: Christine had known the professor *and* had some medical expertise. "I was wondering if we should put together some sort of memorial for him, like on Facebook or in the alumnae mag. Since we were his last students, so to speak."

That statement met with a curious silence. A couple of people exchanged glances. Me, I held my breath. Finally Donna volunteered, "I'm not sure that's a good idea. He, uh, wasn't all that popular."

"Why not?" I asked innocently, although I was pretty sure I knew the answer.

"He was—how should I put this without sounding Dickensian? A cad. He used the girls in his classes. The kind of behavior that wouldn't be tolerated for a minute today. There would be complaints filed with the administration the same day, I'd bet."

"I don't know about that," Pat said thoughtfully. "A lot of young women are insecure, and they might feel flattered, even these days."

"Well, they shouldn't," Rebecca said firmly. "It's exploitation and harassment. It shouldn't be tolerated under any circumstances, especially not in the environment of a women's college."

"You sound like you've had some experience with this kind of thing," I said cautiously. I figured she'd either clam up, change the subject—or spill a lot more information.

"Did I succumb to his obvious charms? No way, but I knew women who did. I bet we all did. And I've worked in a number of counseling centers, both academic and public, since I graduated. Women of that age, even the smart ones, are vulnerable. He took advantage of that. And then he dropped them and moved on, usually pretty fast, which did its own damage. I mean, we probably have all heard stories about the professor who ends up marrying one of his students. It happens. But to hold a hope like that, even as a fantasy, and then to be dropped for the next sweet young thing—that hurts too. You feel stupid, and none of us likes that, right?"

She might have said she didn't have personal experience with this kind of thing, but I wasn't sure I believed her. Still, it would do no good to press. I decided to change tack.

"You know, I must have been totally clueless when I was there. I never heard any of this." It was the truth. If I'd heard hints, I ignored them, refusing to be diverted from my own college path. I was never the one for late-night heart-to-heart sessions in the dorm, over tea or something stronger, which made it ironic that I was trying to re-create that here and now.

"I think a lot of people knew," Bonnie said softly. "We just didn't know what to do about it, so we did nothing. And there was no one to report it to at the college. Not that I blame them—this kind of problem wasn't on anybody's radar back then, not like it is now."

I nudged the conversation back to the big question. "Do you think whatever went on back then might have had something to do with his death last week?" I watched expressions carefully.

The range of responses—micro-expressions?—was interesting. A couple of people showed surprise, and I thought that looked genuine. Rebecca looked triumphant, if only for a brief moment; then she shut down, scrubbing all expression from her face. Christine just looked sad and said, "I wish he hadn't been invited at all. He seems to have stirred up a lot of memories, and they weren't all happy ones."

"I thought I heard that it was Gerry who invited him," I said. "He must not have known. I don't suppose guys talk about things like this." While I knew that Gerry's wife Barbara had attended Wellesley, she was a few years older than we were, so she might have missed the era of Anthony Gilbert's predations among the students.

Rebecca snorted. "More likely they brag about it. Can't you see it? Late nights at a conference gathered around a bar . . . One respected academic turns to another and says, 'Heh heh, what're the pickings like at that girls' school of yours?'"

Bonnie wrapped her arms around herself. "That's disgusting. I'm not going to believe it. Can't we please talk about something more pleasant?"

She was right: I'd pushed far enough, and I'd learned a few things. And then the food appeared and we gave it the attention it merited. The mysterious *farinata* was a big hit, something like a crunchy chickpea cross between a pancake and a pizza. Of course, the pizza on the plate went over well too, as did everything else. No one was going to say we were picky eaters, and I'm sure we would all agree that we were being served great food.

We ate, and we ate. We talked of our families, and trips we'd made in the past, and absent classmates. After a couple of hours, Jane stood up and rapped on her glass again. "I hope you've all enjoyed your meal?"

Enthusiastic clapping and whooping ensued.

"We've got about an hour before we have to get back on the road. Why don't you stroll around and see the town, and we can all meet at the cathedral at three?"

"Can we get a picture of all of us with the staff from the restaurant?" someone at another table called out.

"Of course—what a great idea. Let's do that now," Jane said. So we all trooped over to the front of the restaurant and arranged ourselves under the sign, and a series of people, including Xianling, took pictures, and then we dispersed. Our vineyard gang peeled off together.

"Any luck?" Cynthia asked when we'd separated ourselves from the rest.

"I managed to steer the conversation to our dead professor," I said, not without pride. "I sat with Bonnie, Pat, Christine, Rebecca and Donna. Nobody liked him much. All but one person admitted they'd heard something about his, uh, activities. Christine both took a class from him and did premed, so she could have the expertise. Donna said she enrolled in his class but dropped it because she thought he was pompous. I wasn't sure if you had her on the list."

"But Christine didn't have access to a kitchen," Pam retorted.

"And you know this how?" I asked.

"Jean was at my table. We talked about what other groups rent the estate, and whether an individual could rent a unit with cooking facilities. I got the whole list—Jean would be happy to throw some more business to Barb and Gerry."

So much for that suspect. "I don't suppose she travels with a camping stove?"

Cynthia laughed. "Nope. And I don't think a couple of candles would generate enough heat to do the trick. But everybody was sharing space with at least one other person—it would be easy enough to check with the roommates."

We wandered the bright and still empty streets. A few shop owners had appeared and were unlocking their storefronts, but it still wasn't exactly bustling. "So what have we learned?" I said, a bit dejected that my big clue was a bust.

"That nobody wants to put together any sort of memorial for the guy," Valerie said. "Funny how many people didn't like him."

"But that doesn't help us," I said. "What now?"

"We keep talking to people," Cynthia said firmly. "We've just started. How many do we have left on our list that we haven't talked to?" Cynthia pulled out her cell phone and we all huddled over the small screen looking at the list.

"Her, and her," Pam said, pointing.

"And her," I added one more name.

By the time we were done, we had whittled the list down to six.

"What's the next stop on our itinerary?" I asked.

"Tea with a relative of Jane's. Didn't she say she was an artist? Somewhere near the sea."

"You mean we're eating again?" Connie said.

"Yes, and save room for dinner," I replied.

We all groaned.

"Let's see if we can corner our shortlist of women and get some kind of conversation going," I said. "Isn't there a beach walk or something where we're going next? There should be opportunities for getting people alone, one on one."

"Just don't be too heavy-handed about it, Laura," Cynthia cautioned.

"What, you think I'm totally tactless? I'm going to get in someone's face and ask, 'Did you kill Professor Gilbert?' Give me a little credit, please." How did she think I could do my job if I was clueless about social niceties?

"Sorry." Cynthia was immediately contrite. "I didn't mean to criticize. I think we're all a little on edge. And I hope we can find a way to enjoy what we're seeing without this clouding everything. Take time to savor the moment, please."

I smiled at her, signaling my forgiveness. "Well, we're all definitely enjoying the food."

"And the company?" she said, and I thought I detected a wistful note.

We drifted toward the cathedral, where we could see a number of our colleagues emerging from different side streets. We all went inside to escape the sun, and we dutifully admired the large painted medieval Crucifixion hanging in a chapel in one of the side aisles, and otherwise we milled around aimlessly until it was time to return to the vans.

The window of our poor van didn't look any better now than it had earlier, even though a lot more glass had fallen out on various Italian roads—I hoped that wouldn't create problems for any of the unfortunate drivers who had followed us. I took Brenda aside briefly. "Are you okay to drive? Because no one will hold it against you if you're kind of spooked."

She smiled, sort of. "Don't worry about it. It happened, and there's nothing I can do about it now. And who's going to take over? There are only a few other people here who drive stick, and they're not about to step up. I'll be fine. And thanks for asking, Laura."

Our little caravan took off again, heading for another dot on the map called Montemarcello, the ancestral home of Jane's Italian forebears. Luckily it was a level ride on large roads, which allowed Brenda to steady her nerves. We found the place easily, and there was even a parking lot at the bottom of the (small!) hill with a church at the top. Apparently this artist cousin of Jane lived halfway up the hill.

But before we could begin that trek, I was drawn to the view across whatever harbor or inlet lay before us. On the other side, mountains rose up to the blue, blue sky. One of the mountains was blanketed in white.

"Is that snow?" I asked whoever was behind me.

It turned out to be Jane, collecting the stragglers. "No, that's Carrara you're looking at. Where the marble comes from. All that white is marble rubble."

Oh, my. Marble snow. Tomorrow's excursion to Carrara suddenly seemed a lot more interesting.

We walked up the hill together behind the main group. "You know, Jane, this whole trip is incredible. I never gave much thought to how much work the planning must have taken, but it is so worth it."

Jane smiled without looking at me. "Even with all the catastrophes? We certainly never included a murder in the schedule."

"Not your fault!" I said firmly. "Anyway, it will give us something to talk about for years to come." I wondered briefly how much I should share about our sleuthing efforts — assuming we weren't all painfully obvious anyway. "What are the police doing about it?"

Jane gave a particularly Italian shrug. "Who ever knows what Italian police are doing? I think we have Loredana and her husband to thank for keeping them at bay. Or maybe they're just slow to respond and we'll find them waiting for us back in Monterosso tonight."

"I hope not!" I said, and I meant it.

We'd reached the gate in front of a small house with a small yard in front of it. Yes, there was food.

"I'd better go speak to my cousin. Thanks, Laura." Jane went ahead of me to greet a woman about our own age, who was standing near the house. Loredana was there too, smiling happily. I could swear she winked at me when she saw me looking. What did she know?

Chapter 21

Our classmates drifted in and found seats at the tables arrayed around the yard. I thought we all looked a bit droopy. It was no wonder, since we'd all been on the road for the last . . . how many days? What day was this? It was easy to lose count, especially since we'd been reduced to a near infantile state, with someone else—the mommies, Jane and Jean—feeding and housing us and driving us around or handing us train tickets. And in a weird and unexpected way that felt good. We were all accomplished and responsible adults, but it was nice to let all that go and allow someone else to take care of us, just for a while.

There was tea, and there were cakes, and there were antipasti of varying description. I marveled that any of us could still eat, even out of courtesy to our hostess, who roamed from table to table and in and out of the house, talking nonstop. The house was modern, nestled among others like it, but with views of the white mountains of Carrara in one direction and the sea in the other. I could get used to living like this, although I had to remind myself that I hadn't seen a market or a store of any sort nearby. I wondered how one found the amenities like food. Maybe I could hire a servant—no, a couple, husband and wife—to take care of all those mundane details like cleaning and shopping, while I worked at my computer (assuming there was anything like an Internet connection) or stared dreamily at one view or the other with a cool drink in my hand . . . I realized I was drifting, and Jane was talking.

"There's a nice walk down to the cliffs, over that way"—she waved vaguely down the hill the way we'd come—"and from there you can see Portovenere and the islands south of the Cinque Terre. It's a real path, you won't miss it." Some people lurched to their feet and started meandering in that direction. I figured I might as well join them—it was that or go to sleep in my chair. After all, I had a mission. And I needed to work up an appetite for the no-doubt huge dinner we were going to have in, what, another three hours? I extricated myself from my seat and took off after the herd, not that I was in any hurry to catch up with them, but I wanted to keep them in sight so I didn't get lost.

The path was indeed clearly marked and more or less paved, which made sense after I had walked past several private homes, none of which seemed occupied at the moment, with securely padlocked gates; and what seemed to be a hotel or condos or something larger on the opposite side, where there would no doubt be magnificent sea views. The path ended with what appeared to be a World War II concrete structure, and I recalled dimly that Jane had said something about the Americans shelling this small town during the war. Off to the south was another similar concrete box. Their presence was an unsettling reminder of a more recent past.

Our little band hopped from rock to rock and peered over the chain-link fence (thank goodness for a fence) at the black sand beach far below. I wondered how on earth one reached it. We all duly observed the islands marching off to the distance, each one paler the farther away it was. I had to admit I had a much better understanding now of the history of representing distance in paintings: all those early Renaissance artists had only to look at the views around them.

We all took pictures. A young Italian couple, who had been there all along, completely ignored our little army of middle-aged women milling around them and engaged in a serious make-out session, or whatever it was called these days. At least they kept all their clothes on, and their hands didn't stray . . . too far. For a moment I felt a pang for young love, or lust, that could render them so oblivious to anything but each other. I wasn't sure I'd ever been that focused on another human being. Well, maybe my daughter, when she was very small. Not my husband, and that made me sad.

They were still there and still ignoring us when we began to straggle back to Jane's cousin's house. I realized I had never figured out what her name was, even though she had opened her home to us.

I caught up with Gloria, one of the few women I hadn't talked to before. "I'm glad I don't have a fear of heights!" I said fervently.

"Even a short fall can be dangerous," she said, continuing at her original pace, looking straight ahead, barely acknowledging my presence.

"Like the professor's?" I asked, since she'd left the door wide open.

"Exactly. He couldn't have fallen more than, what, twenty feet? But it's all in the angle. Land the wrong way and it's all over."

"Think we'll ever know what really happened?" I asked. Maybe the question was overly direct, but I was too tired to think of polite ways to sneak up on the issue.

Gloria stopped abruptly and turned to face me. "I for one don't care. I never liked the man."

"You knew him?"

"From one class, a long time ago. I pegged him for a sexist pig right away."

"Did you transfer out of the class?"

"Why would I? It was kind of fun watching him operate. It was a learning experience in its own way."

"But weren't there other people who weren't as . . . objective as you?"

Gloria looked around us briefly. We were alone on the path, or at least there was no one in sight. "You mean the ones who fell for his line? Sure. Was I supposed to play their mother and warn them about the big bad wolf? They had to learn to judge character sometime." She studied my expression. "You don't approve. What would you have done?"

I faced her squarely. "Probably the same thing you did: let them figure it out for themselves. And if the whole experience proved too much for them to cope with, well . . ."

"Then they weren't Wellesley material?" she challenged.

"No, I wouldn't say that. As I'm sure you know, there's a difference between intellectual intelligence and emotional intelligence, and they don't go hand in hand. We had a lot of bright but possibly fragile people in our class back then, and some got hurt."

"But that's life, isn't it? What do you want? Am I supposed to weep for this guy who had a good life getting away with the kind of crap he pulled, and then he retired covered in glory to his dream villa in Italy, and drank too much one night and fell down and broke his neck? I don't think so. And do you think anybody on this trip is really sorry?" And with that she turned on her heel and resumed her brisk walk back to the house.

I followed more slowly, trying to sort out my impressions. I didn't disagree with what she'd said, exactly, but she had been so vehement, so . . . cold. Did that stem from her own negative experience? Or was she just a cold person?

And had she really been so detached, back in the day—or was she lying?

I would have to compare impressions with my vineyard colleagues when I had the chance. Which was not going to be possible on the drive to this castle, wherever it was, where we would eat dinner, since we were in different vans and there was no privacy anyway. I hoped they had made some progress talking to the others on the list.

Of course, there was no way to guarantee that anyone was telling us the truth. They'd had forty years to practice their lies, or craft their rationalizations. Had any of his "girls" ever told anyone what had happened with Professor Gilbert? Friend, spouse, therapist? If it mattered enough to kill over now, it must have affected their lives all through the intervening years. I thought that Cynthia had collected marital statistics on our group, but we hadn't paid much attention to them. What would they tell us, anyway? There were so many variables to a marriage, or a long-term partnership, and it would be hard to point to any one as the major factor in a failed relationship. I should know; I had a list of causes, none of which was large, but the sum of them was too much for the unstable infrastructure my husband and I had cobbled together. And nowhere on my list was sexual harassment, or even workplace harassment. My failings were my own, and I couldn't lay the blame for my doomed marriage on any event or person from my past.

When I got back to the house after most of the group, people were beginning to clean up and count heads, to make sure everyone had returned before we set off on the last leg of our journey for the day. There was a little confusion when one person appeared to be missing, but when we arrived at the parking lot where the vans were parked, she was waiting—and taking pictures. All present and accounted for, so our wagon train moved on to the next meal.

The town of Fosdinovo, home to the soaring medieval castle of Malespina, was not so far as the crow flies, but there were mountains. Again. Our already rattled quartet of van drivers made slow progress on the hairpin turns, and everyone breathed a sigh of relief when we arrived at our destination without further mishaps and parked in an ample parking lot. Dinner was planned for seven, and since it was only six thirty now, we had half an hour to wander around the narrow medieval streets, admire the views, and take more pictures. Once again we scattered in small groups; our vineyard group gravitated together.

"Let's find a place where we can talk," Cynthia said after looking around carefully to make sure no one could overhear. Accompanied by Pam and Connie, we struck off on a road leading to the left—and downward. Most people had gone up to the right, no doubt searching once more for the perfect view. We found a quiet corner with a handy stone wall to sit on—carefully, since as usual the land dropped off steeply to olive groves and vineyards: lean too far back and it was a long way down.

"Where's Xianling?" I asked.

"She's been taking pictures all day, usually on the fringes of a group," Pam said. "She must have quite a collection by now. I hope she'll share them."

"We don't have long. What've you got?" Cynthia said quickly.

"More disgruntled people," I said. "Gloria said she saw exactly what the professor was up to, and too bad for those women who fell for his line. She seemed kind of bitter."

"Nice," Pam said sarcastically. "But then, a lot of people knew—more than we ever imagined—and they did nothing. Does anybody stand out as looking particularly guilty? What are we supposed to do, take each of the people on our shortlist into a small windowless room and intimidate a confession out of her?"

"Is that what the police would do?" Connie shot back.

"Let's not get ahead of ourselves," I said. "We're trying to fix this before the police get too involved. Look, we can do a little more poking around tonight at dinner and compare notes after we get back. Then we can decide what our next step is."

"Laura, tomorrow is our last day," Pam reminded me, as if I needed it. "We've got the excursion to Carrara, and then the big banquet in the evening. Do we really want to mess those up for everyone? And we certainly aren't going to have a lot of time for tête-à-têtes."

"Do we want a killer to go free?" I protested.

"Maybe it really was an accident," Pam replied. "Maybe whoever it was had no intention of killing the professor, but maybe he made a move on her that night and she panicked and shoved him."

"But he's still dead, accident or not. If—and that's still an if—we identify who his late-night date was, are we supposed to turn a blind eye?"

"First we have to find her, Laura," Cynthia reminded me. "Then we have to talk with her. I'm not going to jump to any conclusions. So let's go enjoy this banquet that Jane has set up for us."

We went back up the hill, over cobbled streets. The banquet was held in the main castle but in an adjacent building that had probably started life a millennium before as a stable. It was built of stone, with a relatively low ceiling. There was a small kitchen at the rear and long tables draped with white linen cloths. We shuffled ourselves among our colleagues once again. Wine appeared, along with the antipasti, and the noise level ramped up, making conversation close to impossible. Which was something of a relief: we were off-duty and we could enjoy ourselves.

"This is incredible!" I yelled to Vicky, sitting next to me.

"What?" she yelled back.

I waved my hand around the room. "Incredible!"

"Yes!" She nodded vigorously. We raised our glasses to each other, grinning.

And then the food started arriving. Platter after platter appeared and was handed around the table. I lost count after three different courses, but still they kept coming. It was all wonderful: pasta, fish, meat, whatever. A flock of ravioli appeared on one platter, filled with ricotta and something green. "Spinach?" I asked Donna, on my other side.

"Nettles!" she yelled back.

I never would have guessed. I speared another one and ate it happily.

The next time I looked at my watch it was nearly ten o'clock. The platters were empty, and it had been at least ten minutes since the last one had appeared. More important, the wine bottles were empty too.

Jane stood up. "I hope you've enjoyed your dinner."

Vigorous cheers broke out.

"Let's congratulate the cooks—can you believe they produced all of this wonderful food in that tiny kitchen?"

More cheers and loud clapping. The kitchen and waitstaff

grinned happily. I hoped we were going to leave them a large tip.

Jane pressed on, "I hate to break up such a lovely evening, but we need to start driving back, and you know what the road to Monterosso is like."

A few people laughed. Not the drivers.

"Plus we have to make an early start tomorrow. We're going to visit a marble mine in Carrara, then have lunch in the town, and our final stop will be at the ruins of the Roman town of Luna, where they shipped the marble from Carrara all over the known world a couple of millennia ago. And then back to Monterosso for a final banquet in the vineyard on the hill. And! Since it's a long drive, and the ride up to Carrara is mountainous, we've rented a bus that will hold us all."

Now the drivers cheered. I couldn't blame them.

"So go ahead and finish your desserts, we'll be leaving for the vans in about ten minutes."

I looked down at my plate. It was empty for the first time in three hours. "Isn't it amazing how much food we've consumed in Italy?" I asked Rebecca, seated across from me—and realized that she could actually hear me, for the first time in hours.

She agreed quickly. "And it's all been good. I think I'll have to rethink my attitude toward Italian food. Sadly, most of the Italian restaurants I know don't produce anything remotely like what we've had."

"Isn't it a shame? But any of us can work with fresh tomatoes and olive oil, right? Can't we re-create at least some of this?"

"Sure, why not?"

We emerged eventually into the blue dusk, with swallows swirling around the tower of the castle. The rolling hills below were growing indistinct as the light died. My belly was full and I felt a slight buzz from the wine. Life was good—except for that pesky murder. Which we had only one day to resolve or risk the wrath of the *polizia*. I hoped we could pull it off.

Half the people in the van dozed on the way back. It was dark by the time we trudged back to our vineyard hideaway. Our small group looked at each other. "This is not the time to try to think. Breakfast?"

"Agreed. See you then."

And we went to bed.

Chapter 22

There must be something different about Italian wine, because on this trip I had consumed far more than I would at home, yet I hadn't had anything approaching a hangover yet. Maybe it was all the exercise we were getting. Or maybe all the food sopped it up. Either way I was content, particularly because this morning I needed a working brain.

Cynthia and I bumped into each other on the way to the bathroom. "After you," I said. "I'll go out and admire the view."

"Thanks," she replied. "I can't believe it's our last full day."

"I know, I know."

I went out, dried the dew off the chairs on the patio, and sat, listening to the clucking of the chickens below and watching the mist burn off in the valley. It was early yet, so there were few sounds from the town. A worker went by in a farm truck on a graveled lane below but didn't look up to see me sitting there in my sleep shirt.

On this whole trip my only real regret was that there hadn't been more time to explore Florence. Even though I'd seen it before, a long time ago, one day was not enough to reacquaint myself with it. Maybe I should come back. Maybe with my daughter? We hadn't traveled together in a while.

My happy daydream was interrupted by Cynthia, now dressed. She dropped into a chair. "All yours."

I took a quick shower, dressed, and joined Cynthia again. "I'm going to miss this," I said.

"I know what you mean. Look, Laura . . ."

I turned to look at her. "What is it?"

"I don't want to leave this death hanging over us all. I don't want it to trash our memories of the trip. But there's so little time left, I'm afraid we won't be able to fix this."

"I know what you mean. You still have that diagram?" When she nodded, I said, "Let's go over it again, with what we know now."

"But we haven't been able to talk to everyone yet," she protested.

"We can't afford to wait. Let's fill in what we can and see where we are."

Cynthia disappeared inside and came back with a bigger, better version of her original napkin diagram. The larger size had allowed her to fill in names, which made the overview a lot clearer.

"I see you filled in the circle for who had a kitchen or somewhere to cook," I said.

"Jean said there were three buildings that had cooking facilities, although she thought the one next to the dining room might be too large for one person. And she told me who was in which."

"Would you go back to Capitignano alone? Or were you thinking of the twins?" I arched one eyebrow.

Cynthia laughed. "You're bad. No, I probably wouldn't come back on my own. I think if I returned to Italy my first choice would be to find a nice hotel in Florence and spend a few days there, although Capitignano was a great place to unwind."

"My thoughts exactly. Anyway, what does Jean's information add?"

"Not much," Cynthia said glumly. "Turns out that most of the people on our shortlist were in one or another of them, or had a close friend who was. Can't you see someone popping in, particularly when it was so cold, and asking if she could brew up a cup of tea? It would be that easy. And how can we find out? 'Excuse me, but did you cook anything while you were at the villa? Did you let anyone else in to cook anything?'"

"That's what the police will do."

"We aren't the police. We're trying to *avoid* being the police."

I sighed. "Maybe that's just not possible."

"What, you're giving up? That's not like you."

"I didn't say I was giving up. What I *am* saying is that we set ourselves an impossible task, to try to discreetly interview a dozen or more people about a murder while everybody is wandering off in all directions or we're all jammed together in a noisy space and can't possibly talk."

"Well, if you put it that way . . ."

"I do. But I haven't given up."

I checked the time: still too early for breakfast down below. Then I noticed Valerie trudging in our direction. She didn't look happy.

When she reached our patio, Valerie said, "I have to tell you something."

I waved at the remaining chair. "Sit. What is it?"

She lifted her chin. "I'm the one who gave Professor Gilbert the poppy drink," Valerie said. "But I didn't kill him." She dropped heavily into a chair across the table and glared defiantly at Cynthia and me.

"What?" Questions tumbled around in my head: when, how, and mostly, why. My confusion must have been obvious on my face.

Valerie smiled without humor. "I apologize. When you asked me about the poppy drink, I didn't tell you then that I made it and used it on the professor. I knew I hadn't killed him—the stuff I gave him wasn't strong enough. But after talking with you two, and with the others up here, I realized that I wasn't being fair to the rest of our classmates. If I said nothing, just to protect myself, that would get in the way of finding out who really did kill him. And that would leave us all under a cloud, and I didn't want that. So I figured I should eliminate one variable from the mix and let you focus on what really happened. I take it you haven't shared any of this information with the whole group?"

"No, we've kept it quiet," I said, "although some other people may have put two and two together and guessed. But the police know somebody had given him something, and I'm afraid that was my doing."

"What, you're some kind of international cop?" Valerie asked.

"Not exactly." I wasn't about to give her a detailed explanation. "But I did go so far as to make sure that the autopsy was thorough, or the police would have been content to call it an accident and close the file. When the autopsy results came back, they found out about the poppy stuff, since it set off a drug test. I opened that box, but I think there's a good chance I can close it again, since it's pretty clear that another person was involved. Look, when did you feed the stuff to him?"

Valerie sighed and leaned back in her chair, the tension beginning to drain from her. "Early on, when we were having cocktails before dinner. You know those drinks they were pushing at us? They were plenty strong enough to cover any odd taste—heck, they tasted odd anyway. And the color was helpful too. So I brought Professor Gilbert a drink and made sure he drank it—he was used to women waiting on him, so he didn't think twice about it. And it wasn't his only drink."

"You're saying that the amount he drank and the timing mean that the effects would have worn off by the time dinner was over?"

"Yes, most likely. I wanted him to look stupid during the dinner, maybe stumble a bit in front of everyone. That's all I knew about the properties of Tuscan poppies, and when I got here and learned that Anthony Gilbert would be our speaker, it seemed too convenient to pass up, and sort of appropriately ironic."

"Did it work?" Cynthia asked. "I mean, did it have the effect you wanted?"

Valerie shrugged. "I don't think so, but I don't really know. It gave me the creeps to be near him again, so I sat at the other end of the room. Everybody was drinking, so probably no one would have noticed. And nobody had seen him for a long time—they might just have written the effects off to drink or simple old age. He was pushing eighty, after all. I know, the whole thing was stupid, but when I heard he was coming, I wanted to do *something*."

"Were you . . . I mean, did he?"

"I slept with him, all right? I was the girl of the moment for about fifteen seconds in 1969 and then he lost interest. It hurt, but I survived. It took me a while to realize I was far from the only one, and he was a jerk in other ways too. He was a mean-spirited bully. I wish I'd had the guts to complain to someone, but I couldn't figure out who—the college didn't have a support system in place, like they do now. So I figured the best thing I could do would be to hunker down and get a good education while I had the opportunity. When I saw him at the villa, though, it all came back. There he was, smug and sleek, and that seemed wrong. I knew there were other women there who had had run-ins with him. I wanted to do something, and I figured embarrassing him, attacking his ego, was the best way. So I tried to dope him, just a little, so he looked like a stupid drunk, and bring him down a notch. Am I in trouble?"

I looked at her, searching her face. "The autopsy showed the presence of an opioid in his system, but according to the official record it would not have been enough to kill him. Given what you've told me, it had in fact probably worn off by the time dinner was over. I think we can set that aside."

"Thank you. And I didn't try to get in the way of what you were doing, at any time. I talked to a lot of the other women, and I reported everything I learned to you. I really didn't want to think that I had killed him, and from everything you've said, I didn't. But someone did."

"If we eliminate you, we're back where we started," Cynthia protested, "with a body and a handful of suspects who knew him and/or had a motive to do him harm, and no way to eliminate them. If we go to all of them and ask for alibis, it'll be one unholy mess."

"If the police get involved, it'll be an unholy mess anyway. Should we look for the most damaged person?" I suggested. "Is it easy to hide the kind of anger and hate that lasts forty years?"

Valerie and Cynthia turned to look at me, and I held up my hands in mock surrender. "No, I'm not suggesting we go directly to each person and ask, 'Where were you at midnight on the day and who can vouch for you?' But I think we've agreed that the professor's kind of behavior can cause long-term harm to vulnerable young women. Nobody who came on this trip was expecting to be confronted by him so many years later. There are women who have put that part of their history behind them and it wouldn't matter to them. But there are others for whom it was traumatic, and maybe they wanted to rewrite history, or to make peace within themselves by confronting him after all this time. Professor Gilbert might have misconstrued their intentions, given that he requested that bottle of wine. Maybe in his misguided mind he thought the woman was looking for a repeat performance."

"Jerk," muttered Valerie. "I can't believe I ever fell for his crap, even when I was nineteen."

"You weren't the only one, Valerie," I pointed out. "In any case, if he thought he was going to have an amorous evening, this time he got something else altogether."

"Laura," Cynthia interrupted, "we've got less than twenty-four hours. How do you suggest we figure this out in that amount of time?"

I stood up. "I need coffee. Let's go get breakfast."

"Hang on a moment, Laura," Cynthia said. "Valerie, we'll meet you down there."

Valerie gave us an odd look, but left. I turned to Cynthia. "What?"

"As long as we're looking for confessions, I . . . I've got something to say."

"Don't tell me *you* killed him."

"No, of course I didn't. But the night he died . . ." She looked uncomfortable.

"What? Spit it out, will you? I'm hungry."

"I was with the two chefs, but I kind of, uh, misrepresented our activities."

I cocked my head at her. "You mean no wild orgy?"

"Not exactly. I did spend the time with them, so my alibi holds. But mostly they wanted to practice their English on me — they're hoping to find jobs in a restaurant in Florence and they thought it might help."

"So why did you lie about it?"

Cynthia looked away, out over the steep vineyard. "It made me sad, I guess. I keep trying to pretend I'm not as old as I really am, and maybe I hoped . . . Forget about it."

"Let's go get breakfast, shall we? And please, no more revelations before I've had my coffee."

Did I really think that coffee would help?

We trooped down our steps in single file. Valerie was waiting for us, so I pulled her aside before we reached the patio. "Thanks for telling us, Valerie. You probably would have been in the clear if you hadn't said anything."

"I know. But that didn't seem right. And I want to know who actually had the guts to kill him."

"I understand. I'm glad you came clean with us."

Our breakfast was a quiet affair. I was thinking, or trying to. We'd crossed one more person off our list — Valerie — but as for the rest we were indeed back to square one, except that we'd gotten to know a lot of the women better. Was I ready to point a finger at anyone in particular as a killer? Nope.

I liked these women. We weren't the same people we had been forty years earlier, but if anything we'd improved with age. When I stopped to think about it, this whole event had been extraordinary. We'd all gotten along well. We'd all followed the jam-packed program and apparently enjoyed it. No one had whined or complained or dragged their feet. No one had thrown her weight around or tried to impress anyone else. I tried to imagine a comparable group of men setting off on an expedition like this one and almost spewed coffee. Not in a million years.

Maybe the whiners and the divas had chosen to stay home. Did anyone acknowledge that she was a diva? High-maintenance? A pain in the ass? Wouldn't you know by this point in your life?

Or maybe there were still women who didn't feel complete without a man around, or who had become accustomed to letting a man take care of her. Maybe we were the most independent-minded women of our cohort. Whatever the reason, I liked these women. We were still smart, funny, interesting people. I wanted more and more to erase this stain from the holiday and send everyone home with happy memories.

"Your thoughts?" Cynthia asked as I was finishing my second cup of coffee.

I took a deep breath. "If we don't come up with a name by tonight, I say we throw it on the table after the fun part of the banquet and see what happens."

"God, that sounds like a recipe for chaos. Isn't there a quieter way?"

"If you've got any ideas, now's the time to lay them out," I replied.

"I've got nothing," Cynthia said. "We're heading for some pretty serious caves at Carrara, aren't we? Maybe we can take people into dark corners and force a confession out of . . . someone. Is anyone claustrophobic, do you know?"

"Not that I've heard. But nobody asked, just like nobody asked if we were afraid of heights. We are a fearless bunch, aren't we?"

"That's a fact. We even face weird food without flinching too. But back to basics: where are we supposed to find this bus for today?"

Connie spoke up. "I know the answer to this one! We go up the hill there and get into the vans, and the vans will drive us to the bus a mile or so farther up."

"I bet this bus makes our drivers very happy. So, are we ready?"

"All set. Let's get this show on the road."

Chapter 23

The bus proved a happy surprise: plush seats, plenty of leg room, and a good view from the large windows. That last proved important, at least as we neared Carrara. The town—city?—itself looked modern and prosperous; the only peculiarity was the presence of marble sculptures on every other corner. It was kind of sweet—the Carrarans (Carrari?) certainly celebrated their local product. But we were never out of sight of the looming white mountains inland. We wove our way through commercial and residential streets, and then we began climbing. Again. The large bus went even more slowly than our vans had, despite an experienced hired driver, which gave us plenty of time to admire the vistas around every corner. However, the hairpin turns were scary, and not for the first time I hoped that we wouldn't encounter anyone coming the other way. All the traffic seemed to consist of large, slow-moving flatbed trucks loaded with large chunks of marble.

By the time we were halfway up, I was saying "oh my God" about every fifty feet—and now it wasn't from fear. We were in the heart of the mountains; even the gravel by the side of the road was made up of white marble chips. Looking up, the tops of the mountains were wreathed in cloud, and we were headed straight for them. In some ways it looked like a moonscape—certainly not like any mountain I'd ever seen, because it was nearly monochromatic. And all that white slag that had looked like snow from a distance spilled down the slopes and rested where it fell.

We were maybe two-thirds of the way to the top when the bus driver maneuvered the bus through a narrow driveway and into a parking lot. We tumbled out to find a scene with an air of unreality. There were sculptures in process; some men in masks were sanding and smoothing a few near a flimsy open shed. The workers were so covered with marble dust that they resembled statues themselves. Fragments of abandoned sculptures littered the surrounding ground as well—odd architectural bits and pieces, the occasional arm or foot, broken off or never finished. We humans in our brightly colored clothes looked out of place in this sere gray and white landscape.

There were also two bathrooms, so everybody took her turn. One never knows where the next one will be.

Finally Jane herded us toward another parking area, where there were some smaller vans (covered with white dust) waiting. Apparently we were going *into* the mountain, where we would get up close and personal with marble; we were going to follow in the footsteps of Michelangelo. If anyone had claustrophobia, now was the moment to declare it. Nobody did, or they didn't admit to it: maybe curiosity outweighed panic.

We boarded the vans and headed into a dark, narrow tunnel leading straight into the heart of the mountain. A long, long way ahead we could see where the tunnel emerged on the other side, but we stopped in a large chamber an equal distance from each end. We had arrived.

We stumbled out of the small vans into a dark and dripping world. There were lights strung here and there but they cast huge shadows and left a lot of corners in darkness. A few pieces of large machinery lurked in the gloom, looking for all the world like mechanical dinosaurs, but nobody was using them at the moment. I wondered how much noise marble mining generated.

Once we had regrouped, we were ordered to put on hard hats—there was a long row of tables with various sizes of them waiting for us. We all spent a couple of minutes trying on different hard hats until everyone was satisfied, as though style mattered a thousand feet underground. But there would be pictures, so maybe it did. Then the tour guide, a young, plump woman, stepped up and spoke in accented English.

"You see where we come in? That is four hundred meters away—that is more than a thousand feet. The other end of the tunnel, the same. And the same again of marble below us, and the same above us. You are surrounded by the marble of the mountain."

That was a startling statement. We were standing literally in the heart of the mountain, and the rest of the world was no more than a small square of light a very long way away.

She went on, about how the tunnels had first been built, about how the slabs of marble were cut and allowed to fall on giant pillows filled with marble dust (what else?), about the history of the families who had been carving marble for generation upon generation, even about safety regulations. A lot I tuned out, more fascinated by our unlikely situation. The scale of the space was so unreal, and we humans seemed so small in the midst of it. It was hard to estimate how far above our heads the "ceiling" was. It was even harder to imagine what cutting a multi-ton slab and detaching it from its matrix would be like. How did the workers stand it? I noticed that most of our group was equally distracted, staring up and around, walking through puddles underfoot without even noticing. Good thing there wasn't going to be a pop quiz at the end of the tour, because I was pretty sure we'd all fail it. There was simply too much else to absorb.

We must have spent half an hour inside, poking into dark corners, before we trooped back to the vans. On the way out I snagged a seat next to the tour guide.

"How did they get the stone out of the caves and down the mountain back before there were trains and trucks?" I asked.

"They would slide them. With lots of soap. And many men to hold them back with ropes."

Of course. Giant marble sleds. I wondered how often they had broken loose. How had they warned the people waiting below?

When we had all returned to daylight, we made a beeline for the gift shop. It was funny to see everyone arguing over which piece or pieces of marble—in the form of coasters, statuettes, boxes and so on—to haul home with them, but I understood the desire. I knew I felt different after spending time inside the marble, and I wanted to bring home a keepsake. The matching salt and pepper shakers didn't weigh *that* much, and I would remember the experience every time I sprinkled salt on something.

The next stop was obvious: it was time for lunch. We dutifully boarded the bus and started the tortuous trek down the mountain. We could see huge holes punched in the sides of all the slopes, quarries that had been operating forever and were still going strong. How long would it take the world to run out of Carrara marble? It didn't look as though it would happen any time soon.

In a strange way it was a relief to be back on flat ground, in the middle of the modern world, although the mountains still loomed around us. The bus driver let us out next to a small park and we headed to a brightly lit restaurant a block away—which our group filled entirely. I found myself sitting with more people I hadn't had time to have a real conversation with, but then the food started arriving and I shut the door on conversing to concentrate on what was in front of me. There was no way to speak privately in this melee, and I wanted to give the food the attention it was due.

Where were the restaurants like this back home? I had to admit I didn't go out much. I didn't really enjoy dining alone, no matter how good the food, and since my daughter had moved away there really wasn't anyone in my life I could call on the spur of the moment and suggest going out to eat. All right, here the company made a real difference: I was enjoying being part of a roomful of women who were smart and interesting, and who loved to talk and eat, often at the same time. I had never thought of myself as a "joiner," but maybe it was time to reconsider my position. Or maybe it was time to sit back and enjoy the moment—and eat yet another fantastic multicourse meal.

I turned to the person next to me, someone whose name, Edith, I recognized vaguely from my short-lived foray into the sciences. She was Asian, and back in my college days the Asian women taking biology and chemistry classes were notorious for skewing the curves for the rest of us, who were struggling with those subjects most of the time. I wasn't sure if that group had made many friends, in or out of class—they seemed always to be studying. I was curious to learn about how her life had turned out, and we chatted through a couple of courses. She had indeed become a doctor, married another doctor, was still practicing medicine, had traveled widely and lived abroad, and had led an altogether admirable life. I in return felt I had to apologize for abandoning my once-beloved major and taking on more prosaic work, which I couldn't talk about in any detail anyway. But she wasn't judgmental, and by and large we had a cheerful conversation.

My ears pricked up when I heard the word "professor" from someone at the far end of the table, and I tuned in to that conversation.

"Too bad he had to die while we were there," someone said. I couldn't see her face from where I sat.

"I'm surprised someone hadn't offed him years ago," Dorothy said with surprising frankness. "You know, at the last Alumnae Council meeting, I ended up talking to someone who must have been twenty years behind us, and she said even then he was still up to his old tricks."

"That's disgusting," I heard another voice respond. "Why didn't anyone ever say anything?"

"Well, in our day we were taught not to make waves, right?" Dorothy replied. "We were the 'nice' girls. End of an era, maybe. I'm sure nobody would put up with that kind of nonsense today."

"Let's hope not. Wonder if there's anything in his file about all that?"

"I wonder how the college will handle his obit," Pat said. "Can't you see them dancing around all this? 'Professor Gilbert was truly involved with his students, blah blah blah.'"

The speakers laughed and went on to talk of other things. Had everybody on campus except me known about his activities? What else had I missed? I remembered a solar eclipse one year, and the student strike. But lecherous faculty? Not on my radar.

I sighed and went back to my excellent food.

It was well past two when Jane stood up again. "I hope you've all enjoyed this wonderful meal"—enthusiastic clapping from all—"but we have one more stop to make before we return to Monterosso for our final banquet: the ruins of the Roman port town of Luna, where all that marble you saw today was shipped out to the rest of the world. The town was built in the second century BC and thrived for several centuries. Now it's one of the most important archeological sites in the region. As you will see, it's currently under excavation. And it's spread out over several acres, so you can walk off your lunches!"

Once again we hauled our derrieres out of our seats and set off to find our bus. This time the drive was relatively short, although it took us well out into the countryside, which was quite lovely, with or without historic ruins. Odd how quickly we went from a bustling modern city to the ancient past. To reach the small museum slash ticket desk, we strolled some distance from the parking lot, stopping to admire a handsome flock of black sheep, each equipped with a low-toned bell. When they rang in unison as the flock moved, it was both musical and moving, and I wondered for the first time if my point-and-shoot camera could handle a video with sound. I hoped someone would capture it.

The museum came complete with a couple of cats sunning themselves on the steps—another thing I loved about Italy. This late in the day we were the only visitors. We acquired a tall, distinguished tour guide and set off across the meadows to stare at the foundations of a forum, shops, houses, fragments of the Aurelian Road and the city drain, while listening to the learned guide explain it all. I found if I paid attention I could pretty much understand what he said; my art-historical Italian was still useful. We made a circuit of what would have been the city walls, then headed farther out to the remains of the amphitheater, which, we were informed, could have held the entire population of the town with room to spare.

Once there I peeled off from the crowd and wandered on my own around the outer aisle of the amphitheater, trying to imagine it packed with thousands of cheering people. I found a convenient portion of wall and sat down, just absorbing the ambience, but I wasn't surprised when Cynthia joined me.

"Anything new?" she asked.

"Not really, except I have yet to find anyone who liked the professor or wants to defend his memory. Sad, isn't it? On the surface he was eminently respected, but under it all . . ."

"I know what you mean. So we haven't proved a damn thing."

"Nope, apparently not. What if we did manage to talk to everyone, and then cross-checked every blinking fact with every other, and we came up with no one at all in that intersection of those circles of yours? If they all alibied out?"

"But the professor is still dead!" Cynthia protested. "Somebody killed him."

"Yes, he is dead, but maybe it was really an accident. We've got the explanation for the poppy juice, and if Valerie was telling the truth, it wasn't strong enough to do much harm, and besides, he drank it early in the evening, so it should have worn off by the time he died."

"What about the wine and the two glasses?" Cynthia asked.

"Maybe it was all quite innocent—his date showed up, they talked about old times and polished off the bottle, and then she left and he took a walk to look at the stars. Hell, maybe he got stood up by his whoever it was and drank the whole bottle of wine himself, and then decided to walk it off, slipped and fell, end of story."

I leaned back against ancient stones warmed by the setting sun and shut my eyes, listening and just being. There was so much history here, and yet all those long-ago inhabitants were gone, the site forgotten for centuries. But here we were.

I opened my eyes suddenly. "Cynthia, what if it wasn't one of us?"

"Who else is there?"

"We haven't thought much about that. I guess we were so worried that it could be a classmate that we didn't look much further, plus we'd already left Tuscany. But what if we were wrong?"

"Well, that's a whole new can of worms. You still think there's a Wellesley connection?"

"The timing would suggest that, plus the fact that there was such a handy collection of potential suspects, a lot of whom have motives. Maybe that was the red herring." I was beginning to get excited about my nebulous idea. "What if somebody took advantage of this trip of ours to lure the professor in and kill him?"

"Or what if someone actually planned the trip with that in mind?"

We stared at each other. "But Jane and Jean have been planning this for at least a year! We signed up last summer."

"That works for either scenario. If someone had already waited forty years, what difference did one more make? And that would let whoever it was polish the plan. How long ago did the professor retire to Italy?"

"I have no idea, but I'm sure it was announced in the alumnae magazine. Everyone would know where he was."

"Including Jean and Jane? As you said, they set this up."

"Jean was an art history major. Is either one of them on that list of ours?"

"Both are. Naturally they took one or another of Gilbert's classes."

"We need to talk to them. Who else?"

"Barbara went to Wellesley, but not our year." Cynthia looked contrite. "But I never asked for a profile on her—I guess we were too focused on our classmates."

"Hey, it's early back in the States. Ask now."

Cynthia pulled out her cell phone and walked away to talk. She was back in two minutes. "We should have a report on Barbara by the time we get back to Monterosso."

"And we'll have to find a way to talk to Jane and Jean before the banquet. I hate to pry now, when all we want to do is enjoy our last night."

"We'll all enjoy it a lot more if we can wrap up this murder."

Chapter 24

We all strolled slowly back toward our waiting bus, delaying our departure as long as possible. The flock of black sheep was still there, now in a line, diligently munching their way through a field of lush grass. The shepherd, a man about our age, politely tipped his hat to us as we passed. His dog ignored us, keeping his eye on his charges.

On the bus I watched the scenery unfold as we made our way back to Monterosso, and I thought hard. I wanted resolution for the death of the professor, for all our sakes. Sure, maybe he was pond scum and deserved to die, but murder was murder, and I didn't want to believe any of the people on the bus could have killed him. Nor could I imagine how to sort out the legalities of charging and prosecuting someone in a foreign country, particularly Italy, still smarting from the ongoing Amanda Knox mess. The fact that we were all polite older women might work in our favor, since I'd always heard that Italian men respected their mothers, and we were certainly the right age. But at least some of us had been and were assertive smart women, which might not play so well with the *polizia*.

No, Laura, that's a biased assumption. You haven't had any direct interaction with a local police officer, so you'd better keep an open mind. You'll need it. There were at least a few women on the force these days, weren't there?

But I couldn't talk to them because I didn't speak Italian, and I didn't feel confident of their English capabilities. Worse, I needed to speak to some other Italians, specifically Loredana and her husband, who I hadn't even met. What had he said that had kept the police at bay so long? Would it last? And could he help at all if Cynthia and I did actually come up with a solution?

Strange vacation this was turning out to be!

When I found Professor Gilbert's body back in Tuscany, I had been presented with choices. I could have done nothing; I could have *not* reported seeing the body and waited for someone else to deal with it. Or I could have alerted someone — but not made that phone call. Why had I done that? Because my intuition told me something was not right with the death? I didn't believe in intuition, or gut feelings. The fact that I had been right about his death was little comfort.

It had not been a simple accident, not entirely. Valerie's potion could have played a part in it. Was I obligated to turn her in? To whom? Based on what I knew of the Italian judicial system, I wouldn't want to throw her into that. If only the autopsy had found nothing unexpected, this whole thing would have gone away.

I was sorry that I had fallen asleep so quickly that night. If I had stayed awake reading, as I so often did, I might have heard the footsteps of a second person over my head, might have heard an argument, or at least a heated discussion; might have heard a voice I recognized. Might have heard bouncing bedsprings (no, don't go there—I hadn't looked to see whether the autopsy had made any reference to recent, um, intimate activity). Instead I had zonked out entirely and missed it all. Maybe it was fitting that I had been the one to find the body—I'd fallen asleep on the job. But who goes on a vacation with a bunch of old friends anticipating a crime? I certainly hadn't.

Mentally I reviewed everyone else's behavior following the announcement of the death. To the best of my recollection no one had shown an inappropriate reaction, like whooping with glee or bursting into tears. Of course, we'd all had long practice with putting on a game face. But even after that first moment, no one had gone off skulking in corners and weeping, or had taken to drinking too much—or at least, not any more than the rest of us. If someone felt guilty, she was hiding it well. She must have heaved a sigh of relief when we had departed the scene of the crime.

But I had to admit I didn't know these women well. Why on earth did I think I could figure out what had happened? Even with Cynthia's and the others' help? I was not good at this, and I never had been. My usual reaction to crises was to say something like "how interesting" and then take notes or pictures. This did not make me popular with some people, who would have been a lot more sympathetic if I'd dissolved in tears or had hysterics. Sorry—I'm too old to change. My brain just keeps ticking along, making observations, drawing conclusions. Useful for my job; not so useful in personal relationships.

The ride back to Monterosso took well over an hour, and I'd bet a number of people dozed at least part of the way. We arrived back around six, and those of us staying at the vineyard had the easy walk down. But there was no quiet corner to be found there: the staff was busy setting up for the big dinner. The tables on the patio had all been pushed together to form a single long one, now draped with white linen, punctuated with lush bouquets of flowers. The staff members were adding cutlery, plates and glasses even now. No place to linger.

The six of us looked at each other. "Dinner's not until eight. I don't want to waste time taking a nap," Connie said.

"Back down to town? That means we'll have to walk back up for dinner."

"I don't care. Let's do it," Connie said firmly.

So we did, picking up Xianling along the way. We hadn't seen much of her today, nor had we talked with her, although she'd been in the background, taking pictures as always. The downhill leg was easy; we would deal with the uphill one later. "We need to talk to Jane," I said to Cynthia, watching where I put my feet on the slanting path. This was not the time to twist an ankle. "Do you know where she's staying?"

"With relatives, I think," Cynthia said. "I don't know where."

"So I guess it will have to wait."

We reached the town, where everyone was still out and about on the streets. We wandered down to the shore and found a table at a café and ordered sparkling water—saving our appetites for the dinner?

"Well," Valerie said.

"Exactly," I agreed. I had no idea what to do next.

Xianling, who had accompanied us in silence, finally spoke. "I have something. I don't think you're going to like it, but I believe you need to know."

I sighed and turned to the others. "I asked Xianling to do something for us that she is best suited for. All right, Xianling, let's have it."

Xianling pulled her ubiquitous tablet from her large bag and I wondered irreverently what else she might have in there, like Mary Poppins. "You asked me to collect pictures of the dinner, and the cocktails before," she said.

"I did. Did you find something?"

Xianling was not to be rushed. "I asked all the others whom I knew had taken more than the occasional picture. As you suggested, I told them I wanted to assemble a memory book for our trip, in digital form so that we could all share it easily. Most were happy to contribute. Last night after we returned from dinner I assembled the pictures you requested and identified all the people and where they were at the relevant times."

An impressive effort on her part—and a lot of work. "Thank you, Xianling. It never occurred to me how much of your time it would take."

"I collected quite a few pictures, but most were not relevant to this," she stated in a matter-of-fact tone. "I eliminated the ones that showed much the same scenes. Then I looked to see who had been in proximity with who else and when—during the cocktail hour, and at the dinner."

And then it hit me: she didn't know about Valerie's confession. Valerie had shared the information about her role to Cynthia and to me, but not to the others. Awkward. I wasn't about to reveal what Valerie had said, so I had to let Xianling go forward. Maybe something else useful would emerge.

"Have you come to any conclusions?" I asked Xianling.

She shook her head. "There's nothing conclusive. Of course, it would be nice if someone had captured the moment where someone slipped something into the professor's drink, but no one did."

So nothing pointed to Valerie, I thought, relieved.

Xianling wasn't finished yet. "However, what is perhaps more interesting is the number of people whose expressions were captured while they were looking at Professor Gilbert, when they thought no one was watching."

"Interesting," Cynthia said. "Did anyone stand out?"

"Several, but I found this the most striking shot." She tapped on the screen and enlarged a picture, then handed it across the table. The rest of us leaned in to look.

It was a shot of the head table, taken from an angle off to the side. Professor Gilbert sat in the center, regaling someone out of the frame with a story, his hands gesturing broadly. And on his other side sat Gerry—with a look of pure hatred on his face.

Cynthia and I looked at each other. "Oh my God," I whispered.

"What?" the others asked, bewildered.

I shut my eyes for a moment to collect myself. "Cyn and I were talking earlier . . . We had begun to wonder if maybe we've been looking at this backward."

"What do you mean by that?" Pam said.

"We got so worried that one of our classmates might have done it that we forgot it wasn't all about us. That someone else might have been involved."

Valerie's eyes lit up with something like hope. "You think so?" Clearly she would be glad to be let off the hook.

"Maybe," I said.

Cynthia gave a start. "Oh, crap, I think my brain is fried. Hang on a sec." She found her own tablet and turned it on, scrolling through messages until she found what she was looking for. She clicked on a message, scanned it quickly, then clicked on an attachment. Her eyes widened. "*Merda!*"

"What?" we all said in chorus. Even we could understand that particular Italian term.

"We were right, Laura. About being wrong, I mean. Look." She handed me her tablet.

I peered at the screen, trying to decipher the report one of her people had sent . . . and the name jumped out: Gerry.

I looked up at her. "Why?"

"Keep reading—no, don't bother, I'll just tell you. Gerry had a younger sister who went to Wellesley, after we'd graduated. She took a class from Professor Gilbert. She killed herself the summer after her sophomore year. You can figure out the rest."

"The inference being, she couldn't handle whatever Gilbert had done to her or with her?" Pam asked. Connie and Denise just stared, and Valerie looked triumphant, although she tried to conceal it.

"Probably," Cynthia agreed. "It may not matter, if that's what Gerry thought. I can't believe we were so stupid as to miss that. I mean, most people said he was the one who invited Professor Gilbert to speak."

Pam broke in. "Yeah, and we thought he naively believed he was doing something nice for us that we would enjoy. Instead, he was setting the scene for the professor's murder and using us all for cover."

"Could it still have been an accident?" I asked. "I mean, say he confronted Gilbert about what had happened to his sister. Gilbert probably couldn't remember her at all, and that would have set Gerry off."

"What about the two wineglasses?" Cynthia countered.

"We know that it was the professor who asked for the wine to be taken up to his room," I said. "We were so busy thinking it was a tryst with a woman that we didn't think about alternatives. Maybe he intended it as a thank-you gesture for Gerry."

"Does Gerry's wife know, do you think?" Pam asked.

"I . . . don't know," I said. "They've been married forever, if I remember correctly." Cynthia looked at her tablet again and nodded confirmation. "How could she not know about his sister's death, under the circumstances?"

"Lots of ways," Cynthia said promptly. "She and Gerry's sister never overlapped at college. The sister's probably wasn't the only suicide during that decade. And it didn't happen on campus." She looked at her screen again. "It was over the summer. She was at home."

"So Barbara wouldn't have had much reason to know."

"Oh, come on. Gerry never mentioned it? In all the years they've been married?" Pam said incredulously.

"Haven't they lived abroad for a lot of that time?" Xianling asked. "Did Barbara ever attend reunions? Not everyone does, you know. And husbands have been known to keep secrets."

"So you're saying she might *not* have known?" Connie countered. "Does that make it better or worse?"

"I don't know," I said, feeling deflated. "It's probably not important anyway." I'd been right about it being murder, but I'd been looking in the wrong direction for the killer. Good news, bad news.

"What do we do now?" Valerie asked.

"That is a very good question," Cynthia said. "We have no proof. Even if someone had preserved the crime scene, if they do such a thing around here, Gerry's prints would have been all over — he owns the place. The glasses are long gone, as is the bottle. The physical injuries were inconclusive. I mean, there wasn't anything like the prints of a pair of hands wrapped around Gilbert's neck, right? In fact, the only physical evidence we have is that he had a drug in his system, that you put there, Valerie."

"What?" Xianling said, startled.

"Sorry, it just slipped out," Cynthia apologized to Valerie.

"Don't worry about it. Guys, I brewed up a potion from the local poppies and slipped it to the professor. I'm amazed nobody caught a picture of it. But it was a mild solution—he'd have had to drink a gallon for it to kill him. I just wanted him to look foolish."

"Who else knows?" Pam demanded.

"Just Laura and Cynthia. And now you. You going to turn me in?"

Pam shook her head. "The man deserved it. You're saying it didn't contribute to his death. I don't think the police need to know, if it comes to that."

"Are we supposed to tell them what we suspect?" Connie asked timidly.

"We could wait until they come asking," Cynthia said.

"Will they?"

"I . . . don't know."

Xianling pounced on Cynthia's weak answer. "If they do, will we tell the truth?"

I stepped in quickly. "But we don't have the truth—we have a lot of guesses. And we're in Italy, and we don't understand the local judicial system. I have no idea what the repercussions would be. Pam?"

Pam held up her hands. "Don't look at me! I haven't a clue about how things work around here, and I don't want to find out."

"What do *you* think we should do?" Cynthia asked. "All of you? Look, Laura and I don't have to bring you into this at all, if you don't want. Even you, Valerie—I'm willing to write off your little poppy juice experiment as irrelevant, and as far as I know nobody except us knows anything about it. We can suggest that it was an error in the blood tests or something. Or he did it himself."

"Do we tell our classmates what we suspect?" I asked.

"About Professor Gilbert's killer? No. We never told them it was a murder, and the police haven't been sniffing around. Let sleeping dogs lie. Let them go home thinking it was a sad accident, period," Cynthia said.

I glanced around our little group. "Do you agree?"

They all nodded wordlessly.

I turned back to Cynthia. "Jean needs to know."

We lapsed into silence, stunned by fatigue and sunshine and unexpected revelations. Maybe it was fate that sent Jean walking past our table at that moment. She stopped.

"*Ciao*, ladies!" she said brightly, no doubt relieved that the end of her responsibilities was in sight. "Ready for the banquet?"

The seven of us at the table exchanged looks, and I thought we all nodded. I said to her, "Jean, there's something we need to talk about. But not right here. Maybe we could go into the church where it's cool and quiet?"

Jean looked mystified. "All right, if it won't take too long. I'd hate to be late for our party."

"We'll be quick. Come on." I led the way to the church, which was both open and empty. We gathered at a couple of pews, halfway down the nave, where we could be sure no one would hear us. And we laid out for poor Jean what we thought we knew. She looked increasingly shell-shocked. When we'd finished our summary, she looked away, down toward the altar.

"I had no idea, I swear," she said. "How awful."

"How did you meet Barbara and Gerry?"

"I met Barbara through an Alumnae Council event, several years ago—she wasn't our year, you know. We got to talking about Italy and she said she and her husband had this place in Tuscany that they rented out for groups. I've actually been there a few times, so of course I met Gerry. You might even say that Capitignano was the inspiration for this whole reunion—I could envision all of us in that beautiful place. And then Jane and I got to talking, and she said she had enough connections in this area to set up something along the same lines in Liguria. We had such a lovely time, planning all this . . ." she finished wistfully.

I rushed to reassure her. "And it has been lovely, really. Look, so far most of our classmates still believe it was an accident, and we'd like to keep it that way. We can't let what happened to the professor overshadow what has been a wonderful experience."

"What do we do, then?" Jean asked.

"We haven't figured that part out," Cynthia said. "We'd rather not talk to the police, and I think we agree we aren't going to take this to them. We here are the only people who have discussed this, and we only just figured out what we think happened."

Jean brushed a few stray tears away and said firmly, "We need to tell Jane, just in case, because I don't think my Italian is anywhere near good enough to handle this."

"I agree. Do you know where to find her?"

"I do. Let's do it now, before she gets sucked into the banquet."

Jean led the way to a house halfway up the hill on the way to the vineyard. When she knocked, it was Loredana who opened the door, with an expression more serious than any I had seen on her normally sunny face. When she stepped back to let us in without saying anything, I could see why: Jane was there in the living room, as was the *senatore*.

And a pair of uniformed policemen.

I wondered what the Italian phrase for "busted" might be.

Chapter 25

We made an odd crew, and I wasn't looking forward to trying to explain anything. Jane was the only classmate in the room who spoke Italian well, but Jane didn't know what we'd just explained to Jean. Cynthia and I had the most pieces of the story, but we wanted to keep Valerie out of it if we could, which meant we had to choose our words carefully. Loredana hovered like a mother hen, but we couldn't communicate with her. The *senatore* was an unknown quantity, but the young police officers seemed very respectful of him. And we still had no idea whether we were facing Tuscan or Ligurian police or representatives of another agency altogether. Was it too much to hope that at least one of them spoke reasonable English?

Everybody looked confused. I wondered briefly if we should ask for a lawyer, but if we couldn't find an English-speaking one, that could only make things worse and would no doubt take time. I'd rather this was resolved now, with a minimum of outside intervention. But at the very least we needed to confer with Jane, our lone interpreter.

I stepped forward. "Jane, can we speak with you privately?"

She looked at the rest of us, then nodded. "Loredana, we'll be outside."

"*Si, si.*" Loredana made a whisking gesture toward the back of the house—then followed us out to a stone patio, leaving her husband to deal with the men. We had to speak softly—and quickly. While Loredana meant well, she didn't understand half of what we were saying, so poor Jane had to keep translating for her cousin while listening to us. It was a wonder that Jane's head didn't explode.

Cynthia and I outlined what we'd deduced, in the briefest possible terms. By silent agreement she and I left out any mention of Valerie and the poppies; I said only that the detailed autopsy had turned up something suspicious, and Jane didn't press for details, nor did she ask why I happened to know that. I hoped that nobody had read all the fine print on the autopsy. When we finished, there was a moment of silence as Jean digested it. She was looking imploringly at Jane, maybe hoping she could make all this go away. Cynthia and I held our tongues: we had done what we could, and now it was out of our hands. We had carefully omitted explaining where we had come by some of our information; let them think that we had put all the pieces together through delicate conversations with everyone else. I didn't think anyone would question that.

Jane touched Loredana's arm and drew her aside for a private conversation, not that we could understand anything they said anyway. They spoke quickly and urgently, with much gesturing on the part of Loredana. She seemed incensed, and Jane appeared to be trying to calm her down. While we waited I could hear the rumble of male voices from the living room and wondered what they were talking about. The murder? Sports? Politics? Was the *senatore* handing out glasses of wine? How the heck did one deal with the police in this country?

After another five minutes of heated discussion, Jane and Loredana rejoined our huddled group. Jane looked at all of us in turn.

"Let me get this straight. Nobody has any physical evidence of any of this?"

"That's right," I answered. "But we think it's the only explanation that makes sense. Who are those police?"

"They're local. The Tuscan police got in touch with them and asked them to pay us a call, out of professional courtesy."

That sounded encouraging. "What do they think they're looking for?"

"I don't have all the details, but I gather the general idea is that Professor Gilbert died under suspicious circumstances while we were in Capitignano, and they had a few questions they wanted to ask."

"So nobody is screaming 'murder' and looking to arrest anyone?" Cynthia asked.

"No, so far this is a polite inquiry, nothing more."

"Jane, you know these people better than any of us. What do you think we should do now?" I hated laying this on her shoulders when she didn't deserve it, but she was the only one who could handle both sides.

Jane glanced at Loredana, who nodded her encouragement, then turned to smile at us, still nodding. "Loredana thinks we can make this go away, with her husband's help."

"Is that legal?" I asked cautiously.

Jane nodded. "It's not like we're concealing or destroying evidence. All we have is a lot of guesses. And those guesses are confined to the people here, right?"

"As far as we know," Cynthia replied. "We haven't exactly polled the rest of the group to see what they're thinking. And we only came up with this theory this afternoon."

Jane looked at Jean. "Not exactly what we planned, is it?"

"Jane, Jean—this has all been wonderful," I hurried to reassure them. "You've shown us places we never would have found or even known existed. You've provided us with great places to stay and incredible meals. We all know how much effort you've put into this and we're beyond grateful. You couldn't have foreseen the murder—if it even was a murder, which nobody has proved." I took a deep breath. "We don't want to spoil this for everyone else by dragging the police into this. We've all got arrangements to go home over the next couple of days, and it would be a nightmare to change all that now. We want the banquet to be a happy event, a glorious end to an incredible ten days. So—and I can't believe I'm saying this—if there's a way to make this go away quietly, I think we should take it."

The relief in the room was palpable, although Jane had to explain it to Loredana, who nodded vigorously in agreement. "We will fix this, you will see," she said. I believed her.

Jane smiled at last. "I think we can make it work. Let's go back to the men—wait until you see the *senatore* in action!"

When we returned to the living room, the men were acting like they were old pals. As I had guessed, they each had a glass in their hand, no doubt sampling the vineyard's renowned wines. The police were laughing at some story the *senatore* was telling. He broke it off when we returned.

"*Va bene?*" he asked his wife.

"*Si, si, molto bene.*" She turned to the police, who were struggling to regain their official demeanor, and shot a few questions at them. There was a lot of nodding. Then Loredana looked at Jane and said something, and Jane looked at us and said, "They have just a few simple questions. I'll translate for you. Nobody else here speaks Italian, right?"

We all shook our heads. Maybe for once that was a good thing, since we could easily pretend to misunderstand the questions, and Jane could shade our responses to put them in the best possible light.

"Are they going to, uh, talk to us one at a time?" I asked cautiously.

"No, no, nothing like that. This is not a formal interview, and no one will take notes or record anything. Just information."

We could handle this. We did handle it. The nice policemen lobbed softball questions: Did you know the deceased? We all made noises about knowing him, or at least knowing of him, when we had all been at school together, a long long time before, and everyone had thought he was wonderful (we managed not to gag at that) and wasn't it a shame that he had fallen? Most of what we said was the truth. We hadn't seen him in decades. We hadn't known he was in Italy. It had been a surprise to us to learn that he would be presenting a lecture in Capitignano. Yes, he had been in fine form during his talk and at the dinner afterward, although he might have taken a teensy bit too much to drink. Yes, as far as we knew he'd gone to his room as soon as the dinner was over (which I could corroborate). No, no one else had heard or seen anything of him after that. Yes, I was the one who had found him.

That last bit occasioned an extra question or two. Had I heard anything in the night? No, I was a sound sleeper, and we'd been so busy with our sightseeing and shopping and such that I fell asleep immediately. And Cynthia? She said she'd stayed behind to talk to some of her friends, and I'd been asleep when she returned to our room. What was I doing out so early in the morning? Why, it was such a beautiful day, in such a beautiful place, that I couldn't sleep any longer and I had gone out to enjoy the morning. Yes, it had been awful to come upon the body. I debated about squeezing out a few tears, but I thought that was beyond my meager acting skills.

I did not mention my phone call, nor would they ever find out about it—I had used a very secure line.

The policemen, who indeed were young enough to be our sons, and who had no doubt jumped at the chance to take a jaunt to the Italian Riviera to talk with some harmless old ladies, all but patted us on the head. They apologized for inconveniencing us. They greatly regretted that we'd had to face such an unpleasantness as a dead body in such a wonderful place. Surely it had been a tragic accident that was nobody's fault.

The *senatore* opened other bottle and distributed glasses all around. We toasted the late professor. We thanked the policemen profusely. If I'd been watching the performance from the outside, I would have been nauseated.

And then we sent the police on their way, apparently satisfied. We'd told our stories; we'd done our civic duty. And if anything popped up like an unwanted mushroom, I'd just make another phone call and make it all go away. I did not feel bad about that, because I wanted to spare my friends any more trouble.

When the police were well out of the way, the *senatore* topped up our glasses—and winked. Loredana hugged each of us in turn. Then she looked at her watch. "Oh, the dinner. We must get ready. We will see you up the hill, no? Jane, you stay here a minute?"

Yes, it was time to go up the hill—again—and primp for our final dinner. We said our thank-yous as best we could, then walked out the door.

Jane followed us a short way. "Thank you, all of you. Thank you for coming to me, and for not blowing this all up into a big stinking mess. You don't know what this means to me."

"I think we do, Jane. And we did this for all of us. See you at dinner!"

Jane went back inside, and we turned to the path and started up the hill. This might be the last time we made this hike, and in a perverse way I was going to miss it. After the past few days I could make it to the top without huffing and puffing, no small achievement.

"I think that went well," Cynthia said. "Do you think we're in the clear?"

"I think so," I said.

"What if they come back with more questions?" Connie asked anxiously.

"If they do, I'll take care of it," I said, in a tone that didn't encourage questions, and there were none. "Tonight we enjoy ourselves."

Chapter 26

And we did. Cynthia and I went back to our room and changed shirts and put on fancy earrings, in honor of the party. I know I felt a sense of relief, of calm, about what we'd arranged down below. Whatever the murky legalities were, it felt right. Funny that I had come around to thinking that it was more important to assure that these women — these colleagues, these friends — went home with happy memories, even at the cost of . . . not exactly perverting, but maybe diverting justice. We believed we knew who the killer was, and it wasn't one of us. No amount of official investigation would change that.

The patio had been transformed. The tablecloths were crisp and bright, the silverware gleamed, the glasses — there were three at each place — twinkled in the light of dozens of candles. The cooks and staff stood waiting for us all to appear, beaming proudly. People began trickling in, first in twos and threes, then in a clump, trudging up the last slope of the hill. We vineyard residents gave them a few moments to catch their breath, feeling smug. Wineglasses circulated, but people were reluctant to sit, many of them drawn to the view of the vineyard marching toward the sky above.

But eventually we all found seats. We sleuths scattered among the others. Cynthia sat across and down several seats from me, and she smiled at me when she wasn't busy chatting with those seated next to her. More wine was poured, red and white. It was hard to grasp that it had come from the grapes that grew only a few hundred feet away, had been pressed here, had spent their fermentation in the barrels at the other end of the patio. The olive oil on our antipasti likewise had come from trees that we could see from where we sat. Maybe this was the way food and drink were meant to be, directly from the earth, to be shared with good and amiable friends.

Jane sat at the end of the table nearest me, next to Loredana, across from the *senatore*, flanked by a couple of cousins we hadn't even met before, all somehow involved in the vineyard. Jane looked tired but happy; Loredana kept flashing brilliant smiles at us all, content in her role. She had done — no, exceeded her duty as hostess, averting a potential international incident, appeasing the officials and sending them on their way (I wondered briefly what the *senatore* thought about all of this, but he had definitely come through for us).

The volume of our voices rose and fell. It was a bittersweet moment, rich with recent memories, tinged by regret that it had to end. Before the first platters of food appeared, someone led a round of "Dona Nobis Pacem," and I felt the prick of tears—at the memories, at the soft harmonies of the women's voices. Then somebody launched into our alma mater, and I stopped fighting the tears. I wasn't alone.

The last notes echoed over the valley filled with vines, and then the food appeared and we all dug in. Once again I lost count of the courses—food just kept coming, and it was all good. As the meal wound down, the wines were replaced with *vin santo*, a kind of sweet and heady wine called something unpronounceable and made from dried grapes. A woman across the table leaned toward me and asked, "Have you tried dipping a biscotto in this wine? It's wonderful, particularly if you can find Cantuccini almond biscuits." I nodded affably and promptly forgot the name of the special biscuits, but decided ordinary biscotti tasted just fine with *vin santo*.

And after that, a strong *grappa*. We toasted a lot. We toasted Jean and Jane, with heartfelt thanks. We toasted Loredana and the *senatore* for their magnificent hospitality (and during the toast Loredana winked at me). We toasted Jane's extended Ligurian family for welcoming us everywhere. We toasted each other for having the wisdom to come on this trip. We toasted our absent classmates, who had missed all the fun.

Darkness fell, and people reluctantly started drifting away, claiming early trains or planes. Some were headed to other places in Europe, to meet up with spouses or friends; others were making the long ride home. In a last spurt of energy, Jean and Jane were coordinating rides to the airport or the train station and promising to pick up luggage. I was content to sit and do nothing.

Cynthia dropped into the seat next to me. "I don't want this to end."

I stared into the depth of what was left in my glass. "Neither do I." I sipped at the last of my grappa—strong stuff.

"We ended on a happy note here," Cynthia said softly. "If anyone comes asking, we just tell them the Italian police decided it was an accident and that was the end of it."

"Suits me." I drained my glass. *May you rest in whatever peace you can find in hell, Anthony Gilbert.* "But I think there's something we still need to do, you and I. Do you have to go home tomorrow?"

"No, not really. What are you suggesting?"

"That we go back to Capitignano and talk to Gerry."

Cynthia nodded, slowly. "I think you're right. Rent a car?"

"I'll check it out. As long as I can drive slowly getting out of here, and it's a small car, I can deal with it. And we know the way at the other end."

As it happened, we negotiated the loan of a car from one of Jane's relatives—I wasn't even sure which one—with the promise that their son would drive us part of the way (past the mountains, thank heaven!) and we would drop him at a train station to get home. We'd figure out the back end later.

Our rather loose plans let us sleep in the next morning. We'd said our formal good-byes to Loredana and the *senatore* at the end of the banquet, thanking them (through Jane) for all their help. I wondered how much each of us understood about what the others had done, but we'd achieved a happy outcome, and that was what mattered. We cadged a sketchy breakfast of leftovers and sat on the patio in the sun, waiting for our ride.

Pam, Xianling, Denise, Connie, and Valerie stopped by to say their good-byes. They were all going their separate ways. Valerie's was a shade more heartfelt than those of the others; I still thought we had done the right thing by her.

Xianling was the last to stop. "It's been a long journey from Art 100, hasn't it, Laura?"

"It has. It has been a very unexpected couple of weeks, indeed."

"Keep in touch, will you?" Xianling said. She sounded like she meant it.

"I'll try," I replied—and I meant it.

Finally Cynthia and I were the only ones left. "We don't have to do this, you know," Cynthia said.

"You getting cold feet?" I asked. "I can go alone."

"No, I'll go with you, but I'm not sure what you hope to gain. I mean, do you want to make a case against Gerry? Turn him in?"

I thought for a minute or so before answering. "To be honest, I'm not sure what I want. Closure, I guess. I want to look him in the eye and hear his story. I can understand his anger and his grief and his desire for revenge, but I still resent that he used us, used our trip, to cover up what he planned to do."

"Only because of us—well, you in particular—he hasn't gotten away with it, has he?" She munched on some buttered bread for a few moments. "Nobody ever asked you why you got so involved in this, did they?"

"No. But I think they were trying hard not to think about it at all."

"Can you make trouble for Gerry, if you want to?"

"Officially or off the record? Probably. I haven't decided if it's worth it."

"Laura, how long have we been doing . . . what we do?"

"A long time now. A lot has changed since we started, hasn't it?"

Our driver appeared from up the hill. He was a charming, shy young man by the name of Davido who spoke reasonable English, which he was happy to practice on Cynthia and me. Someone else appeared with a motorized cart to haul our luggage up the hill. We followed more slowly, and I turned to say good-bye to the vineyard view. It would be hard to forget the last few days, for a lot of reasons.

Cynthia came up beside me. "Will you come back?"

"To Italy? Probably not," I said, my eyes not leaving the view. "This was special—it wouldn't be the same the next time. But all this has reminded me how much I like to travel, and that I should do more of it, while I can. There are plenty of places I haven't been yet."

"What, you think you're getting too old for jaunts like this?"

"Not at all, but you never know what's going to happen, right? Seize the day!"

We turned away and made our way up to the top of the path. The car proved to be a shiny new Audi and I almost felt guilty borrowing it, especially since no one had mentioned anything like insurance coverage or even asked if I had a valid driver's license (I did). We traveled perhaps an hour, and then young Davido instructed us to leave him at a train station in a town I'd never heard of, and we were on our own.

The car came with GPS, so we had no trouble finding where we were going. For most of the drive we followed one or another *Auto-strada*, all of which looked like every major highway I'd ever seen, except the signs pointed to exotic places like Florence and Pisa and Genoa. I enjoyed driving like this, on a nice day, with little traffic.

"You planning to retire any time soon?" I asked Cynthia out of the blue.

"Are you a mind reader or what? I've been thinking about it lately."

"Why?"

"I remember when I started in the business, it was all so new, so exciting. There were so many possibilities. Now I'm the old lady of the group, and I feel like I've seen it all. That doesn't mean there aren't innovations, or new and better ways of doing things. But it's not fun anymore. Even the government has kind of tainted it, now that we know they're looking over all our shoulders all the time."

"What would you do with yourself?" I asked. I couldn't imagine an idle Cynthia.

"That's the biggest hang-up—I don't have a clue. No significant other, no kids. Not too many friends—I mean, you're probably my closest friend, and I'm lucky if I see you once a year. All the people I work with seem like children. I don't have any hobbies. I don't garden or fix houses."

"Maybe you could write a book about your company—fictionalized, of course, and lawsuit-proof."

"You mean sit down and do one thing for a long time? I don't know if I could handle that. Like you, I've been thinking of doing more traveling, although not in a pack like this one. I think in the back of my mind I was treating this as a test run. If I could survive a trip with forty other women, I could do just about anything. But I do draw the line at cruises. What about you?"

"Do I want to go on a cruise? No way."

"That's not what I mean, and you know it. You going to quit any time soon? Just hang out for a while? See more of your daughter? I bet you're in line for a nice government pension by now—what's stopping you?"

I drove for another couple of miles before answering. "I guess the same things as you. Apart from my daughter, I don't have a lot of outside interests. And she's got her own life, I can't just piggyback on hers."

"No grandkids in the future?"

"I don't know—I don't pry. But I can't see me morphing into a doting granny. Can you?"

"Not really. What a pair we are! The downside of our outstanding education—we're too dang independent for our own good."

We passed through Borgo San Lorenzo by five, and I was pretty sure I'd recognize the route from there, helped by the convenient road signs. We passed a few rotaries, and then the villa with the whalebone, and a bit farther on the fallen tree where we were supposed to turn. I started up the hill, slowly, both for safety and because I hadn't decided on a strategy.

I think Cynthia felt the same way. "You have any idea what you're going to say?" she asked.

"No. None. I don't know that I've ever confronted a killer before."

"Do you think he'll threaten us? Maybe toss us off a convenient hill?"

"I doubt it. I think he may guess that the game is up, even if the police haven't dropped in lately."

At the foot of the hill below the estate we pulled into the driveway and paused. It was still so beautiful—masses of masonry and stucco crowning the hill, with the row of tall thin cypresses leading the way up the driveway. It was so timeless. But then, this was Italy—and even murder was timeless here. So much history, so much misery.

I hit the gas and we climbed the hill. I parked where the vans had been the last time we'd seen the place. There were no cars in sight, and I wondered if there were any guests in residence, or if Barbara and Gerry had claimed a few days alone after our departure.

When Cynthia and I climbed out of the car, Barbara appeared at the doorway. She didn't look surprised.

"Laura, Cynthia. I wondered if anyone would come back. I assume you want to speak with Gerry?"

She must know something, and again I wondered if she had always known, or if Gerry had been moved to confess in recent days. "Or both of you, if you prefer."

"Come in," Barbara said. "Can I get you something cool to drink? It must have been a long drive for you from Liguria."

"Not too bad. And yes, a drink would be nice."

"Let me find you some iced tea, and then I'll go get Gerry. He's down the hill." She went to the small adjoining kitchen and I could hear a refrigerator door opening and closing, the clink of ice cubes. She returned quickly with two filled glasses. "There you go. I'll only be a moment."

When she'd gone out the door, Cynthia leaned toward me. "You think it's safe to drink this?" she whispered.

"You mean, would she poison us? I doubt it. She would know that Jean knows where to find us — or our corpses."

After a few minutes we could hear the sound of low conversation approaching, and then Gerry came in, followed by Barbara. He gave us a humorless smile. "No police?"

I regarded him steadily. He looked as though he had aged in the few days since we'd seen him last. "No, no police. They still don't know what really happened. But I think we do."

"You know that I killed Anthony Gilbert? I can't say I'm surprised. If your group had come from some nice little junior college, most likely no one would have worked it out."

"Barbara knows?" I nodded toward her.

"She does. She wondered why I invited the man to speak — he'd only just started teaching when she was at your college, but there were already rumors about him and students. Please, sit down, so we can all discuss this like rational adults."

We sat. "Why, Gerry? Your sister?"

"You know about her? Yes, that was it. She was a good deal younger than I was, the baby of the family, and I guess you'd say we all coddled her. We were so happy for her when she went off to a good college — we felt like the whole family had succeeded. And she did really well her first semester. But something changed during the second semester."

"She took Professor Gilbert's class," I said.

"Yes. At first she would write home glowing letters about how much she was enjoying it, and then she stopped talking about him. I was already in graduate school by then, and teaching, so I didn't see much of her after her first year. And then my parents called to say that she was dead."

"How did you work out why she did it?"

"She left a note. Oh, nothing pointing a finger specifically at him, but I'd been reading the letters that came before and it was clear what she was talking about. He had used her, briefly, and then he'd moved on, which I gather was his usual course. She thought she loved him, and that she was special to him. You can guess what happened. But she wasn't strong and she couldn't deal with his rejection. We never saw it coming. My parents were devastated."

"You never told anyone at the college?"

"What could I tell them? That I thought that one of their hand-picked professors had seduced and abandoned my baby sister? I had no proof, just an ugly suspicion. And to make that public, I would have ended up dragging Amy's name through the mud, and my parents would have hated that."

I felt a spurt of anger. "So a lot of other women had to pay the price?"

Gerry looked away. "I suppose that was selfish of me. But your lot — you can't cast stones. I gather Amy was far from the only one he treated that way, and yet nobody else ever came forward."

He had a point: we all shared the blame. So many had fallen victim to Gilbert's charms; so many others had heard the rumors and done nothing. But those were the times back then, indefensible though they might seem now.

"You waited a long time to do anything about it," Cynthia said. I wondered if she was feeling what I was.

"I did. Sometimes I thought I'd laid my anger to rest. And then your group came to stay, and it seemed like a sign. Perhaps it was shallow of me, but it seemed like an ideal way to distribute the blame, so to speak. So many of you could have done it, and had a motive for it, if anyone cared to look."

"You've had the police here?" I asked.

"Of course. They were very polite, and very unsuspicious."

"The wine in the professor's room — that was for you?"

"It was. His way of thanking me for inviting him. He apparently had a delightful time — although he'd failed to snare any of your number for one last fling. He made do with talking to me."

"Did you talk about your sister?"

"No. He hadn't even recognized my surname, so why should he connect it with her? It was a long time ago. We had a glass of wine, we talked about Renaissance philosophy. He drank more than his share of the bottle. We went outside to look at the stars, and I pushed him over the edge. And that was that."

"Did you feel better for having done it?" Cynthia asked.

"Not really. I didn't feel much of anything, just empty. And then I walked away and went to bed."

We sat in sad silence for several minutes. Gerry looked drained and stared into space; Barbara's gaze never left him. Cynthia and I exchanged glances. I was at a loss; I really hadn't planned anything beyond the initial face-to-face meeting. I had no idea what to suggest, much less tell him what to do.

A wordless exchange went on between Barbara and Gerry, and then Barbara turned to me. "I know this must have been difficult for you, and I appreciate both your candor and your discretion. I'd like to request that you give us a little time to consider our options now. We can offer you a place to stay for the night, but you don't have to see us again. And perhaps our minds will be clearer in the morning. Will you agree to that?"

I looked at Cynthia, who shrugged. Up to me, then. If Gerry had planned to bolt, he had had ample opportunity before now. I had to admit that I was ambivalent about the whole situation: there seemed to be no clear right or wrong. Professor Gilbert had deserved to be punished for the pain he had caused so many women. Gerry had taken it into his own hands to punish him, but somehow I didn't feel compelled to penalize him for it. "Thank you. It's very kind of you to offer." Maybe it was strange, to accept the hospitality of a confessed killer. But I doubted that he would murder us in our beds, and I wanted one more night with the spectacular view, even knowing what I did now.

"It's the least we can do," Barbara said. "Forgive me if I don't offer you a meal, but I can direct you to a nice restaurant in Borgo San Lorenzo."

So Cynthia and I ended up staying one last night in Capitignano. The restaurant was fine, if not memorable, and we returned to the villa on the hill before the sun had left the sky — it was, after all, nearing the solstice. We walked up to the church on the hill above the estate and sat on a bench watching the sun set and listening to the flock of sheep below.

"So, what now?" Cynthia asked.

"It's up to me?" I protested. "I'm not good at playing judge. I can't make up my mind whether to forget about the whole thing, now that we know the truth, or to go straight to the nearest police station and try to explain it—which could take days, given my Italian."

"I feel badly for Barbara," Cynthia said. "She and Gerry built a nice life here, but this one event from the past had blown that to bits. I don't know what I'd do in her place. Leave him? Stand by him?"

I shook my head. I had no answers. In the end we walked back down the hill and went to bed early.

In the morning we went back up to the main building to find Barbara alone there. She looked tired but at peace. "Gerry's gone to the police, to tell them what happened."

He'd taken the choice from me, and I was relieved. "I'm glad—it's the right thing to do. But I'm sorry you have to go through this, Barbara. It can't be easy. Look, if there's any way I can help Gerry, I will. What he did, he did out of love for his sister. And if the others knew—and they don't at the moment—they would probably be grateful to him."

"I know. Thank you for offering, but we'll just have to wait and see. And, believe it or not, I'm glad you came back. It's like we've finally tied up the last loose ends that have been dangling for decades. We did truly enjoy having you and your classmates here."

"And we enjoyed our time here as well. Good-bye, Barbara, and good luck."

And we drove away, in our borrowed car, leaving Barbara to grieve.

"What now?" Cynthia asked.

"Well, we've obviously missed our flights. And we have to arrange to get this car back to Loredana and her family. You have any suggestions?"

"I do. How about we treat ourselves to a week in Florence?"

"*Perfetto.*"

Acknowledgments

This is a book I never planned to write.

A year ago, at a Wellesley College reunion, two classmates proposed a trip to northern Italy, where they both have family and friends. They asked if anyone would be interested, and most of the hands in the room shot up, including mine. They could accommodate forty women (no spouses, partners, significant others or offspring invited), and all we had to do was get ourselves to an airport in Florence or Pisa, and they would take care of everything else. There were so many people who wanted to go that they had to hold a drawing to reduce the number to forty. I was one of the lucky ones.

In June we all came together in a small hill town north of Florence, and so began a wonderful ten days, rich in sights and food and wine and scenery and museums and out-of-the-way artisanal shops and more food.

I wasn't going to write about it. I was going to indulge myself in a pure vacation. I didn't have to organize anything, and I was going to sit back and enjoy everything. And then a few classmates realized that I wrote mysteries, and somebody decided it would be a lot of fun to write a mystery wrapped around our trip. This book is the result. Please note: no one died on our trip, and the murder victim is a figment of my imagination.

When we all came together at Wellesley College it was a moment of extraordinary social change, and I wanted to capture something of that era — and also show the impact those changes had on everyone's lives, even in the present. Some of us were friends back in the day, and some of us barely knew each other, but we all shared a very special four years. This book explores the perspectives of the people who were there.

First and foremost I have to thank Sandra Ferrari Disner and Sarah Phelps Smith for working so hard to make this whole trip possible, and for showing us parts of Italy that none of us would have found on our own. They persuaded Lynn and Michael Aeschliman of Capitignano in Tuscany, and Loredana and Luigi Grillo of Monterosso in the Cinque Terre, to arrange for spectacular lodgings (including the one in the Buranco vineyard); they found wonderful restaurants, including one in a castle, that could handle us all; they took us into the heart of a mountain of marble in Carrara; and so much more. Sandy and Sally created an unforgettable experience, enhanced because it was shared.

I won't mention everyone who was there, save to say that it was a pleasure to get to know all of you better. In case you're worried, no real individual is depicted, even disguised, in this book, with the exception of one: Mee-Seen Loong, who was the main cheerleader for this book and who captured images every step along the way.

My years at Wellesley were happy ones, and I hope that I have not maligned the college in any way. The times we all spent there were turbulent, and both innocent and oblivious, and all colleges struggled to adapt to rapid changes. There is no model for the victim in this book, but we all heard stories that may have held some truth. At least no one turns a blind eye anymore.

So here's my tribute to the Fabulous Forty women who made the journey together. I hope I've done you proud and you enjoy the result!

If you'd like to see a full range of photos of the locations mentioned in this book, please see the author's website at www.sheilaconnolly.com.

About the Author

After collecting too many degrees and exploring careers ranging from art historian to investment banker to professional genealogist, Sheila Connolly began writing mysteries in 2001 and is now a full-time writer.

She wrote her first mystery series for Berkley Prime Crime under the name Sarah Atwell, and the first book, *Through a Glass, Deadly* (2008), was nominated for an Agatha Award for Best First Novel; *Pane of Death* followed in 2008, and *Snake in the Glass* in 2009.

Under her own name, her Orchard Mystery Series (Berkley Prime Crime) debuted in 2008 with *One Bad Apple*, followed by *Rotten to the Core* in 2009, *Red Delicious Death* in 2010, *A Killer Crop* later in 2010, *Bitter Harvest* in 2011, *Sour Apples* in 2012, and *Golden Malicious* in 2013.

Her Museum Mysteries (Berkley Prime Crime), set in the Philadelphia museum community, opened with *Fundraising the Dead* in 2010, followed by *Let's Play Dead* in 2011, *Fire Engine Dead* in 2012, and *Monument to the Dead* in 2013.

Her new series, the County Cork Mysteries (Berkley Prime Crime), debuted in 2013 with *Buried in a Bog*. The second book in the series, *Scandal in Skibbereen*, will be released in 2014.

Her first short story, "Size Matters," was published by Level Best Books in 2011, and was nominated for an Agatha Award.

Sheila is a member of Sisters in Crime, Mystery Writers of America, and Romance Writers of America. She is a former President of Sisters in Crime New England, and was cochair for the 2011 New England Crime Bake conference.

Made in the USA
Las Vegas, NV
19 April 2023

70789850R00118